T0121989

Autumn Years

DICKSON LOOS

iUniverse, Inc.
Bloomington

Autumn Years

This is a work of fiction. All of the characters, names, incidents, organizations, and dialogue in this novel are either the products of the author's imagination or are used fictitiously.

iUniverse books may be ordered through booksellers or by contacting:

iUniverse
1663 Liberty Drive
Bloomington, IN 47403
www.iuniverse.com
1-800-Authors (1-800-288-4677)

ISBN: 978-1-4502-7473-9 (pbk)
ISBN: 978-1-4502-7474-6 (ebk)

Printed in the United States of America

iUniverse rev. date: 11/23/2010

Preface

Nearly all the news we read these days is bad. There are devastating earthquakes in which thousands of people die; bloody and costly wars; flu pandemics; economic disasters; and the predicted irreversible destruction of the planet's environment. Yet the truth is that we, here in the United States, are living longer—much longer. When those of us who are now senior citizens were children, we thought people in their sixties were old—and anyone who passed away at the ripe old age of seventy-five was considered lucky to have lived so long and had such a rich and full life. Not so anymore.

This new longevity has produced a phenomenon we will call the autumn years—that is to say, the years we live after we stop working and are no longer productive. We have slowed down some, and we have more physical problems, but we are still active, both mentally and physically, and fully capable of living independently. Medical science, despite the hysteria regarding the cost, has made it possible to enjoy and prolong this period so that it often exceeds twenty-five years. So what do we seniors do during these autumn years?

Many stay in their own homes long after their children have left and try to enjoy the same lifestyle they had during their middle years. Some live with their children—sometimes by choice, but often because of economic circumstances. Some get part-time jobs that may or may not give some sense of purpose to their lives. Also, a large segment of the senior population has the means to live independently and the desire to use these years to start a new chapter in their lives. Our story here is about two people who fall in this category.

Harry and Vera are two elderly people who have lost their long-term spouses and are struggling to adjust and find some way to enjoy life in their autumn years. They are not heroic or unusual people. They resist change and hate to think of themselves as old. Their story is about overcoming the emotional and psychological problems that arise as they adjust to being single again, as well as being elderly. They begin to recognize that old age is not the end of the line, but a chance to develop new friendships and new interests.

The geriatric romance in this story evolves from the impulsive purchase by Harry of an old and dirt-stained painting while he is vacationing in Maine with his daughters. This brings Harry and Vera, who is an accomplished artist, together, and they are plunged into a mystery involving a long-lost painting by a famous artist and the artist's tragic love affair with a beautiful woman during the Civil War. We hope you enjoy their story.

Chapter 1:
HARRY

HARRY WALKER WOKE up with a start on the morning of September 20, the seventy-sixth anniversary of the date of his birth. He rolled out of bed, padded slowly into the bathroom, and sat down to relieve himself.

Years ago, when Harry had been much younger, he had stayed at an old hunting lodge in southwestern Virginia where the gender of the restrooms was identified by two of the most popular hunting dogs in the region. On one door was a large, muscular pointer with his leg cocked up next to a bush. On the other door was an English setter squatting down in a field with her tail sticking out behind her. Well, Harry wasn't much of a pointer now, and that didn't bother him at all. That steady stream his urologist was always talking about had disappeared long ago, so he was now mostly a setter; it worked better that way.

He got up, washed his hands in the sink, and looked in the mirror. Harry did not like what he saw. The image staring back at him was a disheveled old man with a mass of wrinkles on his forehead and deep lines around his red-rimmed eyes and mouth. His bushy hair was white, and his once-powerful physique was wasted, with the flesh on his arms and chest sagging loosely from his body.

"God!" he muttered. "Why doesn't someone take me out and shoot me?" He sighed heavily and went back to his bedroom to get dressed.

He felt tired and dizzy, which was how he had felt just about every morning since his wife died two months ago. Without her, the nights were long and lonely, and he had gotten in the habit of drinking a few scotches after dinner to help him sleep. The alcohol did help him drift off, but it left him with long periods of wakefulness during the night and a mild hangover in the mornings.

Last year at this time, his wife, Mary Ellen, had still been an attractive, energetic woman. A month later, she complained of sudden bouts of dizziness and fatigue. Two weeks of testing confirmed a diagnosis of an inoperable, malignant tumor on her brain, and nothing her team of physicians tried did any good. Finally, Harry called in the home-care hospice to keep her as comfortable as possible until the end.

It was a terrible six months; watching his wife of more than fifty years die while he looked on helplessly left deep marks on Harry's soul. Their home together had been a warm and comfortable place to live; now that she was gone, it seemed so cold and empty. No warm body in bed with him comforted him while he slept; no one offered to listen when he felt depressed or ill. It was strange what a difference one person could make in one's quality of life: with Mary Ellen, his house had been a haven; without her, it was almost like a prison. He had lost his rudder, and he felt lonely and depressed, but he knew he must adjust and move on with his life.

He went in the kitchen to make the coffee. Coffee making was a morning ritual Harry enjoyed. He started making the coffee before Mary Ellen became ill, and it gave him a sense of continuity to perform the same routine now. He began by grinding the coffee beans he had purchased in one of the nearby gourmet boutiques. He then added a teaspoon of dark, rich Kona coffee from the Big Island of Hawaii. He used an old-fashioned percolator and let it perc about five minutes; the result was a rich, spicy, high-octane morning drink—real starter juice, Harry called it, and infinitely superior to the decaf dishwater his cardiologist wanted him to drink.

After two cups of coffee and a quick scan of the morning paper, he began to feel a little better. He boiled an egg and ate it with a piece of toast and orange juice. After breakfast he went out in the backyard and made a list of maintenance projects deferred during Mary Ellen's illness. It was a pretty long list. The house badly needed painting, and the roof over the guest bedroom on the third floor showed signs of a leak. One of the large oak trees had been struck by lightning during the summer and was showing signs of distress. It would probably die, and he would have to call a tree-removal specialist. Several toilets were old and not functioning properly, and the basement had smelled of mildew and dampness for the last several years.

Harry's informal inspection was pretty discouraging. He was looking at a big bill to keep this big house livable just for one person. He should sell it and move into an apartment; and yet this was the place he and Mary Ellen had lived for most of their married life, and this was where he was determined to stay.

After finishing his to-do list, he went over to inspect the garden. Over the past five years, Harry's physical condition had deteriorated; he could no longer play tennis or take hikes in the parklands, and he had had to give up fly fishing in mountain streams, his great passion. He still played golf, but chronic back pain had restricted his backswing recently, so he wasn't sure how long he could continue. His doctors told him that he had very severe spinal stenosis, which resulted in a compression of the nerves that controlled his legs, causing weakness and pain. His condition was unlikely to improve, so the medications he took were designed to control the pain and allow him some mobility. To further complicate his life, he had developed an arrhythmic heart that periodically jumped off its normal pattern and fibrillated wildly. This often caused him to lose control over his arms and legs, further restricting his mobility. So now he had to be content with golf, an occasional fishing trip from a boat, and puttering in his garden.

Gardening was a relatively new hobby he had learned to enjoy in the last several years. At first he had been very unenthusiastic; it was just something to do, and in his circle of friends, gardening was women's work. Gardeners planted flowers, supervised gardens, read books about plants, and arranged flowers—not the sort of thing men did. As he got into it, he found that he really enjoyed it. The wonders of nature had always been a subject of interest to Harry; he always marveled at the instincts of migratory birds and the way salmon returned to the little freshwater streams where they had been spawned. In his garden, he witnessed, close up, some of the other marvels of nature. The blue forget-me-nots he planted along the edges had a habit of spreading out to other places in the garden and outside of it. Out of winter's barren landscape came a wide variety of plants, and exposure to the sun and carbon dioxide let the magic of photosynthesis begin, producing beautiful flowers that attracted hummingbirds, bees, and butterflies. He loved his plants and found himself occasionally talking to them.

He had a spring garden with bulbs and early blooming perennials; a summer garden full of sun-loving annuals; and a fall garden with late-blooming asters and chrysanthemums. A Latino gardener came over once a week to do most of the digging and hard work Harry no longer could do. The other days, Harry worked in the garden, spraying, fertilizing, weeding, and pruning. He usually had a large sack full of cuttings and weeds when he finished. Watching his plants mature and taking care of them took Harry away from his physical and emotional problems and usually put him in a relaxed, optimistic mood.

After working in the garden for several hours, he cleaned up the cuttings and debris, put them in the trash, picked a ripe tomato for lunch, and went inside to take a shower. He had a tuna salad for lunch and then looked at his calendar, which reminded him that he had accepted an invitation to dinner and bridge in honor of his birthday from Eleanor Warren, one of Mary Ellen's best friends. His dinner partner for the evening would be Louise Williams, an attractive widow about five years younger than Harry. He wondered how that would turn out. He and Louise had been very friendly while Mary Ellen was alive and had flirted rather ostentatiously. They were obviously attracted to each other, but Mary Ellen had never been concerned about it, because Louise was a good friend, and she was not after anyone's husband. She just enjoyed attention from men; it was her nature.

After lunch he took a short nap and later talked with his three children on a conference call they set up to wish him a happy birthday. Pat, the oldest, was a lawyer in Baltimore with two children of college age. George, two years younger than Pat, was an investment advisor on Wall Street with three children; and Gwen, six years younger than George, was the baby of the family and the wife of a Stanford economics professor living in Palo Alto with three children. All expressed concern about how he was handling living alone.

Harry assured them he was doing fine, was going to the Warrens' for dinner that night, and was scheduled to play in the Seniors golf tournament the next day.

"So you see," he said. "I'm getting around now, seeing old friends, and my social calendar is filling up."

"Didn't you win something at that tournament last year?" asked George.

"Well, last year I became eligible for the old geezer flight—the super seniors, seventy-five and over. I managed to shoot an 85, which, with my handicap, was a net of 68. None of the others got below 70, so I won. But that was last year, and this year I am afraid my back won't let me take a good swing at the ball, so all I am hoping is that I'll finish."

"Can't ever tell, Dad," remarked Gwen. "Just tee it up, and fire away."

Harry smiled. Gwen was irresistible: beautiful, smart, and so full of fun. It made him feel better just to talk with her.

"I'll do that, Gwen," he said. "Maybe I can squeeze out one last good round and surprise everybody."

Eleanor's dinner that evening was elegant, featuring a beautifully cooked beef tenderloin and some excellent red wine. All six of the other guests were good friends of Harry and Mary Ellen, and all were good bridge players. Harry thoroughly enjoyed the dinner, but found the conversation somewhat tedious. Everyone was politically correct and careful to avoid any subject that might invite controversy. The conversation got around to country-club politics and Harry grew restive. With the war in Iraq, a looming financial crisis, and a burgeoning national deficit, the administration of the country club seemed so trivial.

The recently elected president of the club, Harvey Wittingham, was a third-generation member and had inherited a family-owned real-estate investment business. His title was vice president, but he spent very little time at the office. Most of the time, he was traveling or attending charity functions or golfing.

Eleanor was lavish in her praise.

"Harvey is such a wise man," she said reverently. "He has traveled so much and has such good connections here in Washington. He is just the right person to lead our club and maintain our standards. Don't you agree, Harry?"

Harry could restrain himself no longer. "No, I don't," he said in a loud voice. "He's just a rich stuffed shirt who has never done anything useful in his life. About all he can do is make a good dry martini, and he sure drinks plenty of them. But maybe that's all it takes to be a good country-club president."

After that outburst, the atmosphere of the party changed. James, Eleanor's husband, looked shocked, and everyone else was quiet and restrained; the other guests avoided his eyes when they talked with Harry, and even the bridge game didn't do much to return the guests to a festive mood. Harry tried to be charming and polite when he said good night to Eleanor and James, and he thanked them for a wonderful birthday party.

"It was so much like old times, Eleanor," he said as he squeezed her hand. "The dinner was fabulous, and having such good friends here really made me feel better than I have in months."

"Thank you," she said. "I hope we will see you again soon."

When he took Louise to her apartment building, she was decidedly cool to him. She presented her cheek for him to kiss, squeezed his hand, said how nice it was to see him again, and asked him to please call her sometime—not at all like he had imagined their date would end up. When he was married and unavailable, they really had a pretty exciting time playing footsie under the table, and when they had walked together, she would often take his arm and give him a wonderfully exhilarating feel of her firm, warm breast. But now it was obvious she had very little interest in him; his little tirade about Harvey had not been a good way to increase that romantic interest. But oddly, he really didn't care much about Louise, either. He was, however, very distressed over Eleanor's icy response when he had thanked her for the party.

When he got home, he felt depressed. What had started out as a happy social evening had ended up badly. His host and hostess were embarrassed and humiliated by his outburst about Harvey, and his friends were also uncomfortable with him. He wasn't sure why his remarks about Harvey seemed so offensive. Harvey was considered something of a blowhard and a lightweight by many club members. Probably it was more the way he said it than what he said, but whatever—it clearly had been wrong to have said anything at all unless it was complimentary. He reached for his bottle of single malt and poured himself a generous helping.

"I have got to learn to keep my mouth shut," he muttered.

Chapter 2:
THE SENIOR TOURNAMENT

THE CLUB SENIOR Golf Championship was a one-day, full-handicap tournament and had become very popular in recent years. It included a cocktail party and dinner, after which the winners were announced and prizes awarded. The field was limited to eighty players and, since the senior classification began at fifty-five and more golfers were still playing in their eighties, it was necessary to sign up early in order to get in the tournament. The players were divided into three flights according to age: fifty-five to sixty-four; sixty-five to seventy-four; and seventy-five and over. To be eligible for the Club Senior Championship, all players had to tee off from the regular men's tees. However, the super seniors—seventy-five and over—were allowed to use the front tees and compete for the super senior cup.

The tournament format was a shotgun start at one o'clock with one foursome on each tee and two at numbers one and nine. Time limits were strictly enforced: all players must be finished by five thirty; groups that lagged behind were warned by the marshal to catch up and if they failed to do so, they were disqualified. The club had a large golfing membership, and slow play had become a major problem recently, so the golf committee instructed the staff to strictly enforce the four-and-a-half-hour time limits on weekends and in tournaments. The groups of four were arranged by the staff, and Harry stopped in at the shop to check on who his playing partners were. He was alarmed to see that he was playing with Sam Hardy, Bill Imhoff, and George Adams—all with handicaps above thirty and all notoriously slow players. Harry went inside to talk with Dick Lawrence, the assistant pro in charge of the event.

"Dick, why in God's name did you put all of the slowest players with me?" he asked sharply. "You know we will never finish."

Dick shrugged. "Sam said they wanted to play with you, and he is a retired judge and pretty hard to refuse, so what could I do? But you are a pretty fast player, Harry, and we made you the group captain, so maybe you can speed them up."

"Impossible," groaned Harry. "Sam's a good athlete and was a fine player and can still hit it long, but he has macular degeneration and can't see where he hits it, so I have to spend a lot of time looking for his ball. Bill and George really don't know how to play the game, and they are too old to learn."

"You'll have a fore caddy who will keep track of Judge Hardy's ball, and Bill and George aren't that bad. You'll be fine."

"Yeah, right," said Harry sourly. "And I see you have us starting on the fifth hole, which is the water hole, requiring an over-the-water carry of about 130 yards from the front tee. And you know what? That's where we fall behind by at least one hole, because I can guarantee that at least three of us will be in the water on the first shot ... and maybe on the second shot also."

Dick looked a little troubled by Harry's criticism. "I just thought you older men would like to start on a short hole, and all of you can easily hit it 130 yards."

"Come on out and watch," said Harry morosely. He went out to the practice tee to warm up. He hit practice balls for about ten minutes and then went over to join his group. He was pleased that he had been set up to ride with Sam Hardy. Sam was a real gentleman and could still play some good shots, even if he couldn't see them. Bill and George were nice enough men and had always been cordial to Harry, but they were impossible to play with. They were never ready to play when their turn came, and they dillydallied around the greens until he wanted to scream.

"You know, Sam," Harry said as they were riding out to the fifth hole, "The time limit will be strictly enforced today, and with Bill and George in our group, we don't have much chance of finishing. Why did you ask to bring them in with us?'

"I told Dick that I would like to play with you. We've had some good games together over the years, and you always help me find my balls. Bill and George were standing there, and they said they wanted to be with us. What could I do?"

"Nothing, I guess, so we'll just try to do our best. Unfortunately, I am the group captain here, and I keep the official scorecard … and you know I will have trouble with Bill and George over their scores."

"Yes," agreed Sam, "they do have selective memories, don't they?"

The gun sounded at one o'clock, and the tournament was under way. Harry went first and dumped his drive in the pond. After seeing that, Sam took a longer iron and hit it over the green, into the sand trap behind it. Bill and George also drove their balls in the water. At the drop area, Harry played a nice wedge ten feet below the pin, and George hit his ball in the rough to the right of the green. Bill put his next shot in the water and finally got over the pond on his third try. With his penalty shots, he was lying five on the edge of the green. Harry made a good putt for 4; George took four to get down from the rough, and Bill three-putted for an 8.

"Gosh, that was an awful start, Harry," said Bill. "I guess I'll have to take a 6."

"It was an awful start," agreed Harry, "and you had an 8, not a 6."

"What!" exclaimed Bill indignantly. "I was on in 3 and 3-putted!"

"You went in the water twice, Bill; everybody here knows that. Now get in the cart—there are already two groups waiting behind us on the tee."

The next two holes were uneventful, although Bill continued to protest the score at the fifth hole, and in spite of Harry's prodding, Bill and George continued to take far too much time lining up their putts. Number eight was a long par 5, and Sam hit his drive in the deep rough; neither Harry nor the caddy could find it, and Sam took a lost-ball drop and penalty. He hit his next shot in the rough again and, after using the five-minute time allotment to find his ball, took another lost-ball drop, eventually scoring a 10 on the hole. Bill and George claimed to have made 6, which Harry did not believe. Harry hit three fine shots, getting on the green in 3, but after watching all the tramping around the green by Bill and looking for Sam's lost balls, his nerves were getting a little frazzled, and he four-putted for a 7.

Harry was in a foul mood. By this time, the group ahead was now nearly two full holes in front, and the players were stacking up behind Harry's group. The marshal came up and gave them a warning.

"You'll have to catch up, gentlemen," he said. "If you are still two holes behind when I come around again, I'll have to disqualify you."

"What was that about?" asked George indignantly. "We're not slow; we are moving right along. He has no right to disqualify us."

"Yes, he does," answered Harry, "and if you two guys don't get the lead out of your asses, we're dead meat."

They picked up the pace on the next two holes and seemed to be closing the gap toward the group in front. Bill and George played more crisply and stopped agonizing so much over their putts, but they were not happy about it. George was particularly peeved when he missed a short putt on the ninth hole.

On number eleven, disaster struck. Sam, Bill, and George all drove into the rough. Sam immediately took a penalty drop to avoid delay and hit it into the rough again. This time he picked up, thereby disqualifying himself. Bill and George insisted on looking for their balls beyond the five-minute limit, but neither the caddy nor the players could find the balls. While the men were arguing about whether to take a penalty drop, the marshal rode up and told Harry they were disqualified.

Bill protested loudly. "We can catch up. The reason we're behind is that the fore caddy can't find our balls. It isn't our fault if you give us an inexperienced caddy who doesn't know how to do his job."

Harry turned to the marshal. "The caddy did fine; we just shouldn't be in this tournament. Some of us are past our tournament days, and a couple of us should have given up the game forty years ago."

"That's not a nice thing to say about us," said George heatedly. "We were doing all right, and with my handicap, I think I am in the running to win the super senior flight."

He looked down at the scorecard in Harry's cart. "Hey, I think you got my score wrong on the last two holes. I never got a 7 on number ten!"

"No sense worrying about it now," Harry said wearily. "We are out of the tournament. The only question now is do we want to ride up to the fourteenth tee and play the last holes for fun, or shall we go in?"

The sense of fun and friendship had long since disappeared in Harry's group, so they went in and watched the others finish and post their scores. The super senior flight was won by Ed McKee, a good friend of Harry and a man who was in his early eighties, but still a good golfer, with a solid 18 handicap. Harry congratulated him, and Ed asked him about the disqualification.

"Did you see who Dick stuck me with?" Harry asked.

"Yeah, I saw. I asked Dick why he did that to you. He said he couldn't help it, and he thought you were pretty hot."

"I was, and I still am. I didn't have much chance of winning again this year, but I would have enjoyed trying. I don't see why all of the slowest players were dumped on me."

'I guess no one else wanted them, either, but they are members, and Dick had to find a place to put them. How many holes before you were axed?"

"Just seven. I feel sorry for Sam. He was part of the problem, and he knew it and disqualified himself, so I wouldn't have to look for his balls. At least he tried. But those other clowns shouldn't be allowed on the golf course!"

"Calm down, Harry," admonished Ed. "Bill and George are good men and successful lawyers; they just don't have any coordination and really haven't much idea about how to play the game. But don't get all bent out of shape about it."

After all the players were in and the scores posted, Harry took a shower and got an early start on the cocktail party. He was enjoying himself, telling all his friends about the travails of his group leading to eventual disqualification.

"We lasted just seven holes," he said, "but they might as well have kicked us out on our first hole. That set the tone. Three balls in the water, and another went in on the second shot. Sam and I got 4s; Bill and George got 8s and had to struggle to get that; and then Bill stood on the green and argued with me about the scores. By the time I got him in the cart, there was an open hole ahead of us and two groups waiting on the tee behind."

"What an awful beginning," said Walt McCarthy sympathetically.

"Yes, it was bad," agreed Harry, "but it got worse. Bill and George spent so much time squatting down trying to read the break on their putts I was tempted to goose them. In fact I don't see how I restrained myself. And then Sam started driving into the deep rough, and Bill and George caught the fever. It seemed as if we were looking for lost balls all the time. We took about thirty-five minutes to play number eleven, and that did it."

As the party progressed, Harry's stories about their disqualification got more lurid and more critical of his playing companions, and his voice got louder. During dinner Sam came over to Harry's table. His face was red, and he was obviously agitated.

"We've known each other a long time, Harry, and I consider you a good friend, but you are way out of line criticizing Bill, George, and me like you have been doing all evening. You have ridiculed us and embarrassed us repeatedly, and I want you to know that I resent it, and so do George and Bill."

By this time, Harry had consumed four scotches and two glasses of wine and was a little foggy. He was angry and embarrassed by Sam's comments.

"All right, Sam," he said, his speech slightly slurred, "I'm sorry if I offended you, but you, Bill, and George shouldn't play in tournaments. You can't see, and you can't hit the ball straight. Every other hole, we have to stop and look for your ball—you can't play in four and a half hours like that. And Bill and George should give up the game; they couldn't play in four and a half hours if their lives depended on it."

Sam was surprised at the bluntness of Harry's reply. Harry was generally very considerate about Sam's sight degeneration, but there was no tone of apology in Harry's voice; he looked angry and belligerent.

"You won't ever have to worry about playing with me again," Sam said in a tight voice. He turned on his heel and left.

Harry felt a twinge of regret after Sam left. Why had he been so critical of an old friend who had had the misfortune of losing his sight? He held up his wine glass to be refilled. Before the waiter could fill it, one of his golfing friends came up and took the glass away from him.

"I heard that exchange with Sam," said Jack Barlow. "You have had enough wine. I am going to drive you home, and Ed McKee will follow in your car—now give me your keys." Jack was a small man in his mid eighties, still a good golfer with a very decisive personality. You usually didn't argue with Jack.

Harry handed him the keys. "I guess I came on a little strong, did I?"

"I want to get you out of here before you alienate the entire club," answered Jack.

On the way home, Jack told Harry he needed to develop a new attitude. "I know what it is like to lose your wife, and I went through some very hard times when mine died seven years ago. Most of the time, you are a good man, Harry, and you wouldn't talk like that to Sam. But you are drunk tonight, and you better lay off alcohol for a while if that's what it does to you. Get someone to talk to and help you through this period, like your minister or your children." Ed parked Harry's car in the driveway and put the keys on the kitchen table, and they said good night.

Harry was devastated; he began to weep. "Why did I say those things to Sam, one of my best friends?" he muttered aloud. "Why can't I keep my big mouth shut?"

He staggered over to the bar, poured himself a large scotch, and slumped down on the sofa. He felt the room spinning around; he became nauseated and was dimly aware that he was losing consciousness.

The next thing Harry saw was his daughter, Pat, kneeling on the floor beside him, wiping away some old vomit from his face and shirt.

"What the hell happened?" he asked groggily.

"I've called 911," she said. "They're sending an ambulance, which should be here in a few minutes. Your heart is going like a trip hammer, and you are full of whisky."

"My God," he whispered hoarsely. He tried to get up, but Pat restrained him.

"The medics in the ambulance cautioned me not to move you. They are in contact with the cardiac unit at the hospital and will try to give you something that will slow down your heart, but they may have to detox you first."

"W-w-what!" stammered Harry.

"Get all that alcohol out of your system, because it may cause adverse side effects when combined with your heart medications …"

A few minutes later, the ambulance arrived, and Harry was rolled onto a gurney and placed inside the ambulance, where the medics gave him a blood-thinner shot and a low-risk intravenous dose of heart medication, as directed by the hospital cardiac unit. He was taken immediately into the cardiac emergency room, where Dr. Springer, his cardiologist, was waiting for him.

Pat followed the ambulance in her car and sat in the waiting room until Dr. Springer came out and introduced himself.

"We'll try to get him stabilized," he said, "but it will be a little dicey until all of the alcohol in his system has metabolized. He is in no immediate danger now."

"That's a relief," sighed Pat. "Here is my card if you need to call. I am the closest family member, but it takes me about an hour to get here from Baltimore. So I would appreciate it if you could call me and let me know if I should hire someone to care for him when he gets out of the hospital."

"We'll call you before we discharge him."

"Thank you, Doctor. Do you have some idea about how long he will be hospitalized?"

"I would think three or four days. You should be able to talk to him tomorrow morning."

"I'll call him; we are all very concerned about him, and I hope you can give us some guidance on how we should care for him after he leaves the hospital."

"I think he needs a change. Living alone seems to be difficult, and he needs help to get his drinking under control. I can recommend some detox institutions where he would be supervised by professional people."

Pat looked very distressed as she got in her car to drive back to Baltimore.

She was worried about her father's health and a little angry too. She had a family and a demanding job with a successful law firm and now it seemed that she would also become the person responsible for taking care of a dysfunctional parent.. Supervision in a detox unit was not a viable option; he would never consent to it, and it would be a terrible blow to his already fragile self-esteem if she suggested it. However, something had to be done. He could not continue to live alone in his home; that much seemed clear. But she was not about to decide what should be done by herself. Her siblings had to get involved. They must find a way to care for their father which would give him the independence he craved and the medical attention he needed. They also had to find a way to get him to control his drinking which had become a serious problem since their mother's death.

Chapter 3:

THE FAMILY CONFERENCE

On October 1, ten days after the calamitous events of the Senior Golf Tournament, Patricia Walker Johnson was sitting at her desk in Baltimore, trying to reach her brother, George. Pat was a pleasant-looking woman with a calm demeanor. She had worked nearly all her married life and managed to be a successful working wife and mother at the same time. She was the oldest of Harry's three children, having turned fifty at just about the time her mother passed away.

There had been no landmark birthday party for Pat. The stress of her mother's last illness and making arrangements for the memorial service and burial had left no time for personal matters, and now that her mother was gone, her father had her full attention. Three times since, she had driven to Harry's home in McLean, Virginia; twice she had found him depressed, with a sink full of dirty dishes and newspapers stacked up outside the front door. The last time, after the Seniors Tournament, she found him on the floor, reeking of whisky, his heart wildly out of sync. She had gotten him to the hospital in time to avoid a major heart attack, but it had been a close call.

Her father was going through a difficult period; he couldn't seem to cope with living alone, and his drinking since her mother had died was unacceptable. A different lifestyle for him was necessary, and she needed George and her sister, Gwen, to help decide what he should do, and then persuade him to do it. He was very independent and a born male chauvinist, so convincing him to live with one of his children—not to mention maintaining the peace once he did so—would be a very difficult option. But was there anything better?

When George answered Pat's call, he was on his cell phone. "I'm getting on the shuttle to Boston now, Pat, and I should be able to get through my meetings by three o'clock this afternoon," he said in a pleasant baritone voice. "I agree with you completely that we must get Dad out of his house. He can't live by himself; you would be wearing out the road between McLean and Baltimore every time he failed to answer the telephone."

"Yes, George, I know that," she answered, "but you also know that he doesn't want to move in with any of us."

"The plane is about to board, Pat—I gotta go," said George, speaking rapidly. "I'll be at this number after three. Try to hook up a conference call with me and Gwen at about three fifteen. I'll hang around there until four, and if I don't hear from you by then, I'll call you tomorrow morning. Bye."

Pat hung up and wrote down the number her brother had given her. George was always in a hurry; life on Wall Street suited him. He ran a small but very profitable investment trust for selected clients with serious money. His rigorous work ethic and innate business instincts helped make his business successful, but Pat thought there was an element of luck in the equation also. The sun always seemed to shine on George, as it had the time he hit the jackpot in Las Vegas.

Pat remembered that incident clearly. Her mother and father decided to take the older children on a tour of the western parks. Gwen was only nine at the time, and she opted to go to camp with some of her friends for the summer instead. The rest of the family flew to Salt Lake City, rented a station wagon, and began their odyssey. The magnificent Tetons and Jackson Hole were mind-boggling. Herds of antelope, elk, and mule deer stretched out over a vast wilderness and made a lasting impression on her. Having been born and raised in the congested eastern corridor between Boston and Richmond, Pat had never been exposed to such big country. Everything was big: the animals, the trees, the sky, and the endless mountains and rolling plains. Even the stars in the high, clear atmosphere seemed bigger and brighter than they were back home.

On their way to California, Harry decided to stop at Las Vegas for a couple of nights of "high living." They stayed at the MGM Grand and ate dinner at an expensive restaurant that featured, much to their mother's disgust, a live floor show full of sexual innuendoes and skimpy costumes.

Pat was seventeen at the time and about to enter her senior year at high school, and she was mildly amused by the show but more amused at George's reaction. This was one time his cool demeanor deserted him. He was just fourteen, and the raging hormones of the adolescent male had recently arrived. He became red-faced and wide-eyed, staring at the occasional bare breast of the female entertainers.

After the show, the family stopped in the casino, where George became fascinated with the slot machines and the grim-faced old ladies who seemed to be the major players. When one of the women relinquished the quarter machine, George walked over, put in a quarter, and hit the jackpot. Pat couldn't remember how much money he won— probably a couple of hundred dollars—but she did remember the sirens, bells, and whistles that went off to announce a jackpot winner.

George was that way; good things happened to him. He had come to expect it, and it gave him that cool, confident manner. Pat and George were very close, and he respected her and admired her efficiency and honesty. But they were very different. Pat never hit any jackpots, and the good things that happened to her were the result of good planning and hard work.

Pat wasn't a brilliant, charismatic lawyer, and she never would be great at haranguing a jury or cross-examining witnesses. But she had done well in the pro bono division of her firm because she enjoyed helping people with legal problems, and she was a very good negotiator. She wasn't a beautiful woman, either, but her energy and gracious manner made her attractive to both men and women and inspired confidence from her clients.

Pat called Gwen and left a message to be ready for a conference call at twelve fifteen that afternoon, emphasizing that it was very important.

George Walker boarded the ten o'clock New York to Boston shuttle and settled down for the hour's ride to Logan Airport in Boston. He was concerned about his father. The agony of his mother's illness and death had been a nightmare for all of them, but it had been most devastating to his father. After all the prayers, eulogies, and condolences from family and friends were over, Harry seemed to have no interest in making a new life for himself. The maids Pat hired to take care of the house and fix meals for him lasted at most two weeks; his depressed manner and occasional critical outbursts created such an oppressive environment that they left as soon as they could find another job.

Originally, George had thought Harry could be happy living with Pat. She had two acres of land, and they could easily afford to build him a separate guesthouse that would give him the independence he needed. The more he thought about it, however, the less feasible it seemed. Pat was a calm, charming woman, but she was a charger. She was very fond of her husband, Peter, and they had a good, solid marriage, but Pat made the decisions in that household. Meanwhile, Harry was very much an alpha male, and clashes of personality between them would be inevitable.

It would be very difficult for George to bring his father into his own house, too. His wife, Jean, also had a very strong personality. Early in their marriage, they had some rather serious clashes in which each wanted to assert themselves in areas they considered to be their domain. Such power struggles had led to some pretty disagreeable misunderstandings until they both finally staked out their own territories, and now it was difficult to find a more devoted couple, nor a more solid marriage. Perhaps Harry might work it out with Gwen; she was the youngest, and he could never resist her charming and lively personality for very long. But going to California was a pretty big step for George's father at his age. Just getting him out of his home would be very difficult. The three siblings needed to come up with something in a place that was familiar to him and that would be associated with a happy period of his life.

Harry still owned a lovely old house on the Chesapeake Bay near Salisbury, Maryland, that the family referred to as the "beach house." It was about a hundred feet from the bay, on a grassy knoll that sloped gradually to a sandy beach. Harry had built a fifty-foot pier with a boathouse at the end, where they kept a day sailboat and an outboard motorboat they used for fishing. It was a place the whole family had enjoyed while the children were growing up. It was also near Johnson's Island, a 200-acre marshy island, that Harry had bought when George was about eleven and on which he had built a hunting lodge. That was a project George would never forget. Local workmen were employed to do most of the work, and George had a wonderful time helping to mix the mortar and lay bricks for the huge wood-burning fireplace that provided heat for the living-dining area. He also helped the carpenters set the door frames and nail on the trim. Harry was an electrical engineer and ran a successful subcontracting business, so he had access to the materials he needed to design and install a modest generator system that provided power for an electric light and a pump to provide water for the indoor bathroom. It was a rustic but comfortable lodge, and George and his father loved the duck-hunting trips they took with many of their friends.

George remembered vividly those early mornings on the marsh before sunrise, with the wind in his face, the sounds of ducks quacking, the haunting cries of loons, and the rush of powerful wings as large flocks of waterfowl flew overhead, searching for a place to land. A sense of mystery, almost like a religious epiphany, always came over George when he was alone in the marsh. Watching a pond freeze over was a source of endless fascination. Sudden streaks of thin ice would shoot through the ripples until the pond surface became still, and he could see ice forming on the heads of the decoys. Why did cold water sink to the bottom and then expand and rise to the surface just before it froze? Such behavior defied the laws of physics, but if it were otherwise, life as he knew it could not exist on this planet. To George that was a more powerful sermon than any he had heard in church.

Someplace near the beach house and the hunting lodge on Johnson's

Island might be the answer to their predicament. Harry was lonely and depressed; he needed to get out of his house, but it was where he had lived most of his life. Yes, the house had been host to many happy years when the children were growing up and they all had each other, but the most recent memories were sad and depressing. A move into the beach house might be worth mentioning on the conference call. They could probably get some local couple to move in with Harry and take care of him and the house. Harry would certainly get along better with the bay watermen and their wives than he did with the maids Pat had gotten for him.

George was very fond of his father; they had shared many hunting and fishing trips together, and Harry had taken good care of his family when he was growing up. George was a graduate of Lehigh and Harvard Business School and had never had to pay a single cent of tuition. His sisters had also gone to Ivy League–type colleges and never had to borrow money to graduate. To manage such a sacrifice, their parents had to roll back their lifestyle and forgo some of the expensive trips and high-priced cars that their contemporaries enjoyed. Later, when George was stuck in a boring, secondary management position at a large bank, Harry had loaned him the money to start his own investment business, which his father had predicted "was bound to fail." But George had strong entrepreneurial skills, and his business became very successful— so much so that even George was surprised. It was very important to George that they come up with a workable plan so that his father could regain his zest for living and enjoy the years he had left.

We call them the golden years, he thought, *but getting old is tough, and learning to enjoy life as a single old man will be difficult for Dad.*

At 12:15 p.m. Pacific time, on October 1, Gwen Walker Loukakis was sitting in her sunroom in Palo Alto, California, waiting for the conference call arranged by her sister, Pat.

Gwen was a tall, classic blonde with bright blue eyes and a beautiful, full, feminine figure. She knew how to manipulate people with an easy, self-deprecating manner that made casual acquaintances dismiss her as a pretty blonde airhead. But looks can be deceiving. Gwen was a Phi

Beta Kappa graduate of Middleburg College in Vermont and had been considered a rising star at the Fidelity Investment Group in Boston, where she had worked for two years after graduation. Then she met Nick Loukakis, a newly minted MBA from Harvard who was working for his PhD in business administration.

It started as a casual coffee date after Nick had delivered a lecture to some of the Fidelity analysts on the role of capital markets in the developing economies of the third world. After Nick's speech, Gwen had questioned him about some of the assumptions he made in his talk. They adjourned for coffee and further discussion, and then nature took over, and they were engaged six months later. Nick was the son of a Greek immigrant lobster fisherman in Maine. He was the only one in his family to attend college, and he had graduated with honors from the University of Maine. Much to everyone's surprise, he had been accepted by the Harvard Business School, where he excelled and was urged to stay on as an instructor and work toward his PhD.

The romance had come as a shock to Gwen's mother, who had assumed Gwen would marry one of her many suitors with a background similar to her own—who were more adaptable to the social status enjoyed by the Walker family in Washington. When Gwen and Nick had gotten engaged, Gwen was very apprehensive how her family and their friends would react to her fiancé. At the reception her parents gave to announce their engagement at the country club, Harry took over and treated Nick like another son. He enjoyed telling everyone that this was one Harvard PhD who had his feet on the ground and his head screwed on right. Now, fourteen years later, Nick was a fully tenured professor of economics at Stanford's School of Business and totally devoted to Harry, and so was she.

Promptly at twelve fifteen, the telephone rang, and Gwen heard the familiar voices of her sister and brother. After the siblings exchanged greetings, Gwen asked, "Pat, will you please explain to me what is going on with Dad? Is he in bad shape?"

"He is home now," she answered, "and he assured us that it was just a case where he had a little too much to drink at the party and there is nothing to worry about."

"Tell Gwen what happened and how you found Dad," said George.

"I called Dad at about ten in the evening to inquire how he did in the golf tournament. When I got no answer, I was a little concerned, because I was aware that he had been drinking too much for some time. I had gone to McLean twice before when he failed to answer the telephone, and each time I found him huddled up in the family room beside the bar, with several days' dishes and newspapers stacked up in the kitchen. The whole house smelled of whisky."

"Doesn't he have a maid to come in and take care of the house?" asked Gwen.

"We can't keep anyone working for him more than a week or two," answered Pat. "He seems to drive them away.

"I called again early the next morning," Pat continued, "and when I didn't get an answer, I called one of his golfing friends and found that he had been driven home in an intoxicated state after insulting one of his best friends, so I drove down as quickly as I could and found him passed out on the floor—full of whisky, and his heart beating wildly. I got him to the hospital, but it was a close call."

"So what should we do?" inquired Gwen.

"We must get him out of his house and into a new environment," Pat answered. "He can't cope living alone in that house, where Mother died. It's just too full of memories of her. We must get him into a new and pleasant place, where he can start thinking ahead, not living in the past."

"Agreed," said George, "and I'm thinking beach house. It is a place we all love and is close to Dad's hunting camp. He enjoys the local watermen, and I think we could get an older couple to move in and take care of him and the house. He gets along with them better than he does with the maids we tried to get for him."

"What about you, Pat?" asked Gwen.

"I'm thinking more about these newer luxury continuing-care communities, where there is on-the-spot excellent health care, independent living, and a lot of affluent seniors like him. It would be a place where he can make new friends and maybe enjoy a different lifestyle. He isn't getting along too well with the old country club group; I heard he managed to insult Eleanor and James Warren at a birthday party they gave for him."

"What can I do to help?" asked Gwen.

George answered, "We're thinking of having a family meeting where all of us will meet with Dad and tell him he has to leave his house and move somewhere else."

"Suppose he refuses to meet with us? What do we do then?"

"That would be a problem," agreed George. "So we mustn't make it sound intimidating … and that's where we need you, Gwen."

"I'll do whatever is needed," she replied.

"We'll tell Dad we are all coming down to have lunch with him at his club in Washington and talk about his health concerns," George said, "and we'll tell him you are coming all the way from California to see him. I doubt he will refuse that kind of an invitation."

"Yes," said Pat. "You are the youngest, and you can manage him better than anyone else. It is very important that you be with us."

"When will you arrange this meeting?" Gwen asked.

"We're shooting for 1:00 p.m. next Wednesday at the Metropolitan Club," said George. "I'll check with Dad and make sure he is willing to meet with us and will confirm to you tomorrow."

"Suppose he refuses to leave his house in spite of our urging," said Gwen. "What are we prepared to do?"

"We will have to do whatever it takes," replied Pat. "We can't leave him as he is."

"I'll be there," said Gwen.

Chapter 4:
THE MEETING

ON THE DAY of the meeting with his children, Harry woke up feeling tired and a little dizzy. After the serious heart fibrillation episode caused by his excessive drinking, he had tried to stay away from alcohol, but after a week, he had returned to his old habits of afternoon cocktails and a couple of nightcaps before bedtime.

Harry was not looking forward to this meeting. George had called him and emphatically told him they were all coming to Washington to see him—even Gwen, all the way from California. He guessed they were going to confront him on his drinking habits and try to get him either to live with one of them or go to some nursing home. He wasn't going to do either of those things. He would just have to tell them up front that he was capable of taking care of himself and appreciated their concern, but that they should mind their own business and stop sticking their noses in his affairs. They wouldn't like that, but it was best to get that on the table so they could go on to other things.

He had a light breakfast and put on his best suit. It wouldn't hurt for the family to see that he could clean up nicely.

All of his children were sitting in the lounge of the Metropolitan Club when Harry walked in. In spite of his misgivings about the meeting, Harry couldn't help but admire them. This was one thing he and Mary Ellen had gotten right: all of their children had gown up during the sexual revolution and the drug age, and all of them had survived and were attractive, capable citizens—real contributors to society. He was very proud of them.

They all rose when they saw him and greeted him warmly. It was easy to see that they were genuinely fond of their father, and all of them complimented Harry on how well he looked.

"Thanks, kids," he said. "Although ... you don't look like kids anymore. I feel like I'm having lunch with my lawyer, my stockbroker, and Miss America from California. It's good to see all of you. Let's have a drink before we get down to business and start saying things we don't want to hear." He signaled to a waiter, who came over to get their drink order. Gwen ordered tomato juice, and Pat and George ordered club soda. Harry understood this was an expression of disapproval of his drinking habits, but he was not intimidated.

"Let me have a double of whatever single malt Johnson has open—on the rocks."

"Dad," George said, "don't you think you're having a little too much scotch these days? Didn't Mom talk to you about that a few times?" George was clearly uncomfortable criticizing his father.

"Constantly," Harry agreed. "She was always trying to improve me, bless her."

"Well, are you?" asked Gwen, her blue eyes boring into Harry like a couple of dumdum bullets. "Isn't that what caused your heart attack ten days ago?"

Harry looked at his children sourly at first, and then his eyes brightened up.

"Johnson!" he bellowed. "Hold that scotch. I changed my mind. Make me a gin martini with an olive—straight up."

He turned to his children. "There you are," he said, looking very pleased with himself. "You're right—I think I am drinking too much scotch these days, and I've been thinking of switching to gin for some time. That make you happy?"

"Very funny, Father," said Pat, looking like an angry mother. "Just remember, I am the one who has to drive fifty miles to pick you up off the floor and get you to the hospital, and I am getting sick of it."

"You may be surprised to hear this, Dad," George said, "but we are here because we all love you, warts and all, and we want you to be happy and well cared for in the years ahead. It is very stressful for us when you drink too much."

Harry was not pleased with the way this meeting had begun. "Okay, let's start over," he said. "I admit I have been hitting the bottle lately; as you all know, it's been a tough year, and a drink at lunch for a person my age shouldn't cause anybody any stress. I will deal with my alcohol consumption in my own way, and I promise you, Pat, you will never find me passed out on the floor again. Now let's talk about your agenda for this meeting. The issue must be important for you all to come here from your offices in the middle of the week and Gwen all the way from California. So what's on your mind?"

"What's on our mind is you, Dad," said Gwen clearly and with a surprising amount of force. "We are not going to just sit by and see you so unhappy that you are trying to kill yourself by drinking too much. We're here to help you."

"I'm not trying to kill myself," said Harry irritably. "We have discussed that already. I am not an alcoholic, and I am perfectly capable of handling my liquor consumption without any help from you.

"As for being unhappy," Harry continued, "yes, it's hard for me to adjust to living alone, but I can adjust, and I will determine my future lifestyle, and I will decide where and how I want to live. I appreciate your concern, but we will all be much happier if you direct your attention to your own affairs and stay out of mine."

"You haven't been handling your drinking problem at all well," cut in Pat, looking hard and determined. "It's altering your personality. I haven't been able to keep any household help for more than a week or ten days, and you've managed to insult some of your best friends in the past two weeks. You are not adjusting. You are getting worse."

Harry was incensed. "I'm getting along fine, and I don't need any more sanctimonious lectures from you! I'm getting along with my friends very well, and I intend to get involved in more of the activities around the club. My friends were very helpful to me after Mary Ellen died."

Pat was getting heated up, and she responded in loud, forceful tones. "I talked with Sam Hardy and Eleanor Warren, and they told me about how rude you have been lately—and Jack Barlow urged me to talk to you about it, which I am trying to do."

Harry was also getting angry. "Try to remember, Pat," he said loudly, "I'm your father. I took care of you as a baby and wiped your ass and changed your diapers. I've known you for a long time, and you aren't nearly smart enough to tell me how to live. No one has accused me of being incompetent, and I have a right to live the way I want without any interference from you."

"No one has accused you of incompetence yet," Pat shot back. "But if you keep on sitting around feeling sorry for yourself and losing yourself in the bottle, we'll be forced to have you declared incompetent and have a trustee appointed to take care of you and your affairs. How would you like that?"

Harry was furious. "Are you threatening me?" he demanded "Just try something like that, and we're finished." He was beginning to shout and signaled for another drink. The waiter came over, looking embarrassed, and took his order for a second martini.

"Dad, Pat—calm down," said George. "The members here in the lounge can't help overhearing us, and we will never get anywhere unless we look at this with some understanding of each other's feelings."

Pat immediately took Harry's hand. "I'm sorry, Dad," she said. "I was way out of line. We're here to try to help you not get into a messy argument."

Harry signed for his drink and took a big sip. "I know you want to help, kids, but just stop trying to push me around. I am having difficulties that I'm sure I can resolve, but I'll listen. What do you think I should do?"

Gwen gave a big sigh. "Thank heavens the shouting match is over," she said "So let me weigh in with what I think will make everyone happy."

"What's that?" asked George.

"Dad needs his independence, and he does not like to be alone. He needs to have someone he can talk to and do things with—someone to fill the void now that Mom has died. He can get all those things if he comes out to California and lives near us … and don't you dare tell me you wouldn't like living with me, Dad!" she said, trying to look severe.

"Of course I would like being with you or any of the others, but not on a permanent basis."

"Why not?" asked Gwen.

"Well, it would be your home I am invading; you all have families, and that must be your first priority. I would feel like an interloper—someone who doesn't belong there."

"Yes, I know how you feel, Dad," said Gwen. "You do have a prickly personality, and you like to do things your own way … but Mom had no trouble managing you, and neither would I."

Harry laughed. "So you think I would get along with you better than the others?" he asked.

Gwen smiled. "Well, you and Pat are too much alike; you would clash like you just did, and I can't see you finding some nice little bungalow near George that would cost less than a million dollars, so that leaves me … and you know Nick is devoted to you."

"All that may be true, Gwen," he said. "But I just can't get up and leave this area at my age. I've lived around here all my life, and I just can't see myself living in California or Arizona or Florida or any of those places where old people go."

"What about the beach house?" asked George. "We could probably get a local couple to move in with you and take care of the place, and you wouldn't be alone. You get along with those old watermen better than the maids we have tried to get for you."

"That's a possibility," said Harry. He brightened at the suggestion.

He loved the beach house, and it had been a favorite family vacation spot while the children were growing up. "I might look into that."

"I have another suggestion," said Pat. "Continuing-care retirement communities are becoming very popular these days. I think—"

"You mean nursing homes," snorted Harry. "Places you put old people waiting to die."

"Not true anymore, Dad," Pat said. "There are lots of affluent seniors who are now living into their eighties and nineties. They are demanding gracious independent living along with experienced, on-the-spot medical services."

Harry looked a little surprised. "I don't know about that," he said. "I've visited friends who had strokes or were losing their marbles, and they were confined in places that looked like hospital wards and smelled of pee and Lysol."

"Trust me, Dad," said Pat emphatically. "These places don't even resemble the homes you are describing. Some of them look like college campuses."

"Maybe so," said Harry skeptically. "But there is one alternative you haven't mentioned, and that is staying right where I am, where I lived with your mother for over forty years and where all of you children were raised. Why shouldn't that be the most obvious and workable option? After all, that's what I want to do."

The children were silent for a while. George finally asked; "If we got you someone who was willing to stay with you and take care of the house five days a week, could you manage?"

"I'm sure I could," he answered.

"But would you be happy?" asked Gwen. "Would you enjoy living in that big house by yourself now that Mom is gone?"

"I don't know," admitted Harry. "Right now, it's hard: hard to relax, hard to sleep, hard to think, and … it's so damned quiet!" He glared at his children. "But it is my home," he said. "Mary Ellen and I lived there together for a long time, and I am not going to leave."

"And that's the crux of the problem we face, isn't it?" asked Gwen. "Your house represents the past—the years you were in your prime and you and Mom were together and very devoted to each other. Now your life has changed. Mom is no longer here; you are alone and no longer in the prime of your life. Living in your home makes you think of the past. It's our job to help you find a place where you can think ahead."

"We have discussed three options, Dad," said Pat softly. "Living in California near Gwen; moving into the beach house, or moving into one of these continuing-care communities—and there is one on the eastern shore of Maryland, not far from the beach house. I hope you will at least consider some of these places." She handed him a thick envelope containing several brochures of some of the continuing-care facilities.

"All we can ask, Dad, is that you consider these choices carefully," said George. "I think you really agree with us that staying in your house is not a good idea. You aren't happy there, and it is putting a big burden on Pat to be constantly on alert in case something goes wrong."

Harry suddenly felt very tired. The emotional strain of confronting the issues of his drinking and moving away from his home had left him depressed and disgusted with himself.

"I guess I've been pretty much of a problem these last few months, haven't I?" he said in a subdued tone. "It's been tough on you, Pat, and I should have realized that."

"It's been tough on all of us, Dad," said Pat, giving his arm a squeeze, "but the hardest thing for us is to see you so unhappy."

"I will give serious consideration to everything you've said today," said Harry, "but I have to tell you I do not want to move out of my home, and I'm a little surprised that all of you think staying here won't work for me. Now let's go up and have lunch. I know you have planes to catch this afternoon."

Lunch was a quiet, subdued affair. Gwen tried to keep things light and humorous with stories about Nick and life as a professor's wife on a major college campus. Her anecdotes helped to lighten the mood, but it was obvious that Harry was tired and concerned over his future.

After lunch Harry thanked them all for coming.

"It was not an easy session for me," he said, "but you opened some doors and made me see how hard it is for you if I continue here as I am now."

"Whatever you do, Dad," said George, "we'll support you to the best of our ability."

"If you want to talk some more about this, Dad," said Pat, "I'm just an hour away, and I would be glad to stop over some evening if you're lonely."

As Pat and George were preparing to leave, Gwen announced that she was going back with Harry to their home.

"I didn't come all this way just to have lunch," she said. "I want to see our old home again and have a nice visit with Dad."

"Wonderful!" exclaimed Harry. "We'll go out to dinner at L'Auberge Chez Francois , and we'll eat a lot of rich food and drink some good French wine."

"I'm going to prepare a nice simple dinner at home, Dad," replied Gwen, "and then we are going to talk seriously about these options."

"Good for you, Gwen!" said George enthusiastically. "Work on him—he enjoys arguing with you."

"How long can you stay?" asked Pat.

"I have to leave tomorrow afternoon," replied Gwen. "The president of our company has called a meeting, and all real-estate agents must attend."

Chapter 5:
A NEW BEGINNING

AFTER GEORGE AND Pat left, Gwen went in the cloakroom to pick up her overnight bag, and she and Harry drove back to McLean. This was the first time she had really looked around the old neighborhood since she was married. There was such an emotional strain on the family during her mother's memorial service that she hadn't paid much attention. It was still much the same as she remembered it, except the trees which had grown taller and fuller. The effect was that of an old community with stately homes, green lawns, and quiet streets—an enclave in the midst of one of the most congested areas in the country. She enjoyed driving around with her father and looking at familiar scenes of her childhood. The elementary school she had attended was still there; the homes of friends where she had played and spent many a night were still unchanged; the streets where she and her friends had gone trick-or-treating were very familiar. . Many memories flooded Gwen's mind as she drove through the neighborhood and recalled those happy days of growing up in this lovely community.

At dinner Gwen and Harry talked about their family and reviewed what had happened to their friends and neighbors over the past twenty years. Father and daughter shared a relaxed, warm conversation full of nostalgia and a little sadness that those bright, exciting days were over.

"I think you can see, Gwen, why it is so hard for me to leave this house and this area," said Harry.

"Oh, yes, I do," Gwen replied quickly. "It was so good to drive with you and see all the familiar places. It brought me back thirty years to when I was little and knew all the neighbors and their children. And it was wonderful to sit here and talk to you about it."

"Then I guess you agree that this is the place where I ought to stay?"

"I really don't know, Dad," she replied thoughtfully. "I'm having a grand time reliving my years growing up here, but Thursday I'll be back in the real world, thinking about my children, my husband, and my job. I will enjoy remembering our life here in my youth, but most of the time, I will be thinking about what is happening now and in the future. Can you do that here, Dad—start a new life and put the past behind you?"

"I don't know," admitted Harry. "I guess I'm not doing so hot right now, am I?"

Gwen laughed. "Getting drunk and insulting your best friends isn't exactly the way to start a new life. But I heard what you said about the new club president, and I suspect it was true … and you told Sam he shouldn't play in tournaments, which also was true … so what you said wasn't very bad."

"It was the way I said it," replied Harry. "I just have to learn to keep my mouth shut."

They talked well into the evening and again the next morning, after breakfast. Gwen made sure Harry understood why his children admired and respected him; she reminded him how he had helped all of them and how he had made Nick feel like part of the family when she had announced her engagement over her mother's initial opposition. She emphasized his need to start a new life—one that did not necessarily entail the same lifestyle he had had with Mary Ellen. When Gwen left at noon on Wednesday, Harry was feeling much better.

After Gwen left, Harry began to think of what he should do to begin a new life. He was surprised by the intensity of concern over his welfare expressed by his children. Taking time off in the middle of the week and coming to Washington to see him showed how worried they were that he would be unable to cope living at home by himself. He was a little amused by their obvious relief that he had not chosen to live with any of them, and a little insulted that they were so sure he couldn't continue in his present lifestyle. He hadn't seriously considered moving out of his home, but he understood that he was now a problem—particularly for Pat, who lived closest to him. It was important that he show them that he could control his drinking and that he could take care of himself.

Harry called an employment agency and asked that they send over a housekeeper who could work from eleven in the morning until seven in the evening. A smiling Latina lady came the next day, and Harry tried to interview her but quickly found out that she spoke very little English. After much talking and using sign language, he thought she understood what was expected of her and hired her.

His next project was to get back into the social circle in the country club.

After Harry's retirement from business six years ago, Harry and Mary Ellen had enjoyed an active social life centered around the country club. Harry had organized two golfing groups, which met in the afternoon on Mondays and Wednesdays—times when there was minimal play on the golf course. He enjoyed playing in the matches and having a couple of beers with the men afterward. He and Mary Ellen also participated in a mixed doubles tennis game late in the afternoon on Thursday, followed by a leisurely dinner at the Sports Grill. Usually they were invited for bridge and dinner at a friend's house over the weekend, and once a week, they had friends in for dinner at their home. It was a relaxed and satisfying lifestyle.

Then, about two years ago, Harry's health problems had begun. His back caused him a lot of pain, sometimes immobilizing him for several weeks. His heart ailment also curtailed his physical activity at times. Several times he was hospitalized for electric-shock procedures to restore his heart to its normal rhythm.

Then Mary Ellen had been stricken by cancer, and he had gone through six months of emotional turmoil.

All told, Harry had enjoyed very little physical or social activity during the last eighteen months. His attempts to get back in the club social schedule and back to playing golf in September had been pretty dismal, but he was determined to try again.

For the next three weeks, Harry tried to re-establish himself in his old country-club group. He thought he might be accepted as a single man who could serve as an escort for the many widows around the club. He called Louise Williams a few times, but she was always busy. He gave a lovely dinner party at the club for five couples with whom he still had cordial relations and got Phyllis Conway, an attractive widow, as his date. But he never heard from them again, except for a couple of polite thank-you notes for the party. He tried to get back in with his old golfing friends and played a few times, but the pain in his back made it difficult for him to finish eighteen holes.

By the end of October, he was pretty discouraged, and when the Latina maid he had hired gave him notice that she was quitting, he was ready to throw in the towel. He started thinking more about the other options his children had suggested. Leaving home would be a big change, but maybe it was time for a change.

Harry opened the envelope Pat had given him and began reading the brochures about continuing-care communities. He also put in a call to Ed Strong to see if he had any ideas about getting live-in help for the beach house, in case he decided to go down there to live.

Ed Strong was a contemporary and close friend of Harry's son, George. He was one of a group of young teens Harry used to take on hunting trips to the duck club and on fishing trips in the bay. Ed was personable and a good companion, and Harry had grown very fond of him over the years. He wasn't much of a student and graduated from a local community college without much distinction. But he was very alert and possessed an acute business sense that some of his more educated friends lacked. Harry described him as a "used-car salesman with street smarts." After graduation, Ed had gone into the real-estate business on the eastern shore of Maryland, not far from the town of Cambridge. His business had grown slowly but steadily, and he was now well-known in commercial circles and was involved in many enterprises on the eastern shore.

When George moved away and Harry began to get older, he found the task of running and maintaining the duck club to be too much for him, so he leased the club to Ed in a long-term deal. It was a good move; Harry and George were always welcome whenever they wanted to hunt, and Ed made many improvements to the clubhouse and entered into a state wetlands project with the Maryland Environmental Agency that resulted in a dramatic improvement of the marshes around Chincoteague Bay and significantly improved the hunting at the duck club.

Ed gave him a list of possible couples who lived around the beach house and also raised some questions about the wisdom of such a move. The beach house was a great family retreat; spring, fall, and early summer were the times Harry's family generally came down to the bay. But the beach house was situated near the large, marshy areas at the mouth of the Pokomoke River, which were prime breeding grounds for flies and mosquitoes. July, August, and September were mostly hot and buggy—not fun months to live at the beach house.

Harry remembered being attacked by a swarm of mosquitoes on a summer day when he and George had been out in the marsh, building duck blinds. It had been pretty terrifying; thousands of mosquitoes covered their faces and hands, and the droning noise sounded like a small airplane. They were forced to run for the clubhouse to escape, and the duck club was in the same general area as the beach house. Some of the old watermen loved to tell stories about how big the mosquitoes got in that area. Harry particularly remembered a description by Roy Stevens, a retired market hunter, who fished with Harry occasionally. He said in his high, nasal twang that, by the end of summer, the mosquitoes got "so big they could stand flat-footed and screw a turkey."

Ed also pointed out that the beach house was pretty isolated in the winter months, which were generally cold, windy, and damp. The nearest hospital was in Salisbury, which was nearly forty miles away.

After his long conversation with Ed, Harry's enthusiasm for the beach house option had declined sharply, and he began to look more closely at the retirement communities. He visited some of the places Pat recommended.

There seemed to be two broad classifications: life care and continuing care. Life-care facilities generally charged a high monthly fee, which stayed the same whether you were in independent living units or in units requiring assisted-living care or skilled nursing. Continuing-care communities usually charged a lower fee for independent living and sharply increased fees for units requiring a higher level of care. In most cases, the incoming resident paid a substantial entrance fee that entitled him to live in the particular house or unit that he selected and then paid a monthly fee of four or five thousand dollars, which was supposed to cover all the services the facility offered.

The system was very confusing, and the concept of paying hundreds of thousands of dollars for a small house or apartment and having no ownership interest in it seemed almost fraudulent to Harry. On top of that, paying four of five thousand dollars per month for the rest of his life just to live in a unit for which he had already paid a big price did not sit well with Harry.

Money was very important to Harry. He had been born in 1930 and had thus lived through the Great Depression. His father had a midlevel job in the Department of Agriculture, and his mother taught first grade at the local elementary school, and they were able to hang onto their jobs throughout the thirties.

They lived in a comfortable row house in northwest Washington, and while their combined incomes were modest, they were better off than some of the prominent businessmen who suffered ruinous losses during those bleak and desperate years. Harry didn't remember much about the Depression, but it had a significant impact on Harry's character. He was a fiscal conservative and very uncomfortable with debt. It was the reason his business had never gotten bigger: he was waiting for the next calamity. Harry believed implicitly in Murphy's Law, which postulated that whatever can go wrong will go wrong. His conservative instincts had also affected the way he invested. When he sold his business at age seventy, he ended up with approximately $4 million in cash. He hired a very conservative investment advisor and, although he had listened to George describe investment opportunities that yielded high returns but with added risk, he very seldom took a flyer on anything involving much risk. So getting into a situation which involved paying a substantial entrance fee for something he would not own and then paying a heavy monthly service charge for the rest of his life was of great concern to Harry. He met with his lawyer and financial advisor many times before becoming convinced that he could afford it.

After looking over facilities in the Washington area and not finding any he liked, he decided to look at Bay Watch, which Pat had recommended. It was located on the eastern shore of Maryland, near Salisbury and not far from the beach house. It had a large central building that housed the clinic, the main dining room, a grill, and an activities center. Behind the main building were two three-story apartment houses connected to the main building by covered walkways. The independent-living villas were located about four hundred yards from the main building in four separate clusters. The newest cluster had the largest and most elaborate villas, but all were comfortable and well maintained.

The administration building, where Harry had his appointment, was unobtrusively located near the main entrance. He was greeted by an attractive, pleasant woman.

"Welcome to Bay Watch," she said.

"Thank you," answered Harry. "You have a fine-looking development here, and I like the area. It is close to a summer home I own, and I am hoping this might be a good place to settle down."

For the next two hours, Harry toured the "campus," as his guide called the 140 acres on which Bay Watch was situated. He was impressed. There was a state-of-the-art fitness center with an Olympic-sized swimming pool, an auditorium, and a well-equipped assisted-living and skilled-nursing facility. He thought one of the older villa locations was particularly attractive, since it overlooked a tidal creek and a heavily wooded area. He decided to put his name on the waiting list and made a deposit of $2,500.

By the time the meeting was through, it was early afternoon, and he was feeling pretty good on that fine mid-November day. He called Ed Strong and made an appointment to stop by his office on the way back to Washington. Ed sometimes appeared to be an old-fashioned snake-oil salesman, but Harry was fond of Ed and valued his advice and counsel.

When Harry drove up to Ed's office, which was located in a little brick building a few hundred yards off Route 50, he was greeted warmly.

"Always great to see you, Harry," Ed said, shaking his hand with a viselike grip.

"Let go of me, you ape!" said Harry, rubbing his hand. "You got that grip grabbing other people's money, didn't you?"

"Now, Harry, you know I don't do that. Actually, people do throw their money at me, and I keep trying to give it back. So what did you think of Bay Watch?"

"I liked it," he said. "Now what do you know about it?"

"Quite a lot. I sold them the land on which the newest residences are located, and I am on its board of directors."

"So what am I getting into here?" asked Harry. "I don't want to get involved with a shaky enterprise that collapses after I buy into it."

Ed explained that Bay Watch was a financially sound, conservatively operated facility backed by local eastern shore businessmen. It was operated by a nonprofit corporation and was unlikely to sell to an out-of-state corporation that owned multiple retirement communities and operated them in order to make more money for its stockholders.

"This will stay local, Harry," Ed explained. "Most of the directors are local businessmen like me, and having a bunch of affluent seniors in our community is good for business. You buy your cars here, eat at our restaurants, and shop at our stores, and your visitors stay in our inns and motels. It's a good choice, Harry."

Ed's comments reinforced Harry's initial judgment that, if he did make a move, this would be the place he would go, and he returned home feeling rather pleased with himself. While he had been engaged in researching and visiting the various continuing-care communities, subtle changes were taking place. He no longer felt lost and unappreciated; he still missed Mary Ellen, especially at night, but he was now absorbed by a new project. New challenges lay ahead if he decided to move to Bay Watch. He would be moving away from the metropolitan area of Washington, where he had lived all his life. He would be leaving his old friends, his doctors, and his clubs to begin a new and different lifestyle.

Would he like it? There would be more regulation and regimentation of his life and less independence. He would have to eat at certain defined times, and he would have to get permission to make any alteration to his house. How would that be? He had no friends at Bay Watch; he would have to make new friends and participate in different activities. Would his new neighbors accept him? These were troubling issues, but the excitement of dealing with them was gradually replacing the emotions of self-pity and despair that had caused his long bout with depression. He was also becoming less dependent on alcohol.

The morning after returning from Bay Watch, Harry went out in the backyard to work on his garden. He took his weeding hoe and cut out some of the summer annuals that had died during the heavy frost the previous week. He loved his garden and the familiar setting in his spacious backyard. He worked for about an hour and then sat down on a nearby bench to rest. It was a warm Indian-summer day in November, and most of his summer plants were dead or dying; it was time to dig them up and clear the space for a little winter fertilizing. He reflected on his life here in McLean and in this house, which he and Mary Ellen had called home for more than forty years. It had been a wonderful life, and they had raised three outstanding children. He had many happy memories of their life together … but his life had changed in the last several years.

He no longer played tennis or golf, and his back problems prevented him from taking long walks along the nature trails in the nearby parklands, which he had enjoyed so much after his retirement. It seemed clear that he was no longer part of the social activities at the country club, either. Part of that was his fault, because he had behaved so badly last September, but he also sensed that he wasn't the country-club type. He enjoyed the activities—tennis, golf, swimming—but he had no reverence for the club. The country club enjoyed a social prestige that few other clubs could match. To be a member gave a person social status, which was very important to many of the members. Harry didn't feel that way; since he couldn't engage in any of the athletic facilities, he had no urge to go to the club and hang around. If it weren't for Mary Ellen, he probably would not have been elected as a member.

At seventy-six, Harry was no longer middle-aged. He looked and felt old. Most people disliked being called old and came up with modifying terms like "senior" or "mature." Call it what you will, Harry was an old man now and well into the final stage of his life. This was how the world worked: everything born, hatched, or sprouted went through the same cycle of growth, maturity, reproduction, old age, and death. He looked around his garden. This was autumn; the plants, like Harry, had matured and were growing old, and soon they must die. There was nothing anyone could do to change that cycle, and Harry thought he might as well accept that he was in the last stage of his life and make the best of it.

Harry called Bay Watch and asked how soon he could move in if he decided to buy into the community. He was told there was a villa in the section he liked that would be available in April of the next year. He had several friends in the real-estate business and decided to call Dick Stevens and tell him to put his house on the market.

"Time to make a change, Dick," he explained. "Do you think it will sell quickly?"

"I hope so, Harry," said Dick, "but the market is very soft right now. Prices are falling, and there is talk of a housing bubble, so we better get started right away."

Chapter 6:
THE HUNT

THE NEXT SEVERAL weeks were very frustrating for Harry. He had to downsize drastically, since the villas in Bay Watch were much smaller than his home. Many e-mails between Harry and his children helped him determined what he would keep, what the children wanted, and what he would have to sell. The process was depressing; he would have to part with many tables and chairs, bedroom sets, and his favorite leather sofa in the family room. It was like leaving old friends, and he didn't like it. Then there was the negotiation for a villa in the location he wanted. Bay Watch wanted him to pay the entry fee immediately; otherwise he might lose the home he had selected. But Harry wasn't going to do that. There was some talk about a real-estate bubble, and he was much too conservative to buy into the community before he sold his home. After a period of negotiations, the two parties entered into an uneasy compromise in which the care center would hold his villa for six months, and he would increase his deposit to $15,000, which would not be refundable.

While Harry was deeply involved with his preparations to sell his home and move to Bay Watch, Ed Strong called and invited him to a duck hunt at the clubhouse on Johnson's Island.

"You need a break, Harry," he urged. "George is coming down, and it will be good for you." Harry accepted immediately. The trip dates were set for Tuesday, December 10, to Thursday, December 12. Ed had a party of six, including Harry and George, and it was agreed that they would assemble around three o'clock on Tuesday afternoon at the boathouse on Rattlesnake Landing, an old commercial fishing dock. Charlie, the guide and caretaker Ed had hired, would then take them to the island in his boat.

When Harry arrived at the landing, he found George already there, talking to Charlie. They loaded his gun and equipment on the boat and waited for Ed. He arrived a few minutes later with his brother, Chris, and two of Ed's business associates. Charlie very efficiently stowed the gear of the other four men in the boat and then carefully packed the food and beverages Ed and Chris had brought in a dry place. By four thirty, they were at the clubhouse.

It was a relaxed and congenial group. Ed and George were the cooks. Chris, who had the reputation for being a deadly wing shot, took care of building the fires and lighting the kerosene lanterns. Although the house was equipped with a generator system with enough power to run electric lights and a pump installed in the indoor bathroom, the soft glow of the kerosene lanterns was more suited to the charm of an old-time hunting camp, and Harry and Ed liked it that way. There was only one bathroom in the clubhouse, but there was also a one-holer outhouse that Harry always used because he said the odors the other hunters generated in the bathroom were so overwhelming that the outhouse seemed like a pleasant refuge.

Harry loved the excitement of preparing for the hunt: taking out the guns, checking the mechanisms, and setting out the ammunition and warm parkas they would use in the morning. This was all part of the ritual he enjoyed so much. So was the conversation. He knew all of the hunters were well-educated family men with responsible jobs and were reserved and well-spoken—at least until they left the boathouse at Rattlesnake Landing and embarked on the mile-and-a-half trip across open water. It seemed they shed the veneer of civilization and parked it in the boathouse, because when they arrived at Johnson's Island, they had morphed into good ol' rednecks. Four-letter words became more frequent, and the conversation shared while they sat around the fire before dinner was pretty basic and earthy. By the third round of drinks, the main topic of interest centered around women and included many lurid testimonies regarding sexual prowess.

"Hey, Harry," Chris called, "tell us about how it was in the olden days. I bet you were a horny old bastard."

Harry laughed. "What you boys are going to learn, sooner than you think, is that sex is an overrated indoor sport; it is nowhere near as satisfying as taking a good crap!" This brought loud protestations from the younger men, along with many stories of unusual (and unlikely) sexual events and conquests.

After a delicious dinner prepared by George and Ed, the poker game was organized. Each of the men bought $20 worth of chips, and the game went on until one person had won all the money. The victor then had the honor of placing the $120 in a coffee can for the cleanup crew who came in and cleaned the clubhouse after the hunters left. Cleaning up the mess created by six hunters resembled the labors of Hercules, and the crew earned every dime of the donation.

Harry always did his best to lose quickly, so he could get to bed and fall asleep before the younger men got into the bunk room and started snoring. But that strategy was not entirely successful, because he had to get up several times during the night to relieve himself. The nocturnal noises emitted through the nose and mouth, and other orifices, by five healthy young males who had drunk too much whisky defied description. Harry wondered if one or two of them were about to strangle on their own windpipes.

The morning began at five when the hunters had a snack of doughnuts and coffee and gathered around the fire to put on warm clothes and wait for Harry.

"Where is he?" asked one of Ed's friends.

"He's in the outhouse, taking his morning constitutional," replied Ed. "He'll be ready in a few minutes. He loves getting out in the marsh before sunup."

Chris and Harry were assigned to a blind on a small pond about a quarter of a mile from the clubhouse. Chris went on ahead to set out the decoys. As Harry walked down the path through scrubby pine woods, he paused near the edge of the marsh. It was just shy of 6:45 a.m. and still dark with the beginning of a pink slash in the east. He listened to the wind and the faint call of a hunting owl; off in the distance, a dog was barking, and overhead he heard the mournful "herrr-onk" of geese moving out of the bay and into fields where they would feed. He felt alone and at peace. He was aware that time was running out for him, and he savored this moment of stillness before dawn; he had a strange feeling of detaching and becoming an integral part of his surroundings.

Then he heard Chris splashing around in the pond, setting out decoys; the spell was broken, and he started wading in the marsh toward the blind. The walk in the marsh was not long, but even so, Harry had a tough time negotiating the holes and extricating himself from the thick, heavy mud that clung to his waders. Chris had the decoys all set out when Harry finally stumbled into the blind. He stood up and surveyed the marsh and the decoy spread. They would be hunting marsh ducks, which normally overshot the decoys and landed upwind of them, so Chris had set out most of the mallards and black duck stools downwind, with two oversized birds right in front of the blind. The setup looked very realistic, and the decoys looked as if they were feeding on the pond weed, which was very thick that fall. Harry was particularly fond of his black duck decoys. The large decoys had been handmade by some of the master decoy carvers who had flourished right after World War II. Three had been done by Ira Hudson of Chincoteague, Virginia, and two by Madison Mitchell of Havre de Grace, Maryland. The symmetry of design, the graceful curve of the neck and head, and the way they sat on the water, bobbing in the wind, made them stand out among the others in the set.

Harry had purchased them from a dealer about the time he had built the clubhouse and paid $300 for the five. It was an uncharacteristic extravagance, but he was fascinated at how these rough old watermen could fashion these remarkable images of ducks from a block of wood using mostly hand tools. In addition to being beautiful decoys, Harry thought they were pieces of art. In recent years the market for hand-carved decoys had increased rapidly, and Ed Strong estimated Harry could get several thousand dollars for them if he wanted to sell.

It was an exciting morning; Harry loved the pungent smell of the marsh and the noises coming from birds and small animals as the day was breaking. He could hear the shirr of wings beating overhead and the sounds of loons calling on the bay. As the sky brightened, he glimpsed small knots of ducks flying around the marsh, looking for a place to land. The feeling of anticipation was overwhelming. This might be his last hunt, and he hoped the ducks would fly.

And fly they did. The morning was cold and windy, with a hint of snow in the air and, as the visibility increased, he was able to see swarms of ducks coming in off the bay to seek shelter in the marsh. The men were ready when sunrise came: guns loaded; duck calls handy; and Sky, Chris's young black Labrador, perched on her seat, poised for action. Out of nowhere, two mallards dropped out of the sky and swept over the decoys. Chris dropped both of them with two shots.

"Not bad," observed Harry. "I can see why they call you 'the assassin.'"

"Just dumb luck," said Chris, "and now we're going to get you a duck."

"That won't be easy," grumbled Harry. "We only have three or four seconds to get up, aim the gun, and shoot. By the time I get off my ass, the ducks are half a mile away."

Although many opportunities arose, and Harry did manage to get off a couple of shots, he didn't hit anything. By nine thirty, Chris had his limit, and the ducks had pretty much settled down and stopped flying. Harry waited outside the blind while Chris picked up the decoys. Harry did not know what caused him to look up at that particular moment, but some instinct pushed his alert button, and he looked up just as five big, black ducks—the wariest birds on the marsh—with their wings set were about to land in the pond, even though Chris was standing there picking up the decoys. Harry threw up his gun and fired; a big, black drake folded up and fell into the marsh with a loud thump. Sky was on it instantly and brought it to Harry.

"Great shot, Harry!" Chris shouted.

"Were you surprised?" asked Harry.

"Yes," admitted Chris.

"So was I," said Harry. "Why would those ducks try to land in the pond with you right there in the middle of the pond?"

"That's how those birds act sometimes. Most of the time, they will spook if you blink your eye, but sometimes they make up their mind to land, and they'll do it even if you are in plain sight, waving at them."

At breakfast, after a round of Bloody Marys, Harry told the group about his miraculous shot and the strange way the black ducks decoyed with Chris in the pond.

"But why did you only shoot once?" inquired Ed. "You said there were five of them ready to pitch in."

"Are you kidding?" snorted Harry. "I was so surprised when I saw that bird drop, I was almost paralyzed." The other hunters told of their experiences; nearly all had gotten their limit of four ducks. Most were mallards and wigeon, but there were also a few black ducks and pintail mixed in the bag. Altogether, twenty of the best game birds that fly hung on the walls of the clubhouse; it was a very good morning shoot.

The afternoon hunting was typically not very good on the marsh, so they opted not to hunt in the afternoon. They were pretty close to their daily limit, and it was also good to let the birds get back in the marsh and settle down for the night without being disturbed. Some of the hunters, including Harry, took naps; others worked around the clubhouse making minor repairs and getting out the decoys they would use Thursday morning. Later in the afternoon, the men cut some brush and rode out in Charlie's boat to some small outer islands that Ed had acquired, where they had several shore blinds for hunting the big water-diving ducks. These were mainly Greater Scaup, which the local watermen called broadbills, and canvasbacks, which had been making a recent comeback after years being on the no-hunt list. At sunset they finished work on the blinds and returned to the clubhouse.

Ed and George cut up some duck breasts, grilled them for about five minutes over a hot fire, and served them on crackers as appetizers. They were delicious and went very well with scotch whisky. The conversation, while spirited, was more subdued than the previous night. The men had been up since five o'clock and had spent many hours sitting out in the cold marsh and brushing up the shore blinds on the bay, so they were tired. No poker game materialized after dinner, and Harry turned in early and fell asleep almost immediately .

At five the next morning, Harry had to drag himself up and into his clothes. He felt as if he could sleep another twelve hours, but he didn't want to miss a shot at the big-water ducks.

About forty-five years before, when he had first started hunting in Chincoteague Bay, there were still large flocks of broadbills and canvasbacks that came down late in the season in big bunches containing three or four hundred ducks. The technique of hunting them was different from marsh-duck shooting. Usually they flew over the decoys at high speed, and there were normally fifty or more ducks in the flock, so it was hard to pick one out, get on it, and lead it sufficiently. More times than he would admit, Harry had picked out a bird and seen one drop about fifteen feet behind the one he was aiming at. It was exciting and very difficult shooting. Over the past thirty years, the habitat of the eastern flyway had changed, and the big water ducks no longer came into the bay in such large numbers, but there were still enough left for several days of good hunting, and the game refuges around Johnson Island, which Ed had encouraged, brought the birds close to the hunters' blinds.

At six thirty, all the hunters got into Charlie's big work boat and set out for the shore blinds. It was very windy, with gusts up to thirty knots, and the ice-cold spray drenched Harry a couple of times on the way out, but his parka was water repellent, and he kept it buttoned up, so the water didn't get inside and get his clothes wet. The sunrise was spectacular; dark, ominous clouds went scudding downwind as the sky turned from pale pink to a flaming orange color. Plenty of activity swirled around the islands as small strings of butterballs came in to seek shelter in the lee of the islands and several large bunches of broadbills passed them high overhead. The shore blinds were larger than the marsh blinds and easily accommodated three people. The wind was northeast, and the blinds were situated on the south shore of the islands, so the wind came from behind and from the left. When the divers decoyed, they usually landed downwind of the decoy set instead of flying over the decoys, as the marsh ducks did. So this time, the set was upwind of the blind, leaving the space in front of the blind as an inviting place to land. But wild ducks almost never are predictable, and they had seen a lot of blinds where bad things happened during their long migration from Canada and had become wary of those funny-looking boxes with bushes all over them. So they usually made a couple of passes to look over the decoys and then come roaring downwind, at full speed, over the set to land about a quarter of a mile away. The trick was to judge when they were making the last pass and blaze away, hoping to hit something.

They set out thirty-six decoys at each blind, and Charlie put his boat out about 300 yards in the bay between the blinds, where he could watch them and pick up any crippled ducks the dogs couldn't get. This time Harry hunted with his son, George, and Ed. There was a hole in the front of the blind with a platform for the dog, and Ed had his big male Labrador, Buster, sitting on the seat and ready to go. At about seven thirty, they heard some shots from the other blind and saw three ducks fall. The wind had kicked up quite a heavy sea where the ducks fell, but little Sky, Chris's dog, negotiated the waves with apparent ease and retrieved all three.

"I was a little worried about her," commented Harry. "She seems so young and small compared to Buster; I wondered how she would do out here."

"These dogs are all water dogs and great hunters," replied Ed. "I think they are a little too compact and big in the chest for show dogs, but that extra room in the chest makes them bob around like corks, even in the roughest weather."

"Look out!" whispered George urgently. "Here they come!"

"My God!" whispered Harry. "Look at them!" About a hundred

broadbills were coming in off the big bay water from the east, sweeping in close to the shoreline of their island. The birds were riding the wind and going very fast, but they saw the decoy set and cut their wings about fifty yards past the blind and swung around for another look; this time they passed a little closer. Nobody in the blind moved; the ducks swung around again, and this time it looked as if they were going to fly right into the blind.

"Take 'em," said Ed, rising out of his seat. As the ducks came by, doing at least sixty miles per hour, they were so close that Harry could see the big, broad, blue bills and the yellow eyes on the big drakes. He got off three shots, and so did Ed and George.

"I can't believe this!" exclaimed George, gesturing toward the water. "We didn't kill a single duck. Nine shots ... and zilch!"

Harry shook his head. "I guess we better get Chris over here."

Ed chuckled softly. "They will really razz us when we get back to the clubhouse. I hope we get another chance."

Half an hour later, they got their second chance. This time the flock was much smaller, maybe twenty to twenty-five ducks, and they got five, which Buster enthusiastically retrieved. And just before they were ready to quit, another thrilling flock came out of nowhere and buzzed over the decoys. The roar from the wings of the large flock sounded almost like an airplane, and the unmistakable white they showed on their backs when they turned identified them as canvasbacks, the most prized waterfowl on the eastern seaboard.

This time, the hunters kept their cool and managed to drop four out of the flock. *Another memorable morning*, thought Harry. If this were to be his last hunt, he would go out in style.

After lunch they said good-bye and gave Charlie a generous tip. Ed took the ducks, all properly tagged and amounting to four short of their two-day limit. He said he would take them to a place nearby where they would be plucked, dressed, quick-frozen, and held until they wanted them. It had been a delightful hunt and had included some quality time for Harry with his son, George. He returned home feeling invigorated and resumed his work on preparing his house for sale with renewed energy.

Chapter 7:
MOVING ON

GETTING HIS HOUSE ready to sell was a lot more complicated than Harry anticipated. There was a lot to do. Dick Stevens insisted that some exterior painting was essential, even though it was the wrong season to paint. Also, the plumbing in some of the bathrooms had to be upgraded and the interior walls painted with more modern colors. Roofers were called in to patch up several places that were leaking, and some concrete contractors were hired to waterproof the basement floor. For nearly a month, continuous activity buzzed and pounded and sawed around his house, and Harry barely noticed the Christmas season. He went up to Baltimore for a few days to have Christmas with Pat and her family, and the latter were surprised to see that Harry was so fully occupied with the process of moving that he showed no signs of stress over being alone during the first Christmas season after Mary Ellen passed away.

By mid-January, Harry was ready to sell. Dick wanted him to wait for another six weeks, until the end of winter, and also wanted the kitchen upgraded at a cost of $35,000, but Harry refused. He had already spent close to $20,000, and he wasn't going to spend any more. His house was a large, spacious home with over half an acre of land in one of the choice locations in the Washington area, and he was confident that it would sell easily. After some haggling, he and Dick agreed on an asking price of $1,450,000.

By this time, the credit and financial crisis had deepened, and one of the hottest real estate seller's markets had morphed into a buyer's market. Weeks went by with no serious offers. Harry had to endure the embarrassment of having his lovely home picked apart by critical prospects who were bottom shopping. In the end, he had only one serious prospect who really wanted his home, but they were very conscious of their position of strength and made many demands and revisions in the contract of sale. At one point, Dick suggested Harry take it off the market and try to rent it, but Harry was very much opposed to entering into a contract with Bay Watch before he sold his home, and by this time, he was committed to moving as soon as he could, so they endured the long negotiations and finally settled on a price of $975,000—a reduction of $475,000 from his asking price. It was a bitter pill to swallow, but the ordeal was over, and Harry now had just forty-five days to get out of the house and turn over possession to the new owners.

Harry felt a lot of pressure to get things marked for the movers to take to Bay Watch and decide what would go into storage for later distribution to his family, and one of the most vexing problems he faced was the lack of cooperation from his children in picking up the items that were too valuable and too fragile for the movers to handle. They had to be individually wrapped and carefully packed. Some valuable pieces of jewelry and silver needed to be picked up and distributed among the three families, along with some very rare and valuable china sets and figurines. He kept asking when his children would pick these things up, and they kept putting him off.

One evening, as Harry sat glaring at three sets of antique china, two complete sets of sterling silver flatware, and various tea services and silver pieces Mary Ellen had accumulated over the years, he got to thinking about the selfishness of his children and their insensitivity to the time pressure he was working under.

"Christ," he muttered to himself, "these things are worth a lot of money, and I am trying to give them away, and none of the kids are interested enough to come and pack them up and take them away." He poured himself a generous shot of MacAllan single malt and thought about what he should do. After several more scotches, he thought he had a plan that would attract their attention.

The next morning, he called McCall, one of the premier auction houses in the Washington area, and asked them to send someone over to look at some items he was thinking of selling. When the appraiser came out, Harry showed him the set of Meissen china and asked him how much he thought it would bring.

The appraiser looked a little startled and asked, "Do you really want to sell this? It is a very nice set of eight place settings; doesn't anyone in the family want it?"

"Apparently not," answered Harry. "What do you think I should get?"

"I would say at least $4,000 and perhaps more."

"What's my cut?" asked Harry.

"Our fee is 15 percent of the gross sales price," he answered. "You keep the rest."

They made arrangements for a pickup time and set an auction date of about ten days later. After the packers came and packed the Meissen and took them to the McCall warehouse, Harry called the family and told them what he had done and suggested that they arrange to have the other items picked up if they really wanted them. This brought a flurry of angry phone calls from Pat, Gwen, and Jean, George's wife, telling him he had no right to sell such a precious heirloom. They were all busy with their daily lives, they said, and would get over to pack up the china and jewelry as soon as they could. Harry told them that was fine, but they better do it quickly.

As Harry anticipated, the rest of the valuable items were picked up quickly by Pat and stored in a secure storage area to be divided up later, and he turned his attention to making some renovations in his Bay Watch residence. The place he selected needed some repairs to the exterior, and he added a patio and had the maintenance department install a garden where he could grow plants and vegetables. The occupancy date was set for May 10, and his date for surrendering occupancy of his old house was May 8.

The whole family came down to help with the move. George and Peter, Pat's husband, were the technicians arranging for broadband internet service and hooking up his computer, his slimline TV, and his stereo sound system; Pat and Jean supervised the move from his former home in McLean; and Gwen strode around the new residence barking out orders to the movers like a veteran top sergeant. The process took two days, but it was done. Just a little more than eight months after the memorable meeting at the Metropolitan Club, Harry had given up his old home, moved away from the area where he had spent all his life, and was now installed in a new place with a decidedly different lifestyle. He felt both apprehensive and excited; this was a big change, and he was surprised at how few regrets he had about leaving the Washington area.

George broke the silence and suggested that it was time for a little celebration.

"Let's have a big shot of your best scotch, Dad," he said. "I think we've earned it."

"Yes, we have," agreed Harry. "Now, where the hell did we put the whisky?"

"It's in the cupboard above the bookcase," said Pat, pointing to a two-door cabinet built into the wall. "But it's locked."

"Well, where's the key?" asked Harry, beginning to feel that he had lost control in his own home.

"I've got it," replied Gwen with a smug smile. "I didn't want the movers helping themselves, so I locked it up and put the key in a safe place." She reached inside her sweater and took the key out from her bra. "Here you are—nice and warm."

Harry laughed heartily. His younger daughter was a real live one. "That's a strange place to hide a key," he commented.

"Oh, I knew where it was," said George with an exaggerated leer at sister. "Her sweater is so tight I could see the key outlined perfectly."

"You haven't changed at all, George," said Gwen amiably. "You are still disgusting."

Harry opened the cabinet and poured them all a generous portion of his prize eighteen-year-old MacAllan scotch whisky.

"Thanks, kids," he said, raising his glass. "I couldn't possibly have made this move without you."

"It took a little time, Father," said Pat, "and a little persuasion from us, but in the end, this was your decision and your choice, and we are all very proud of you."

"This place was your discovery, Pat," he said, "and when I get settled in, you and the family must come down for a visit."

"We'll do that, Dad ... and I know if you don't like it, we'll hear about it."

"That you will, dear," he said, giving her cheek a warm kiss.

Chapter 8:
BAY WATCH

Living at Bay Watch was very different from Harry's lifestyle at McLean. His house was small compared to his former home. He had two moderately sized bedrooms, a small kitchen, a good-sized living room, two bathrooms, and a powder room. There was also a small family room where he kept his desk in the corner and his slimline TV mounted on a wall. He got his own breakfast; lunch was from eleven thirty to one o'clock; dinner was from five thirty to seven thirty; and absolutely all activities had ceased by eight thirty at night.

After the turmoil and emotional strain of moving, Harry was exhausted. The first few nights, he slept pretty well, and he spent the days getting familiar with his new home and learning the routine of living in a continuing-care community. But very soon, the reality of his new life began to sink in. He did not know a single person at Bay Watch. He did not possess the easy social skills that Mary Ellen had used so effectively in establishing themselves in Washington society, so his attempts to get acquainted were awkward and initially unsuccessful. He began to have doubts about his decision to leave Washington, and he returned to alcohol to help him blot out the present and bring back happy memories of his life in the Washington area. But the past moments of happiness he relived carried with them a sting. Along with the remembrance of past achievements came the painful realization that those happy days had been in another phase of his life that was now over.

During the process of moving, Harry had been very busy. He had had no time for introspection or depression; his thoughts were focused on the move, and his reliance on alcohol diminished. He still enjoyed two drinks of scotch before dinner, but there were no nightcaps or midday drinks during that period. As he struggled to adjust to his new lifestyle, Harry began to analyze his drinking problem. He had an addiction to alcohol; it was a mood modifier, and he craved it when he was lonely and depressed. When he used alcohol to excess, his demeanor changed; he became surly and outspoken and, in general, a pain in the ass to his friends. He would have to do something about his drinking if he were to succeed in establishing himself at Bay Watch, and he was determined to give it his best shot.

Harry struggled for a while, but eventually got his drinking under control and tried hard to focus on the challenges that lay ahead. Fortunately, learning to live in Bay Watch did not allow much time for reflection; getting started in a new lifestyle turned out to be a difficult challenge. Eating dinner and lunch alone made him feel embarrassed and self-conscious. He asked to be seated at an open table, so he could meet more people, and he made some nodding acquaintances that way. There were also resident committees whose job was to help new arrivals like Harry assimilate into the community. They invited him for cocktails before dinner with a small group of his neighbors so that he could get better acquainted. The process was slow and somewhat discouraging, but he was making progress and beginning feel more comfortable in his new surroundings.

Like in so many retirement communities, the women at Bay Watch outnumbered the men. At first, Harry thought most of the women were pretty sad looking; they were either emaciated or too fat, and they all looked old. The men he met seemed nice enough, but they too looked old, and some had serious mobility problems caused by arthritis or other more debilitating diseases. He joined the fitness club and a duplicate bridge group where he got to know some of his fellow residents pretty well. One of his new friends was Jim Pyle, a retired Foreign Service officer who had lived in many exotic places in the world. He had been ambassador to two obscure West African countries that had become of some importance because of new oil discoveries. Jim explained that the high-profile ambassador appointments usually went to big contributors of the ruling political party who had zero experience, while professionals like Jim were generally sent to Africa.

Jim's wife was a hatchet-faced, severe-looking old broad, and Harry didn't like her when they first met. But after they got better acquainted, he found she had a dry sense of humor and a keen intellect, and when she smiled, it lit up her whole personality. He became very fond of the couple, and they all ate dinner together frequently.

As he got to know them better, Harry found the residents to be interesting and friendly. Some had serious health issues, but they were coping as best they could, and he heard very little complaining or discussion of symptoms and illnesses by people who "enjoyed poor health." They were not living in the past, telling stories about themselves; they were living in the present. There may not be much of a future for some of them, but they were enjoying today. The attitude was infectious, and for the first time in several years, Harry could feel a sense of optimism growing inside of him.

Many of the residents had interesting backgrounds. Harry once remarked to Kathy Douglas, one of the many feisty widows living in Bay Watch, that he enjoyed hunting and had built a rustic lodge on an island in Chincoteague Bay. She asked if Harry had ever hunted big game, and when Harry said no, she told him that she had gone on a moose hunt during her honeymoon. It seemed she had married a somewhat eccentric Norwegian immigrant who loved the great North Woods of Canada. So he had taken his new bride way back in the bush of northeastern Ontario to a primitive hunting camp, where they shot a moose the first day. Together they field-dressed the animal, quartered it, and packed the meat out of the woods to the camp, where they engaged in the highly romantic occupation of butchering it, hanging it to properly age, and finally bringing about three hundred pounds of fresh moose meat out of Canada and back to civilization.

"It was some honeymoon, Harry," Kathy explained. "That moose weighed about a thousand pounds, and when we gutted him, I can tell you truthfully that we were standing up to our knees in blood."

"I believe you," muttered Harry, looking dazed.

He later found out that the marriage to the Norwegian gentleman had been short-lived and that Bill Douglas, her second husband, had been a much longer-lasting and conventional (if less exciting) husband and had just recently died.

Another of Harry's new friends was a neat, compact man with a scholarly manner and conservative appearance. Harry judged he was a retired professor or schoolteacher. It turned out that David Kimball was a former Navy carrier fighter pilot, having graduated from the Naval Academy in the class of '43. He had seen action in three wars, and when he retired, he had undertaken a second career with military intelligence and become the head "spook" (as David called it) in the Hong Kong station. After retiring again, he still was not done. He went to law school, passed the bar exam, and practiced law for ten years in Salisbury. Somewhere along the way, after his wife passed away, David met Cherry Roberts, a recent widow, and a lovely geriatric romance bloomed. Cherry was a charming, vivacious woman in her mid eighties with snow-white hair and a wonderful sense of humor. She also possessed that streak of femininity that some women never lose. There was definitely a boy-girl attraction between them, and they were devoted to each other.

Harry was also invited to join a men's bridge club that had some colorful members. One member, George Atkins, held himself out as a retired farmer. But he was also the best bridge player in the group, and Harry wondered how he had learned to play bridge if he spent all his time plowing the fields. After some diligent cross-examination, he found out that George had been a director on the local bank board and a director and part owner of a good-sized construction company. George may have done some serious farming in the past, but he was an astute businessman and quite wealthy, although he didn't want anyone to know it. Others boasted (or downplayed) equally successful and exciting backgrounds, and Harry was beginning to think his career at a small business was, perhaps, the dullest in the community.

Harry's other bridge group, the duplicate bridge game, was much more serious, with good players who had a real love of the game. It met once a week and was very competitive, requiring lots of concentration. Harry was pretty bad at first, but with the help of the other players, he had soon improved his game so that he could play at their level most of the time.

Harry acquired a regular bridge partner, an eighty-one-year-old widow named Joan Stanton. She was a good player and a good instructor, and as they got accustomed to playing with each other, they became quite competitive, winning some of the competitions a few times. Joan was small and round, with a face so full of wrinkles it reminded Harry of a dried-up prune. But she had sparkling brown eyes and soft white hair that she kept well-groomed. Her voice was lovely and soft, with a hint of South Carolina in it. She smiled a lot, and Harry thought she was an attractive woman; he felt some vague romantic vibes when they played together. They became good friends and often ate dinner together, were invited together for cocktails, and went out together to local concerts and the theater. It made Harry's social life much more enjoyable.

He often thought of his old friends in Washington, living as long as they were able in their old homes and trying to enjoy the same lifestyle they had during their active years. He supposed they were happy, but he was very glad he had been enough of a realist to admit that the old times were over for him and had moved on to a new phase in his life.

Bay Watch was near a local community college that was part of the Maryland State University system. It was small and attracted most of its students from the eastern shore of Maryland. Some retired teachers and professors could be found among its faculty, and it offered a continuing-education program for seniors. Harry was introduced to it by one of his neighbors, Jay Osborn, who was a retired English literature professor and taught courses on English literature in the senior program at Salisbury

State. Jay was a wonderful teacher and an enthusiastic supporter of the program.

.In mid-June Harry signed up for a course on global warming, taught by a retired physics professor. Harry had heard many conflicting theories about global warming and thought it would be instructive to hear from someone who might know something about the subject. The seminar met on Mondays and Thursdays from ten a.m. until noon and lasted six weeks. Harry always packed a sandwich and a can of beer in a cooler and, after class, ate lunch in a lovely park near the campus. It was a restful place, and he enjoyed watching the people and reflecting on what he had learned in class.

Global warming was a pretty complicated subject. There had always been climate changes; undisputed evidence existed of recurring cycles of warmth, during which the oceans rose beyond the current levels, followed by ice ages, when glaciers covered most of North America and seas retreated, and all of this had happened before man entered the equation. The professor said the prevailing scientific thought was that these cyclic changes had something to do with the earth's orbit around the sun. Harry thought this was an interesting theory but difficult to prove. These cycles lasted many thousands of years, so observations had to be based on geological data; it wasn't like gravity, where the effects of the phenomenon were immediately available and the evidence was so overwhelming that the phenomenon in question was no longer a theory but a law.

What really interested him was the relatively recent introduction of man-made gases into the atmosphere. He learned that the world consumed about 88 million 55-gallon barrels of oil each day and about 10 billion tons of coal per year. He remembered from his high-school biology class that matter is not destroyed when it is burned; it just changes its form. Mostly the consumed fossil fuels found their way into the atmosphere as carbon-dioxide gas. That was a lot of gas; such excessive pollution was a new factor that hadn't existed when the older warming and cooling cycles existed. It was an interesting concept, and Harry was enjoying the course.

During the first few weeks of his course, Harry noticed an old woman painting a landscape near a brook that ran through the park. He was curious about what she was painting, because there didn't seem to be anything unusual about the landscape, and yet she seemed to be working very hard at it and staring intently at something in the brook. He didn't know her and felt he would be intruding if he came up and asked what she was painting, so he pretended to walk casually by and sneaked a look at the canvas. She was painting a scene where the brook ran over some rocks, making a pretty waterfall with trees in the background, and some trash cans on the near side of the brook. What struck him as strange was that the scene in the painting didn't look like what he saw in front of her.

After several weeks of this ritual of espionage, Harry saw that she was nearly finished with the painting, and he was determined to ask about it before she went away. As he walked up to her, she turned to him and smiled broadly.

"Hello, there," she said. "You have been looking at my picture, haven't you?" He was a little startled by her warm and direct manner.

"Why, yes, I have," he said. "I have been following your progress for several weeks now, but I didn't think you noticed."

"I always notice when attractive men are looking at me." She laughed at Harry's obvious embarrassment. "It's almost finished now, and I'm glad you came over to speak to me."

"I am curious as to what you find so interesting here. You've been working very hard on it for a long time; do you come here every day?"

"No," she replied. "I come only on Monday and Thursday. How about you—do you come here often?"

"We must be on the same schedule," he said with a smile. "I come on Monday and Thursday, too, after my global warming class over at State. I pack a lunch and have it here in the park after class is over. That's when I started watching you."

She smiled and took his hand, leading him close to the easel. "Let's look at it together," she said, continuing to hold his hand. "What do you think?"

"I don't know much about art," protested Harry. "I'm an engineer, and engineers don't get involved with art."

"Maybe I could teach you," she said, giving his hand a squeeze. "That's what I do: I'm an art-history instructor at State and teach a class on Monday and Thursday mornings. Now tell me what you see," she said, still holding his hand.

"Well," said Harry, "your picture doesn't look like what I see. The brook over there is so pretty and bright, and your painting is kind of sad."

"But don't you see the man-made scars on that pretty brook?" she asked.

"No, I don't," answered Harry.

"Those huge trash barrels on the bank are an eyesore and an invitation to throw things in the brook. Look at those old, rusty cans on the edge of the brook ... and that awful plastic bag plastered on the rock on the waterfall. It's hideous! And the trees! Can't you see they are dying? Their leaves are turning brown, and they are falling on the ground, and it is only early July. Pollution is all around us, and nobody is doing anything about it. They don't even notice—like you!" She had drawn herself up very erect, and her remarkable hazel eyes were flashing.

"Don't hit me," he said, throwing up his hands in mock surrender. "I guess you are making a statement with that picture."

"I'm sorry," she said with a shake of her head. "I sometimes get carried away—something to do with my Mediterranean ancestors, I guess."

"I would love to know more about art and pollution," he said, this time taking her hand. "Will you come and have lunch with me next Monday? I'll bring sandwiches and a bottle of wine."

They talked for a few more minutes, until she said she had to go. She agreed to meet him for lunch and then left. As he was driving home, Harry had a vague feeling they had met before. Those big, sparkling eyes with a hint of mischief in them seemed familiar, but he couldn't think how they could have met, since he didn't know any artists. One thing was clear: Harry was looking forward to next Monday. He suddenly remembered he didn't know who she was.

"For God's sake," he muttered aloud, "I forgot to ask her name."

Chapter 9:
VERA

VERA ANTONELLI HARRISON was in an upbeat mood when she walked into her small condominium, located near the Salisbury State University campus. She was feeling better than she had for many months. She had finally met the man who had been watching her paint for the last several weeks, and she was sure she knew who he was. She had flirted with him a little and knew he was interested.

"Harry Walker," she said out loud, "you don't look like such a big stud now." Indeed he seemed a little melancholy and eager to talk with her. She wondered what had brought him here and where he was living. Vera was sure he didn't recognize her, but why did she recognize him? Harry had been two years ahead of her at Wilson High School, and they had dated only three or four times. She liked him well enough, but he was much too full of himself to suit her, so there had been no long-term relationship. She would find out more about him on Monday, but right now she had some other tasks to do.

Vera spent three afternoons a week working in a small art gallery in town. Salisbury was not home to an active art market, so there was not much activity in the shop, but she liked the owner, and it gave her a place to hang her paintings and store her art materials. So she had taken the job at a minimal salary that gave the owner, Elizabeth Leroque, some free time to see her family or go shopping. Vera put the painting and easel in her 1998 Honda and drove to the shop.

Elizabeth greeted her warmly. "Hi, Vera. How's the picture coming?"

"Just about done," replied Vera, unwrapping the canvas and spreading it on the table. "I think I will frame it tomorrow. Can I hang it in the display window?"

"I guess it will attract some attention," said Elizabeth, eyeing the painting critically. "I can't say it makes me feel uplifted, though. What have you done to our pretty little park? It looks like a junkyard."

"I didn't change the landscape very much," replied Vera. "I just emphasized the things most people don't notice. I enlarged the trash cans and added some junk spilling out over the top, and I enlarged those rusty cans in the brook, so you can't miss them. Then I painted the plastic bag in the waterfall a dirty yellow green, so it looks like it's filled with putrid material. It stands out, so your eye comes to that as well as the pretty waterfall."

"What about those trees?" asked Elizabeth. "Last time I looked, they were green and healthy, but in your picture, they look as if they're about to fall over."

"Those trees are not healthy, Elizabeth," said Vera. "The leaves are curling around the edges and turning brown. A lot of them have fallen on the ground. All I did was emphasize the browns in the leaves and the leaves on the ground. I made one minor change and painted the branches as drooping instead of reaching up. These are all minor changes for emphasis. I didn't add anything … but the effect is dramatic, don't you think?"

"What about those dead fish in the pool below the waterfall?" asked Elizabeth. "Are they real?"

"Well …" Vera smiled. "That was kind of an afterthought. Maybe I should take that out. I am trying to express how pollution has invaded us and is destroying the natural beauty of our surroundings. I would like to do a series of environmental pictures showing what is happening to the natural resources we have around Salisbury, like the Wicomico River."

"It would be nice if you could sell one or two of them, so we could make a little money," observed Elizabeth.

"Yes, it would," said Vera. "I wish I could get a grant from one of the environmental agencies or one of the environmental organizations concerned with pollution. It would make the project a lot more stimulating and rewarding. It would be effective, too. Nobody reads those boring articles about the environment, but something like this will attract lots of viewers."

Elizabeth sighed. "Go ahead and hang it," she said. "Gloom and doom doesn't sell well, but after you are famous, we can point to this as an example of your work during your depressed period."

"I'm not famous, and I'm not depressed. I met an old high-school acquaintance this afternoon who was interested in my painting. I know who he is, but he doesn't know who I am yet, and I am having fun with him"

"Good!" exclaimed Elizabeth "God knows you could use a little fun and distraction. Was he an old flame?"

"Not really," said Vera. "He was one of those hotshot high-school jocks who thought he was God's gift to women. Not my type."

"Too bad," said Elizabeth. "But I'm sure you will have fun revealing your identity and reliving your youth. How is John?"

Vera sighed. "Pretty much the same. He seems to be getting a little weaker and sometimes doesn't know me."

John Harrison was Vera's husband. He had had a serious stroke two years before, which had left him paralyzed from the waist down and unable to speak coherently. Vera visited him every day at the nursing home and usually read to him for about an hour and then helped him with his dinner. It was a grim routine, but Vera never complained and managed to stay calm and cheerful throughout the ordeal. Elizabeth thought she was a remarkable woman.

After leaving the gallery, Vera drove to the nursing home, located just north of Salisbury.

She spoke to the floor nurse: "How is he today?"

The nurse shook her head. "Not so good today, Vera. He isn't eating much, and he is sleeping a lot. He may not know you."

"I'll see if I can wake him up, so I can read to him. Will you be bringing dinner soon?"

"In about thirty or forty minutes. If he is enjoying your reading, we can delay it."

Vera went in the room and kissed him softly on the cheek. John's eyes opened, and he tried to speak. She could see he was frustrated.

"Hello, darling," she said. "Don't try to talk now—just lie back and relax. I brought our book, and I'll read to you until dinner."

The book was one of Ruth Rendell's mysteries, set in an English coastal village on the North Sea. John loved mysteries, and this was a good one. By the time dinner came, she had read three chapters, and John was sound asleep. The nurse propped him up, and together they were able to get some chicken soup and sweetened tea in him.

"Not much nourishment," said the nurse, looking worried. "This is one of his bad days, and I don't think there is much you can do for him this evening."

"I'll stay a little longer," said Vera. "Maybe he will wake up, and I can talk to him."

Vera sat for a while and tried talking to John but got no response. After about ten minutes, she walked over to his bed and kissed his hand. "I'll be back tomorrow," she whispered.

After returning home, Vera sat for a while on her small balcony, surveying the stars and enjoying a light breeze on her face. She remembered the strong, energetic man she had married and their long, often exciting life together in the Foreign Service. This was a terrible way for him to go: paralyzed, unable to speak, and suffering all the indignities of not being able to control his bodily functions. And the lifestyle she was living now was certainly not what she had expected.

This is what the marriage commitment means, she thought. *You stay with your mate in sickness and in health.* No sense complaining about it; the tired old cliché "you play the hand you are dealt" certainly applied to her. Lots of people had it worse. She was living in a comfortable place close to her husband; he was well cared for, and most of the expense was covered by long-term-care insurance; she had a lifetime of memories and three wonderful children; and she had a job where she could teach and paint, which was her great passion.

On Monday, at a little after noon, she walked over to the park, knowing Harry was likely to arrive after his class. She saw him sitting on a bench with a large picnic basket beside him. She went over to the bench and sat down. Harry's eyes lit up when he saw her, and he smiled broadly.

"Hello!" he said enthusiastically. "I was afraid you might not come. I don't even know your name."

"Yes, you do, Harry," she said, trying to look sad and disappointed, but Harry could see that her eyes were sparkling, and he had a feeling that she was teasing him. "I am very disappointed that you didn't know me after all we went through together."

Harry was embarrassed. "All right," he said. "You have an advantage over me, and you are enjoying it. Now tell me why I should know you, and how you knew my name."

Vera was having difficulty suppressing a very girlish giggle. "Think back to your school days, Harry. Who was the girl of your dreams?"

The light slowly began to shine in Harry's brain: those big expressive eyes … that lovely contralto voice … the confident way she had taken charge of him last Thursday … he knew who she was.

"Antonelli!" He shook his head ruefully. "I should have known it was you."

Vera was delighted. "See, I always knew I was the girl of your dreams. But why didn't you recognize me Thursday?"

"You look different," grunted Harry.

"So do you," she said. "You are old and gray, and you look kind of subdued—not like the egotistical, macho Harry I used to know—but I still recognized you. What's so different about me?"

She looked so animated and pleased with herself that Harry couldn't get angry at her, but he decided he would have a little fun also.

"Well," he said, "your ass isn't as tight as it used to be, and your bazooms are sagging and not sticking straight out like they used to … and I remember you were a snappy dresser—always wore tight sweaters and short skirts—and here you show up in an old shirt and baggy pants. How was I supposed to recognize you?"

Vera glared at him; this time she was really annoyed. "Don't you ever see anything but a woman's body parts?" she snapped.

It was Harry's turn to laugh. "Come on, Antonelli. You were having a great time leading me on. I was just trying to get even."

"All right," Vera sniffed. "So we're even, but I want you to know this old shirt is a real silk blouse, and those baggy pants are designer jeans. I was trying to look nice for our meeting."

"You do look nice," said Harry. "Better than nice. Now let's go over to the table and eat this lunch I fixed with my bare hands."

They sat down at the table, and Harry took out two fat Reuben sandwiches he had picked up at a nearby deli and opened the bottle of wine. "Help yourself, Vera, and tell me what you have been doing since our torrid romance."

"It wasn't very torrid, was it, Harry?"

"Not my fault," said Harry. "Last I heard, you graduated and went up north to some fancy college—Vassar, I think."

"Wellesley," replied Vera. "I got a full scholarship and studied art history and studio art; after I graduated, I worked for a while in a museum in Boston; met John Harrison; got married; had three kids; and traveled all over the world in the Foreign Service. John retired, and we came down here, where he got an appointment as a professor of political science and I got a job as an art-history instructor. End of story."

"You said your husband teaches at State—does he come here to watch you paint?"

"John had a stroke two years ago; he is paralyzed and can't speak. He is in a nursing home nearby, and I visit him every day." Vera looked steadily at Harry while she was talking. She was outwardly calm, but Harry could see this was a difficult subject for her to discuss.

"I am so sorry, Vera," Harry said gently. "I know something about what you are going through. My wife, Mary Ellen, died a year ago. It was hell watching her fade away knowing there was nothing I could do about it. She lasted six months, and I nearly went crazy. But two years! You must be exhausted."

For the first time, Vera seemed to wilt. Her face sagged, and her eyes became dull and vacant. "It's not a pleasant experience, Harry, and you are right: it is terrible to know there is nothing you can do."

"I didn't realize you were going through such an ordeal," said Harry. "I hope you understand those silly remarks I made were in response to the fun you were having teasing me. Tell me how I can help you."

"Well," she said slowly, "I doubt that I will ever forgive you for those rude remarks about me, but it is exciting to see someone I knew when I was a teen, so I'll try to overlook them for now."

"I'm pretty lonely, Vera," he replied. "Let's try to meet here in the park for lunch on Mondays and Thursdays. I'd like to get to know you again. Maybe you really are the girl of my dreams!"

They continued to meet for lunch until the summer term ended in the first week of August. Their discussions were always animated, and Vera found she enjoyed Harry's attention and his understanding of her problems. He never made any improper suggestions or tried in any way to be anything but a friend. Yet she knew he was becoming very interested in her, and it was flattering and reassuring. Harry was curious about her passion for art.

"What do you teach these kids?" Harry asked.

"In my course, we define visual art and chart its development throughout history. Art affects everyone immediately. It is defined by its emotional impact. You don't need to know how to read or write to appreciate art. The walls of some caves in France are home to some pretty well-developed art that dates back over 17,000 years. Art is found in every culture and in primitive as well as advanced societies. Understanding art is very important, Harry."

Vera's great love of art had developed early in her childhood. Her father was an Italian stonecutter who had come to America to work on the National Cathedral. Like many Italians engaged in construction work, he loved beautiful things and encouraged his daughter to paint. He also loved music and had married Vera's mother, an accomplished pianist, shortly after he came to the United States. Her mother was of English descent and was calm and reserved, while her father was flamboyant and demonstrative. Vera's personality was decidedly more Italian than English, but she had her mother's tall, elegant figure; fair skin; and beautiful, expressive eyes. She had been a strikingly attractive girl in high school. It was not only her beauty that made her stand out among other pretty girls at school; it was also her charm. She possessed a lively, irreverent wit and knew how to make her classmates feel good about themselves. Vera also had a keen intellect and was an easy person to talk to. Harry had been very interested in her in their youth.

"I keep reading about paintings that sell for huge sums of money," said Harry. "What makes a painting worth a million dollars?"

"Some of it is sales hype. Rich people hear about an artist the media says is great, and they immediately want to own those paintings. But the really great artists, the ones whose work has been admired for generations, are those who find new ways to express themselves—like Monet, who started the Impressionist movement, or Picasso, who ushered in a new form of modern art that emphasizes colors and shapes."

Harry shook his head. "Mary Ellen took me to an exhibit of modern art a couple of years ago, and I don't get it. I really think I can do a better job than they did."

Vera laughed. "Well, go do it, and I'll sell it for you for two million dollars." Vera stared at Harry for a few minutes and then leaned over and planted a robust kiss on his cheek. "That's for being a nice guy," she said. "I've really enjoyed getting to know you again, but now I've got to go, and I won't see you for a few weeks. I have to grade a lot of papers and meet with the art department to talk about the fall semester."

Harry took Vera's hand. "Wouldn't you like to have dinner with me some evening? There are some very nice seafood restaurants not far from here, and I would love to show you Bay Watch."

Vera smiled a little sadly. "No, Harry. I am married, and I think we should just keep things as they are and have lunch. I'll call you when I'm free."

Harry gave her his telephone number and walked her to her car. "Call me as soon as you can, Vera, I think I'm going to miss you."

One week later, when Harry returned from a workout at the fitness center, he saw his message light flashing. He picked up and heard Vera's voice. It sounded strained and a little faint. "Harry, John died this morning. My family is all here, and we are leaving tomorrow for California for a memorial service in Oakland, where his family and our children live. I don't know how long I'll be gone. I will be staying with my daughter, and her number is 805-277-0567. Please call me."

Harry was a little stunned. John's death was not entirely unexpected, but nobody is ever really ready for death. Vera was leaving for California, and he had a sinking feeling she wasn't coming back.

Chapter 10:
MAINE

HARRY WAITED TWO days before calling Vera. A man answered the phone and identified himself as a friend of the family who had volunteered to take calls and give information about John Harrison's memorial service and interment in the family plot in the local cemetery. Harry offered his condolences and left his number for Vera to call if she had the time.

He wasn't at all sure he would ever hear from Vera again. They had never been close, and their interests were pretty far apart. She was an accomplished artist, and he knew virtually nothing about art. Moreover, he could see that she was an ardent environmentalist and was greatly concerned over pollution. Harry was definitely a nature lover; he loved the bay and the salt marshes where he hunted ducks; and the green fields and wooded hills of western Virginia where he hunted quail. Pollution was bad; Harry didn't like the smog or the urban noises or the acid rain that was killing the trout in his favorite streams of northeastern Pennsylvania and Maine. But he was resigned to the fact that pollution was a natural byproduct of civilization. Every time you turned on the lights, you were using energy created at some generation plant burning fossil fuel. Pollution was like taxes; you didn't like it, but you couldn't avoid it. Vera was different; she really cared and might even be a real activist. Normally Harry had no use for protesters who marched around the White House protesting nearly everything. But Vera was different;

she was sincere, and she also was a very attractive woman, and that altered the way he felt about her passion for the environment.

The first time he had seen her in the park, she had just seemed like an elderly woman painting a landscape. She was fairly tall and somewhat overweight, with gray hair cut very short. But when they had finally met, he had been a little startled how different she seemed; her face radiated energy and animation. And those eyes! They conveyed all sorts of emotions and suggestions. Add to that the seductive contralto voice and the warm, feminine personality, and the result was a very unique and attractive lady.

She had had a reputation of being a red-hot date in high school, but Harry wondered about that. Men seemed to make an automatic correlation between physical attractiveness and sexual promiscuity. Just because a girl was really stacked didn't mean she would hop into bed with you. He had never gotten very far with Vera, and he doubted that anyone else had, either.

Summer was passing by too quickly. It was now August 16, and many of Harry's new friends had left for the shore or the mountains to escape the summer heat. He missed Vera more than he cared to admit. He had some travel brochures featuring a variety of cruises around the Maine islands, New Brunswick, and Nova Scotia, and he thought one of them would be a pleasant diversion. While he was mulling over his options, he got a call from Gwen.

"Dad, how are you doing in your new surroundings?"

"Just getting older and more cranky," he replied.

"Dad!" Gwen exclaimed. "You are not getting older, you are getting better, and there is no way you can get crankier than you already are." After reviewing the exploits of her children and life on the Stanford campus, she invited him to spend a couple of weeks with her family in Maine. "We've rented an old house with five bedrooms and four bathrooms overlooking Penobscot Bay, close to a tidal creek. Nick wants our children to see what God's country is really like. Our lease runs from August 18 to September 8, and we all want you to come—especially Nick."

Harry liked Gwen's husband. He was a quiet, genial man with an infectious sense of humor. He admired Nick for his determination and academic achievements, both of which had led to his present position as a full professor at Stanford. He remembered vividly when Gwen had announced her engagement to Nick; he was so refreshingly different from her other suitors.

"And, Dad," continued Gwen, "Pat and Peter have rented a cottage close to us and will stay for a week. And George and Jean and two of their children will come over from Nantucket for five or six days, so we will all be together."

"What a great thing to do, Gwen," Harry said. "I certainly want to come, and I promise not to be too grouchy."

"Just be yourself, Dad," Gwen answered. "We would all be nervous if you behaved yourself."

"I was just thinking about one of those small boat cruises up around the Maine islands and New Brunswick, but this tops that. Is Pat going to fly up?"

"Yes, she is leaving on the twentieth. Why don't you see if you can get on the same flight and fly up with her? We'll meet you at Portland and drive you to our place."

"I'll give her a call right now," he said. These travel plans were the tonic he needed. The thought of losing Vera just after they reconnected was depressing, but the prospect of being with his children and grandchildren put him in a much better mood. He called Pat and made arrangements to meet her at BWI airport. He was able to get a ticket on her flight but had to pay full fare and get up at five in the morning to catch the puddle jumper from Salisbury, but it was worth it.

Harry packed carefully. Informality was the dress code in Maine, but he would wear a jacket and good trousers on the plane and pack a tie in case they wanted to go to a fancy restaurant. He made sure he had a three-week supply of his pills. His doctors had given him many lectures on the importance of his medications, but he wondered if they did him any good. What would happen if he stopped taking them? He would probably feel the same, but he decided it wasn't worth the risk to find out.

He got to thinking about where they would be staying. It was on the coast but only a short distance from Lake Sebago. That was an interesting place. It was a large, very deep lake with a robust fishery of lake trout and smallmouth bass. Harry had fished there several times and enjoyed the variety of effective techniques: casting popping bugs for bass around the rocks on the north side of the lake; deep trolling using light tackle and a heavy weight (which kept the line near the bottom, but snapped off when the fish struck); and—his favorite—fly-fishing at dawn in the shallow water. Harry called George and had a brief conversation, and then he took out his duffel bag, in which he stuffed his favorite fly rod, fishing tackle, and wading boots. He had heard that there was a sustainable fishery of landlocked salmon in the lake. He had never caught one, but somehow he and George would give it a try on this trip.

When he finished packing, he put a steel thermos filled with his favorite scotch whisky in the duffel bag and locked it. There had been no further discussion of his drinking habits since the meeting at the Metropolitan Club, but the problem had not disappeared. At times, Harry knew he had had too much to drink; he was working on it, but when he was alone and feeling depressed, he felt a very powerful urge to turn to alcohol as a mood modifier. When he was feeling good and with other people, his craving was not so strong, but it was there. Rather than cause stress by ordering too many drinks in front of his children, he would keep the jug in his room in case he needed it.

He met Pat and Peter at the airport at seven, in time to board their 8:15 flight to Portland. For once, the flight took off on time and arrived in Portland on schedule. Nick met them at the baggage-claim area, and the four of them drove to the big, old-fashioned country house Gwen had rented. She was presiding over the kitchen, directing her brood where to store the groceries she had bought at the local store.

"Where are the kids, Pat?" she asked.

"Both unavailable," sighed Pat. "Mary is on an archaeology dig in the Canary Islands sponsored by the Smithsonian, and Josh is trying out for the varsity football team at Bucknell and is in training camp."

"Good for him!" exclaimed Harry. "Did I ever tell you kids that I was the all-high left tackle for the Wilson Raiders?"

"Many times, Dad," said Gwen, rolling her eyes. "Now you all get cleaned up and settled in, and I'll serve you some homemade clam chowder. Henry and Nick went out early this morning and dug about a hundred littlenecks, so they are nice fat, fresh clams." Henry was Gwen's oldest, and he was a sturdy, lively twelve-year-old who was the image of his father, Nick.

It was a great beginning of the family vacation. George, Jean, and two of their three children were due to arrive on Saturday and would stay in the local motel for a week.

"How are they getting here?" asked Peter.

"George has rented a camper," said Nick with a broad smile. "They are taking the ferry from Nantucket to Woods Hole and will pick up the camper and drive up here."

"Why a camper?" asked Pat.

"I suspect that someone told him about great fishing at Lake Sebago, and he just wanted to be prepared," Nick answered.

"How many people are in on this conspiracy?" asked Gwen sharply. "This was your idea to come to Maine, and you are not going to run off and leave us for some wild fishing trip in the woods!"

"Take it easy, Gwen," said Nick. "I'm going to be right here and will enjoy showing you all around this part of Maine. My cousin is a part-time guide on Lake Sebago, and he has volunteered to take care of the party. I think the idea is to take Henry and Patrick, and the four of them will leave on Tuesday and fish Wednesday and Thursday morning. They can be back here for dinner on Thursday."

"What a great idea!" exclaimed Harry. "I'm glad George set this up with Nick. I will enjoy it; I haven't fished Sebago in a long time, and I hear it's still pretty good."

"I think we all know where this idea originated, Dad," said Gwen, still trying to appear indignant. "You are always running off fishing or hunting, and George and Nick are willing collaborators. But it's nice that Patrick and Henry will get to know each other, and I don't think you will get in too much trouble." Patrick was George's youngest and was about the same age as Henry, and Gwen was pleased that they would have a chance to get acquainted on this trip.

Nick was having a grand time introducing his family to his relatives and boyhood friends. He hadn't been back to Maine in fifteen years, and the trip amounted to a real reunion for him. His older brother, Spiro, owned a very up-to-date lobster boat and was president of the local lobster fishermen's association. Harry was fascinated by the extent to which the lobster fishermen had recognized how the fishery was being depleted and had promoted a largely self-regulating system that had stabilized the lobster population and was providing the fishermen with a steady income. They were years ahead of the Chesapeake Bay watermen, who were suffering because of the depletion of oyster and blue-crab stocks.

George and Jean arrived late Saturday afternoon in a well-equipped camper loaded with supplies.

"Was the traffic bad getting up here?" asked Pat.

"Terrible!" Jean replied. "We took the earliest ferry from Nantucket to Woods Hole, hoping we could get around Boston before the mob hit the road, but it didn't work."

"The airports are going to be pretty bad this weekend, I think," said Pat. "Dad isn't going back until after Labor Day, but Peter and I are scheduled to leave Saturday at four fifteen in the afternoon. I suppose the Portland airport will be like a zoo."

"George and I are not going to fight the weekend traffic if we can help it. We are making arrangements to extend our stay until Tuesday."

"Good idea," said Pat thoughtfully. "I'll talk to Peter and see if we can take a little more vacation time and change our airline reservation. I'd like to stay a little longer, too. It's such fun to see you and Gwen and the kids, and Dad looks better than he has in a long time."

Harry greeted George warmly. "That's quite an outfit you have there," he said, looking over the large, well-stocked camper. "How'd you arrange this trip with Nick? Is Jean upset with me? Gwen seems sort of peeved at the idea of us taking off for a few days."

"Jean thinks it's a great idea," said George with a big smile. "She wants Patrick to get to know Henry, and believe it or not, she thinks it is great for us to have an outing together. And don't worry about Gwen—she'll like it once she gets used to the idea. She just likes to be in charge and doesn't like it when she's not in the loop."

"Well, it is such a pleasure to be included in her vacation family, I don't want to be the one who spoils her vacation plans."

"Don't worry about it, Dad. Henry is going on the trip, and she is thrilled."

The next few days were filled with activities: exploring the town, roaming the beaches, and meeting Nick's friends and relatives. Henry and Patrick became best friends almost immediately, and Kathy, George's fifteen-year-old daughter, was introduced to the nice-looking sixteen-year-old son of one of Nick's friends. Kathy was blooming into a real charmer and was just beginning to learn how to manipulate boys. The boy immediately asked her out for a sail on Sunday. Gwen's younger children, Julia and Pat, ages six and eight, were captivated by digging for clams and swimming in the icy Maine waters. The bay had warmed up to sixty-five degrees, which seemed to invigorate them but was much too cold for the adults.

On Monday, Harry and George began laying out the fishing equipment and clothing they would need for the fishing trip. George had a large cooler in which he loaded milk, eggs, butter, bacon, and other perishables. They packed enough for two breakfasts, two lunches, and one dinner. The other dinner was going to be "fish or go hungry," announced Harry. By Tuesday they were ready to go.

"You boys try to keep Granddad from falling in the lake," ordered Pat.

"Have a good time, you guys," called Gwen. "And don't bring a lot of smelly fish back here to mess up my kitchen."

It was about a two-hour drive to the campgrounds, where they found a nice, secluded spot to park the camper and set up the tent. They had a large masonry fireplace with a steel grill and a sizable stack of firewood nearby. George and the boys got busy setting up the tent and blowing up the air mattresses. Harry opted to sleep in the camper and carefully laid out all the clothes and fishing tackle he would need in the morning. He also called Nick's cousin, Tic, who would be their guide for the next two days. They made arrangements to meet at seven in the morning.

George was well equipped. As evening approached, he got out four folding chairs and a Coleman lantern, which he hung on a tree branch near the tent. Next he broke out the cooking gear: a large skillet, a reflector oven, and some large spoons and spatulas. The boys built a big fire and settled down to rig up their fishing equipment. George soon had the hamburgers sizzling in the skillet, foil-wrapped potatoes baking in the coals, and foil-wrapped biscuits, carrots, and peas cooking in the oven.

Harry took out his thermos jug and poured himself a generous drink of scotch.

"Still need that drink in the evening, Dad?" asked George, looking a little apprehensive.

"Yes, I do," replied Harry, "and I bet you would like a little pop, wouldn't you?"

George laughed. "Okay, Dad, pour me a shot. If there ever were a place where a man could enjoy a good drink of whisky, it would be right here."

The dinner was delicious, and cleanup time negligible. They all visited the latrine, put a couple of big logs on the fire, and listened to Harry tell stories about fishing Lake Sebago in the old days. Harry sat up for a while after others had crawled into the tent and tied up the mosquito netting. The soft moonlight was hypnotic, and the light breeze in the pines made a low sighing sound that was like an old-world lullaby. He poured himself another drink, and a thousand memories rushed through his mind. He thought of the early days with Mary

Ellen, the children, the many excursions they took together, and the fishing and hunting trips he had taken all over the country. It was with great reluctance that he crawled into the camper; he could hear the loons calling on the lake and the coyotes beginning to tune up.

The next morning, Harry awoke to the smell and sounds of coffee percolating, bacon and eggs frying, and two excited boys chattering.

"Tonight we will be eating fish," George told the boys.

Tic met them at seven and drove them to a boat ramp nearby, where he already had his boat in the water.

"We'll see if the lake trout are active this morning," he said as he rigged up four trolling lines. "We'll try them at different depths to see where they are feeding, and this afternoon, we'll go across the lake and try casting for bass."

The morning was productive, and the lakers were very active. They hooked about twenty-five fish and got twelve to the boat, of which they kept four. One was for supper that evening, and Tic promised to fillet and quick-freeze the other three to take home. They were all nice fish, in the seven- to ten-pound range.

In the afternoon, Tic took them across the lake into a rocky cove sheltered from the wind. The boys used light spinning tackle with surface plugs, and George and Harry broke out their fly rods and tried some bright-colored, large streamers. For a while, the action was fast and furious; the bass were scrappy and acrobatic, sometimes coming completely out of the water to throw the hooks. The fish they were able to bring to net were released, and the boys had a lively competition for the most and biggest fish. After a couple of hours of fast action, the fishing began to slack off, and Harry questioned Tic about the landlocked salmon.

"They're here, all right," he said. "But catching any this time of year is pretty unlikely."

"Aren't they starting to school up now for the fall spawning run?" asked Harry.

"Maybe," answered Tic. "You thinking about going after one?"

"Yes," said Harry. "What would be our best chance?"

"There's a big pool at the mouth of Buckley's Creek, which is a major spawning stream for the salmon. With this full moon, I think some of them may be collecting in that pool to feed before they go up to spawn. But most of them are down deep in this warm weather—a hundred feet or more."

"What's the best time?" asked Harry.

"We would have to be on the water by five at the latest. When the sun comes up, they will go down deep again."

"I'll talk to the others and let you know this evening," said Harry.

That evening, while the trout fillets were baking in the oven, Harry discussed the salmon expedition with George and the boys.

"Tic thinks there isn't much chance of getting a salmon this time of year," Harry explained, "but I'd like to try it. I've never caught a landlocked one, and this might be my last chance. Does anyone else want to go?"

Getting up at four in the morning wasn't very appealing to the boys, and George thought this would be a good opportunity to teach them how to use a fly rod. A small creek a few miles away was a great brook trout stream, and they opted to fish there instead.

Harry called Tic and made arrangements to be picked up at four thirty. Waking up and getting himself ready at four in the morning was a chore for Harry. He kept waking up and had to visit the latrine several times during the night and, after the alarm went off, it took a while for Harry to get oriented, find his clothes, and pick up his fishing tackle. He wasn't nearly as quick in the early morning as he used to be, but the urge to get on the water and try for a big salmon was as strong as ever.

Tic came around at exactly four thirty, and Harry was ready. He put his rod and tackle in the truck, climbed in the cab, and gratefully accepted a steaming mug of coffee from Tic.

"We just may get lucky this morning," Tic observed. "The moon was bright all night, and that might lure a couple of the big ones out of their deep holes to feed on the minnows and grubs washed down from the creek."

"When they spawn, do they stop feeding like the ocean-run Atlantic salmon do?" asked Harry.

"Don't really know," replied Tic. "They get awfully picky, though, and I think we should use something big and ugly that will make them so mad they will bite it even if they aren't eating."

"I have some of those," said Harry. "I'll use a sinking tip on the line to get it down fifteen or twenty feet."

"That might do it," replied Tic optimistically.

The misty air carried a chill when Harry got in the boat heading for Buckley's Creek; it was getting light in the east, but sunrise was a good forty-five minutes away. Tic cut the motor as they drifted into a large pool into which a broad, gravelly creek was flowing with a surprising amount of current for this time of year. Harry tied on a big, bright streamer, flicked it out about forty feet from the boat, let it sink for a few seconds, and then began his retrieve in short, sharp jerks. After about five minutes, Harry thought he felt a bump.

"Uh-oh!" he muttered softly. "Something's down there." He gave the rod a few twitches and felt the sudden unmistakable jolt of a major strike. He resisted the urge to rear back and dropped the tip of his rod down to the water before pulling back. The rod bent double, and Harry could feel the powerful surge of a big fish circling the pool.

"Yahoo!" bellowed Harry. "Here she comes!" A large, beautifully colored fish shot out of the pool at least four feet in the air and dropped back in the water with a booming splash.

"Hang on, Harry," Tic yelled. "That's a big one!" For the next five minutes, the big fish savagely tore around the pool, alternating spectacularly high leaps with powerful dives to the floor of the pool. Suddenly it turned and shot out of the pool and into the channel on Buckley's Creek; Harry's line promptly snagged on a rocky outcropping by the edge of the channel. The line could still move out, but if the fish turned, the leader would snap. Tic drove the boat as close to the snag as possible and threw out the anchor.

"I'll clear that line for you," he said.

"No," grunted Harry. "If I get this son of a bitch, I am going to get him on my own. Help me get out of the boat." With Tic's assistance, Harry started wading up the shallow gravel bed; the rocks were slippery, and the current pulled hard against his legs,

but somehow he made it to the snag and cleared the line just as the fish turned and came roaring downstream and back into the pool. It took another ten minutes of expert rod and boat handling to keep the fish in the pool and tire the fish out so they could net it.

As the big salmon lay on the boat deck, its fierce jaw opening and closing, Harry was overwhelmed with its power and beauty. Its bright color with pink dots on its skin was spectacular, and the long, torpedo like body was built for speed and strength. Nothing in the world matched catching one of these. Harry judged that the booming strike could be heard at least a quarter of a mile away.

"Jesus," he breathed, "I thought for sure we had lost that bastard at least five times!"

"He is a big one," observed Tic. "Might go about fifteen pounds. Want me to fillet him and quick-freeze?"

"No," said Harry. "Just gut him and pack him in ice for me, and I'll take him home. I want everyone to see this guy, and we'll poach him whole with an apple in his mouth."

Harry was physically and emotionally exhausted when he got back to camp. George and the boys hadn't returned yet, and Tic put the salmon in a big Styrofoam cooler with two bags of ice.

"What a great trip, Tic!" Harry exclaimed. "We all had a wonderful time, and you certainly made the trip for us. How much do we owe you?"

"Nothing, Harry," replied Tic. "Nick took care of everything."

"Did he now," said Harry. "Well, I love that old, downeast Maine skinflint, but I'm sure he didn't pay you what you are worth. Here, take this," ordered Harry, handing Tic two fifty-dollar bills.

"Now, Harry, I can't take this. Nick—"

"Stop arguing with me," interrupted Harry. "You earned it, and we'll do this again if I'm ever up this way."

After Tic left, Harry crawled in the tent, lay down on one of the sleeping bags, and promptly fell asleep. He awakened to hear loud shouts of dismay from the boys.

"Granddad, you did it!" shouted Patrick, sticking his head in the tent.

"Did you ever doubt that I would?" replied Harry with a big smile.

George and the boys had had a good morning also, and had come back with four nice brookies, which they filleted and fried along with some big buttermilk pancakes.

"The boys are really getting the hang of fly casting, Dad," said George. "We were using dry flies, and these little suckers were hungry. We must have netted fifteen or twenty, and these four were the biggest."

"Dad says he's going to get me and Henry fly rods for Christmas," Patrick exclaimed.

"Let me take care of that," said Harry. "Your father doesn't really know anything about fly rods. I'll get you something you can really handle."

For the next several hours, they cleaned up, put away their tackle, and broke camp. They arrived home at about three in the afternoon, tired but full of stories about their adventures. During dinner Harry entertained the family with his stories about catching the salmon.

"This fish was big and ornery," Harry told them. "He must have jumped fifty times, and I swear he cleared the water by at least eight feet on some of those jumps."

"Eight feet, Dad?" asked Pat skeptically. "No fish can get that high."

"Hey, you weren't there," answered Harry. "Eight feet is conservative! It may well have more than ten feet!" Harry was enjoying himself hugely, and so was his audience.

"How are we going to cook this creature if we do him whole, like Harry wants?" asked Jean.

"That's right," observed Gwen. "The oven is pretty small, and we don't have any thirty-two-inch poachers around here. "

"I'm sure you will think of something," Harry said with a yawn.

"I caught this fish, and it's up to you women to figure out how to cook it."

Jean shook her head. "Harry, you are such an unreconstructed old chauvinist!"

"That's me," said Harry. "And I'm also a tired, elderly man, and I am going to bed."

Chapter 11:
THE PAINTING

"WHAT A LOVELY day!" exclaimed Jean, admiring the rising sun over the sparkling, deep-blue water of Penobscot Bay. "I hope it lasts until next Tuesday, when we have to leave."

"It is gorgeous," said Gwen. "Nick says the marine forecast shows a high-pressure system stalled just offshore, and it's supposed to last for another week."

"He was up early this morning," Jean observed. "I was up around seven, cleaning out the camper, when I saw his car go by. Where did he go?"

"He took the girls and went out with his brother to fish the lobster pots this morning. He's going to pick out a dozen nice ones for the clambake he's planning for Monday evening—our last night together."

"What a treat!" exclaimed Jean. "I have never had a real downeast Maine clambake. What is he going to do?"

"I don't really know," replied Gwen, "but he's been talking about digging a pit, lining it with stones, and bringing in driftwood and seaweed and all sorts of stuff. It is quite a ritual."

"And that reminds me," said Jean, "we have Dad's salmon out there in the garage, covered with ice. What are we going to do with that?"

"Hi, guys," called out Gwen just as Pat and Peter came into the kitchen. "Grab a cup of coffee and sit down and help us decide what to do with Dad's salmon."

"Well," said Pat, pouring out two mugs of coffee for herself and Peter, "I don't see how we can do anything except throw it on the grill and hope for the best."

Peter was walking around the kitchen, checking out the old-fashioned range and primitive oven. "I see only one modern appliance in here, and that is the dishwasher ... and I think it is big enough to hold the salmon."

"What are you talking about?" asked Gwen.

"Yes," chimed in Jean, "you're not going to wash it, are you?"

"No, no, nothing like that," explained Peter. "When Pat and I took the kids to Alaska several years ago, we got a fish and game cookbook, and one of the recipes was for a dishwasher-poached king salmon, and I have always wanted to try it."

"Are you serious, Peter?" asked Gwen.

"Yes, Gwen, I am. Let me give it a try—I think it will work."

"Okay, Peter," said Gwen, "you are now in charge of preparing the salmon, although I don't see how it can possibly work."

A few minutes later, George straggled into the kitchen, along with Kathy, Patrick, and Henry, all looking very sleepy.

"Good afternoon, sleepyheads," Jean said, throwing an exaggerated look at her watch.

"It's not that late," grumbled Patrick.

"It's after ten o'clock, and you are still not awake," said Gwen, addressing them all and trying to look stern.

"We're tired, Mom," muttered Henry. "Camping is hard work."

"I wouldn't know, and I do not expect to find out," declared Gwen. "But why do you look so tired, Kathy? You weren't out in the woods with these crazy men."

"Kathy had a late date last night," said Jean. "We had a little talk about that when she got in."

"Oh, Mother, I just went to the movies with Paul after dinner, and I came right back to the motel."

"And sat outside in Paul's car until I turned on the lights and went out and stood in the doorway," said Jean, giving her daughter a hard look.

"Ah," said Pat with a broad, knowing smile. "The clash of wills between mother and daughter begins when boys and girls discover each other."

"Oh, come on," muttered Kathy, turning a deep shade of red. "Can't we talk about something else?"

"Where's Dad?" inquired Pat.

"I heard him in the bathroom when I came in," said George. "He was pretty tired out last night."

"And he put away a lot of wine, too," observed Pat. "If he doesn't come down soon, I think I'll go up and see how he is." At that moment, Harry shuffled into the kitchen, looking very old and tired. "Good morning, Dad," said Pat. "I was just going up to see if you were among the living."

"I'm still here," grunted Harry, reaching for a cup of coffee.

"We were just talking about those fishy fish stories you were telling last night," said Gwen.

"That's right," chimed in Jean. "It's really too bad this one didn't get away—then I'm sure it would have weighed at least thirty pounds."

"Everything I said was the gospel truth," said Harry. "In fact, that fish probably weighed about thirty pounds when I hooked him; he just lost a lot of weight with all that jumping."

"Right, Dad," said Gwen, rolling her eyes. "Want some breakfast?"

"No, just coffee and a little juice. So what's on the agenda today?"

"Nick and the girls are out on Spiro's boat," said Gwen. "Peter is in charge of cooking the salmon; it looks like the boys are going to take a nap; and we ladies are going down to the beach to dip our toes in that icy water. Want to come?"

"No, thanks," said Harry, "My heart is a little out of sync this morning, so I'm just going to hang around here and take it easy."

"You had a lot of wine last night," said Pat carefully. "Perhaps if you exercised a little more restraint, your heart wouldn't act this way."

"I don't need any more lectures from you," Harry said sharply. "I had a good time last night, and I will be the judge of how much wine I will drink!" He turned his back on Pat and addressed Peter. "So, Peter, you are in charge of preparing my salmon. How are you going to do it?"

"In the dishwasher," replied Peter, smiling broadly.

"Say again?" barked Harry, looking startled.

"The dishwasher," repeated Peter. "I will bring the fish up close to room temperature; then I'll make a lemon-dill-butter spread, which I will put on both sides of the fish; I will make a foil envelope to hold the fish; and I'll add a cup of wine and kosher salt. Then I will seal up the envelope tightly and heat it on the drying cycle, so the envelope is hot, and then turn the washer on full cycle, which will last about an hour. It will cook slowly, and you will have the best poached salmon you have ever eaten!"

"For God's sake!" exclaimed Harry. "That's the stupidest idea I ever heard of."

"Peter is an excellent cook, Dad," said Gwen firmly. "He has volunteered to do the job, and that's what we will do."

"But it can't work, Gwen," protested Harry. "The water temperature in a dishwasher never gets above 180 degrees, and you can't cook anything with that!" The argument went on for several more minutes, with Harry and George flatly opposing the notion, and Gwen and Jean firmly supporting Peter.

"Okay!" said Harry. "I give up, but you better have some hot dogs handy for dinner."

After having coffee and a little glass of tomato juice, Harry went up to his room to rest. His heartbeat was very irregular, and he felt weak and a little dizzy. He took an extra half capsule of his heart medication and lay down on the bed. He felt uncomfortable about his flare-up at Pat. It was not so much what she said that set him off—it was, after all, just a gentle reminder not to drink so much wine when he was having a good time.

The problem was that he knew she was right; he had drank too much the night before, and that had led to difficulty getting to sleep and certainly contributed to the problems he was having with his heart. He finally dozed off and was awakened several hours later when Nick and the girls came in. He could hear their excited chatter as they told their mother about their adventures.

"Mom," shouted Patti, "You should see our lobsters! They are huge."

"Yes, and one of them pinched my thumb," said Juliet, holding up a heavily bandaged finger. "They have these huge claws and can really bite!"

"Daddy showed us how to hold them so they don't get you," Patti said. "You have to get them right behind the claws, so they can't reach back."

"Sounds like it was a great trip," Gwen said, addressing Nick.

"It really was," said Nick. "The girls were all over the boat and couldn't keep their hands off the lobsters. I was afraid they might get a really nasty bite, but one of the lobsters caught Juliet's thumb and gave it a little tweak, and after that the kids were very respectful."

"Is it a bad cut?" asked Gwen.

"No," answered Nick. "We got it off before it could do any serious damage. We have a dozen real nice ones in the holding rack beside Spiro's boat."

"Wonderful!" exclaimed Gwen. "Henry is up, but he looks pretty tired. Says camping is hard work."

"It is," said Nick. "How's Harry?"

"Upstairs resting. His heart went out of sync this morning, and he took some extra medication and is hoping it will get back on track before the big salmon feast."

"He was in great form last night," chuckled Nick. "He has fish stories down to a fine art. I know he's not going to miss this dinner tonight. How you going to do it, on the grill?"

"No," replied Gwen. "Peter is going to do it in the dishwasher."

"What?" Nick asked incredulously. "No way—that's a big fish, and the heat in the dishwasher won't do anything but warm it up."

"I have my doubts, too, dear, but Pat says Peter is a very creative cook, so we're supporting him."

"I hope it works," said Nick, shaking his head.

"So do I," said Gwen. "Dad and George have been razzing him pretty hard."

By five thirty, everyone had returned from the day's activities. Kathy and Gwen set the table; Nick brought in a big cedar plank that he had soaked and heated on the grill so that it would be moist and hot for the salmon; and Peter wrapped the fish in foil and got the dishwasher going full cycle. George brought out the drinks and was acting as bartender.

Harry looked over at Pat and was wondering if he ought to apologize for his outburst that morning when she surprised him by coming over and giving his arm a warm squeeze.

"I know you don't like me nagging you about drinking too much," she said softly, "but we are all so very fond of you and concerned over your health, and we think overindulgence in alcohol is very dangerous for you. I seem to be the only one who will talk to you about it."

"Ah, Pat," said Harry, kissing her cheek. "I'm sorry I snapped at you this morning. I know I drink too much at times, but I'm not an alcoholic, and I have it under control most of the time. Don't worry about it."

"You certainly are not an alcoholic, Dad," she said, looking him directly in the eye, "and you are in control nearly all the time, but I have seen what too much alcohol can do to you, and I shall continue to worry about it."

"You sound like Mary Ellen," said Harry, giving her a big hug.

"I am a lot like Mom," said Pat. "Now go over and have a nice drink of scotch and have some wine with dinner, but remember: Mama is watching!" She laughed and gave him a playful swat on the rear as he went over to the bar.

"How's the heart, Dad?" asked George.

"It's calmed down a lot, but I think I'll take it easy this evening. Just give me a light scotch and a little water."

"What's light, Dad?"

"Well, if Pat isn't watching, make it about four ounces," he said, looking furtively around the room.

George laughed. "She's in the kitchen, giving Peter moral support, but what if I start you off with one shot of one and a half ounces?"

"That'll do," said Harry. "So what do you think: will we have salmon or hot dogs tonight?"

"Peter is pretty nervous now," said George with a chuckle. "He says his whole reputation is riding on this dinner tonight."

"That it is," said Harry as he went across the room to talk to Patrick and Henry, who were still reliving the fishing trip.

At seven o'clock, Pat came out and informed them that dinner would be on the table in five minutes. She maintained a poker face, but her eyes were bright and shining. The air was electric with tension and excitement; anticipation was very high.

"Where are the hot dogs?" Harry asked loudly.

"Outside on the grill," answered George.

Gwen came in with a big bowl of sweet corn, which she put on the sideboard, followed by Kathy, with a huge platter of homemade potato salad. Jean came next with a pitcher of a light, pungent egg, wine, and garlic sauce. There was a dramatic pause, and the room fell silent as Peter and Nick strutted into the room carrying the cedar plank with a beautifully decorated salmon in the middle and a small crab apple in its mouth.

"Voila!" exclaimed Peter. "Break out your cameras!"

For the next five minutes, cameras popped, and everyone congratulated Peter. When the commotion died down, Peter took over the job of carving and serving the salmon, and Kathy acted as waitress. Everyone was served promptly, except Harry and George.

"Hey," George protested. "Is there any left for us?"

"Yeah," said Harry. "I caught this fish, and I should get the biggest piece."

Kathy took her time with their plates, carefully putting on the corn and potato salad, and then went over to Peter, who very ceremoniously put two hot dogs on each plate.

Kathy brought the plates over to the table and said very sweetly, "There you are, gentlemen: hot dogs, just what you ordered."

The whole room erupted with laughter and loud protests from Harry and George, followed by catcalls from the boys. Finally Peter relented and served each of them a generous slice, beautifully done and seasoned to perfection. It was indeed a feast to remember, and many toasts recognized Peter for his culinary artistry.

On Saturday, Nick commandeered all the men and the children to prepare for the Monday night clambake. A pit had to be dug in the sandy soil in back of the house. Then the pit had to be lined with rocks; driftwood had to be found and carried over to the pit; seaweed had to be gathered; and clams had to be dug. It was a two-day project. Harry was still a little shaky from his heart episode and decided to go shopping with his daughters and Jean.

"Where are you going?" he asked them.

"We're going to check out some of the antique shops," said Jean. "There are four or five of them around here. Spiro says they carry mostly junk they hope to unload on unwary tourists, but he says there may be some interesting things. This is an old fishing village, and you never know what may turn up."

"It's exciting, Dad," said Gwen. "Pat collects antique wedgewood pieces, and Jean is looking for an antique mirror for her bedroom, so we have some objectives."

"What are you looking for, Gwen?" asked Harry.

"I don't know, maybe some small trinket or painting we can mount on the wall to remind Nick of Maine. Come with us—you'll enjoy it and maybe find something for the beach house."

Harry marveled at the techniques his girls used in shopping. He always felt obligated to buy something whenever he entered a store, but not these women. They were always polite and affable and looked things over very carefully, but they were absolutely impervious to sales talk, and they felt no embarrassment when they walked out of the shop without buying anything after taking up the owner's time for over an hour. They bought nothing in the first three shops, but in the fourth shop, many very nice pieces could be discovered interspersed with the junk. Pat found a dark-green wedgewood pitcher, which she held up to the light to study the markings underneath. The price was $250.

"That's a ridiculous price," Pat calmly told the owner. "I'm a collector, and I know the value of these pieces. This is very nice, and I will give you $85 for it."

The owner, a shrewd old Yankee, also was well aware of the value. He made a valiant effort to justify the price, but in the end, he sold it to Pat for $100.

Jean also hit pay dirt. She found an antique mirror with a walnut frame and, after a brief discussion, settled on a price of $75.

"I am certainly glad I didn't have to do business with you girls," said Harry, shaking his head.

"It was perfectly obvious that old, foxy grandpa was a very knowledgeable buyer," said Jean, "and we knew that he knew his prices were jacked sky-high. When he found out that we knew something about antiques, he didn't mind coming down."

"And it's late in the season," said Pat. "I'm sure he is trying to get his inventory down for the winter, so it wasn't very hard."

"Well, you got what you came for, so let's go home. I'm getting a little tired."

"One more place, Dad," said Gwen. "I still haven't gotten something about Maine for Nick to hang on the wall."

The last place they went was a converted barn that held lots of dusty furniture and fishing paraphernalia and some rather nice seashore pictures. Gwen was very much attracted to a scene on a dock with fishermen unloading their catch into barrels full of seaweed. With the yellow oilskins of the fishermen and the red and green color of the lobsters and seaweed, it was a very colorful piece.

While Gwen and the others were busy haggling over the price, Harry sat down among a lot of old dusty pictures in a corner of the barn. He was looking through them when he noticed one rather large landscape that had nothing at all to do with Maine. He held it up to the light; it was dusty and dirty, but there in the middle of the picture was a large beech tree, and in the background, the muted shades of brown, green, and red were the unmistakable colors of fall in the foothills of the Alleghenies.

"Sweet Jesus," muttered Harry. "I think I know where that is!"

He took the painting up to the owner, who was just finishing the transaction with Gwen.

"Where did you get this?" he asked the proprietor.

"Let me look at my book," he said. He went into his office and a few minutes later came out with a file containing many invoices and bills of sale. He rummaged through the file and finally came up with a slip of paper that appeared to be an auctioneer's receipt.

"Let's see," he said. "This was one of several paintings I bought in an estate sale in 2003. Mrs. Perkins, who died at ninety-three, had a number of these in her garage. I have sold three of them, and this is the last."

"How much?" asked Harry.

"Well, I'll let that one go for $200."

"That's outrageous!" exclaimed Gwen.

"Yes," said Pat, "You would have to pay at least that amount to get the picture cleaned."

"Here are two Bennies," said Harry, handing over two hundred-dollar bills. "And give me a copy of the estate-sale receipt; I'd like to know who painted this."

When they were in the car driving home, Jean asked Harry why he had bought that picture. "That was a lot of money for an old picture like that, but he could see you wanted it, and you paid full price. Why?"

"Because I think I have been to that very spot," he said. "That's in southwestern Virginia, on an old bean field near Farmville. I was hunting quail with my old hunting buddies years ago when I still had Junior. Do you girls remember Junior?"

"Yes," replied Pat. "He was a huge old pointer who didn't like anyone very much except you."

"That's the one," said Harry, smiling broadly. "He loved me and was the best bird dog I ever saw." Harry paused for a moment, thinking back on the days when he and his friends enjoyed some of the best quail hunting in the east. One of Harry's contractor friends had arranged it. He had leased the hunting rights over an area of old, farmed-out fields and woodlands covering about twelve hundred acres. They stayed at an old, rustic inn, hunting all day and telling stories, playing gin rummy, and drinking lots of good whisky at night. They were all gone now, except for him.

"This looks like the field where we flushed the biggest covey of quail I ever saw," Harry continued. "Junior spotted them for us and froze. It was a sight! When he pointed, he kind of crouched down with his ass up in the air and that big tail sticking straight up like a flagpole. That's why I wanted this picture. We must have killed fifteen quail out of that covey when we got done hunting down the singles."

"But you will have to get it cleaned, Dad," said Pat. "The colors are so blurred you can hardly tell what they are. Do you know anyone who can do that?"

Harry thought for a moment and smiled. "You know," he said, "I might just know someone who can do that. Yes, sir—I think I do."

Chapter 12:
VERA RETURNS

The long-anticipated clambake on Monday evening was almost an anticlimax after all the complex preparations involved. After the pit was dug and lined with rocks, a steel grate was procured and placed about eighteen inches above the bottom layer of rocks; driftwood was piled on the grate, and a fire burned continuously for over twenty-four hours; when the fire began to die down, the embers were shoved through the grate, making a very hot layer of coals, and to keep it hot for the evening, Nick dumped a bag of charcoal on top of the embers. George and Peter borrowed some sawhorses from a neighbor and laid two twelve-foot two-by-fours on each end and covered them with one and a half sheets of plywood, making an outdoor table of twelve feet by four feet. The table was covered with newspapers, which were anchored by stones and two hurricane candles.

At about five thirty, as the evening began to cool, Nick took a big bundle of seaweed and dropped it on the grate. He then put the twelve lobsters on the seaweed, followed by more seaweed and twenty ears of corn in the husks, along with a half dozen franks for the girls, who announced they were not going to eat those "poor lobsters"; another layer of weed was topped off with a bushel of cherrystone clams. He then dumped about two gallons of seawater on the pile and covered it with a tarp. As the cold water hit the red-hot coals and rocks, great clouds of steam rose up and escaped under the edges of the tarp.

"We'll just let it steam for twenty minutes or so," Nick said, "and then you'll have the best eating you ever had."

Pat and Gwen came out with three bowls of a rich butter-lemon-wine sauce for the clams and lobster meat, and everyone brought a chair from the house and awaited the great moment.

"The time has come," sang out Nick as he pulled back the tarp. "Come and get it!" A pungent odor of salty seaweed, seawater, and clam juice pervaded the atmosphere around the pit.

"It smells like the bay at low tide," exclaimed Kathy.

"Let's eat!" declared George. Wearing long, heavy gloves, the men raked the clams out of the pit and dumped them in the middle of the table; next, the corn was taken out and husked and dumped in a mound next to the clams; finally Nick took out the lobsters, sliced the tails with a sharp knife, mashed the claws with a wooden mallet, and placed them next to the mounds of clams and corn. The long buildup, the salty fresh air, and the pungent smell of the clams and seaweed stimulated their appetites, and they had no difficulty clearing the table. Very little remained when Harry pulled the last lobster over to his place at the table.

"Anyone want to split this with me?" he asked. "I don't think I can eat it all."

"You eat it, Dad—it will be good for you."

"I don't know about that," said Harry, dipping a big chunk of rich lobster meat into the butter sauce. "I can almost feel my arteries hardening."

"Have another beer, Harry," said Nick, handing him a cold Beck's. "That will help blow your arteries out."

"Thanks, Nick," said Harry. "I'll have that for dessert. It's always nice to conclude a wonderful dinner with a healthful, nutritious dessert."

The sun had set when they finished eating, and the cleanup was wonderfully simple: it involved rolling up the newspapers with the shells and corncobs inside and dumping them in the trash barrels and then rolling the barrels out to the street to be picked up the next morning. After cleanup, the candles were lit, and everyone talked well into the night. At about nine thirty, a roll of thunder boomed loudly, and streaks of lightning began to show up in the west.

"Looks like that front has started moving in here," observed Nick. "We're due for a change, but we sure had a great two weeks, didn't we?"

"That we did!" Gwen agreed, giving her husband a warm hug and big kiss. "And we all absolutely love Maine!"

George and Jean and their two children left early the next morning to drive down to Woods Hole, and Nick drove Pat and Peter to Portland. Gwen and Harry sat in the kitchen, drinking coffee.

"This has been a really wonderful trip for me," said Harry earnestly. "I wish Mary Ellen could have been here with me, so that she could enjoy all of you the way I did."

"So do I," said Gwen. "Mom was such an upbeat, fun, loving person. I can just hear her razzing you about those hot dogs at the salmon dinner."

"She would have rubbed my nose in it," he said. "She always liked Peter more than me, but I have to say he showed me something, hanging in there with that crazy dishwasher scheme and then actually pulling it off."

"Peter is just right for Pat, Dad," said Gwen. "In this family, we are all different, and you will have to learn to respect our differences."

"I'm learning," he said. "And I am feeling better than I have in a long time."

"How is the heart this morning?" she asked.

"Much better," he answered. "And I think I'll take my picture and walk down to the FedEx office and ship it to Bay Watch to hold for me. It's a nice walk, and I think it will do me good."

"Oh, that reminds me," she said, looking at him quizzically, "Who is this person you said might clean up that old picture for you?"

"Just an artist I met. She teaches art at Salisbury State, and I think she might know how to restore an old painting."

"She?" asked Gwen with a broad smile. "Dad! Do you have a girlfriend?"

Harry felt his cheeks start to burn. "No, nothing like that. Girlfriends are a thing of the past. Nothing could take the place of your mother."

"Why, Dad!" Gwen let loose a delighted giggle. "You are blushing! Don't you let any woman get her hooks into you until I see her and check her out. I think Mom would approve of your having lady friends, provided they are the right type."

Gwen was obviously enjoying herself, and Harry felt he was losing control. He stomped out of the room, saying, "For God's sake, Gwen, this is just an old woman who happens to be an artist, and that's all!" He picked up his picture and hurried out of the house before Gwen had a chance to say anything else.

After the other family members left, Harry spent a relaxed few days getting to know Nick and Gwen's children. Living as they did on the West Coast made it difficult to get together, and except for the memorial service when Mary Ellen died, Harry had seen very little of Gwen's family since they had moved out about twelve years ago. He loved playing games with the girls and talking to Henry, who had become a very enthusiastic young fly fisherman.

Two days after Labor Day, Gwen drove Harry to the airport in Portland.

She gave him a big hug when she dropped him off and said, "We loved having you with us, Dad, and I hope you will come out to Palo Alto and visit us. The children adore you, and we would have such fun showing you the Stanford campus."

"I'll try to do that, honey," he said. "It makes a lot more sense for me to travel across the country than the five of you, but as you know, I'm not a great houseguest."

The flight to BWI was uneventful, and the long wait for the commuter plane to Salisbury was tedious, but Harry made it back to Bay Watch before ten. He fixed himself a big drink of scotch and warmed up a frozen TV dinner. After the noisy excitement generated by his family in Maine, his villa seemed very small and empty. He checked his voice mail and was disappointed to find no messages from Vera. He decided he would call her in the morning. Surely she must be coming back to sell her condo and pick up her things, even if she had decided to move to the West Coast., and he hoped the project of restoring his picture would entice her to stay a little longer.

On the morning after Harry returned to Bay Watch, Vera was sitting alone in the kitchen of her daughter's home in Oakland, California. Nancy was driving the youngest of her four children to preschool, after which she would do some shopping, return home to have lunch with Vera, and then take her oldest son to soccer practice, pick up Barbara from preschool, and return to organize the after-school activities of her other children. It was a busy schedule, and Nancy sometimes looked very tired and frazzled.

This was not a happy situation for Vera; she was truly on the horns of a difficult dilemma. All her children lived in the Bay Area of San Francisco and wanted her to leave Salisbury and live near them. Vera wanted to be near them; they were her closest relatives: her children, whom she dearly loved, and her grandchildren, whom she barely knew. At her age, it was the conventional and logical thing to do. But where would she live? She had been in Nancy's home for over a month, occupying one of the children's rooms. She was aware of the increasing tension her presence was causing in the household. Robert, Nancy's husband, had a good job with the Bay Area Rapid Transit Authority, but taking care of a family of four children stretched their budget pretty tightly, and, while Robert was always cordial, she knew he would be glad to see her leave, so he and Nancy could have more time to themselves.

Vera's son, Jim, worked in the trust department of a large bank and lived with his wife, Betty, and their two children in a comfortable apartment that had zero extra room. Her younger daughter, Melonie, was something of a swinger and lived in San Francisco in a trendy, loft-style studio apartment. Neither the space nor Melonie's lifestyle were conducive to Vera's presence. She had spent a good deal of time looking at condos in the area and even some small, ranch-style houses in the suburbs, but all were way past Vera's rather modest financial means. She also investigated the possibility of getting a job teaching art in some of the schools and universities, but there was nothing there for Vera. The school system and the universities were large, bordering on huge, and so was everything else in California. It was a big state; the Bay Area seemed endless; the traffic jams were monumental; and everything was frightfully expensive. She felt she didn't belong there, and that nobody really wanted her. She was very depressed and on the verge of tears when the telephone rang.

She answered it and heard a familiar voice. "Vera? Is that you?"

"Harry!" exclaimed Vera. "How wonderful of you to call."

"I wasn't sure you were ready to talk to me yet," said Harry. "It takes time to get your affairs settled, but I just had to find out how you are getting along."

"Well, I'm glad you did," she said. "I haven't called you because I feel so lost. My kids seem to want me to stay out here, but I just don't feel like I belong."

"Come on back here, Vera," said Harry with a little catch in his voice. "You have lots of friends here, and we all miss you."

"Do you miss me, Harry?" asked Vera.

"Yes, I do," he replied. "And I have something here that I think you can help me with."

"What is that?"

"I bought a painting when I was up in Maine with the kids," he said. "It's real grimy and dirty, and I hoped you might be able to restore it for me."

"Why did you buy it if it was in such bad shape?"

"Because it reminded me of a great place in southwestern Virginia where I used to hunt quail."

"And you found it in an old antique shop in Maine?"

"Yes"

"How odd," said Vera, sounding a little puzzled. "Well, I'm coming home. You have helped me make up my mind. I do have to sell my condo and pick up my things, even if I do move out here. I was so low that I wasn't thinking straight. I feel so kind of lost and out of touch here … I'll try to explain when I get home."

"Call me when you know your flight into BWI, and I will pick you up and drive you down."

"Wonderful!" she said.

After he hung up, Harry felt much better; Vera would be back in a week or two, and he thought he had a good chance of persuading her to stay for at least another year. After his two weeks in Maine, Harry had lost touch with his new friends at Bay Watch, and he decided that the best way to get back into the normal activities was to host a dinner party for some of the special friends who had been very helpful in getting him acclimated in the community. He called a catering service Ed Strong had recommended and decided on September 20, his seventy-seventh birthday. His dining room was large enough to hold ten people comfortably, and he told the caterer he would supply the main dish, which would be some of the lake trout fillets he had brought back from Maine. Then he called his social mentor and bridge partner, Joan Stanton; he got no answer, and her voice mail did not pick up, which he thought was strange. Next he called George Atkins, the shrewd man who called himself a retired farmer, and invited him and his wife, Amy, to come to dinner.

"You are the first one I called," Harry told him. "I tried to get Joan Stanton, but got no answer. Is she away?"

"Ah, Harry, we didn't know how to reach you," George said softly. "Joanie had a massive stroke two weeks ago and died two days later. It just wasn't the kind of message we wanted to leave on your answering machine. We had a memorial service for her here last week."

"My God," whispered Harry. "I really liked that woman. We did everything together." Harry felt dazed and a little nauseated. Death was so final and so inevitable; no one was ever prepared for it. "Maybe I should cancel the dinner party."

"Well, that's up to you, of course, but I think it would be most appropriate for you to have a dinner honoring Joanie's life on your birthday. This is a community of older people, and things like that happen all too often. She slipped away from us with very little fuss and suffering, and that is how we all hope to go."

Harry thought for a moment. "Okay, George," he said. "I think you are right. I'll have some of her special friends to dinner, and I'll say a few words about her, since I wasn't at the memorial service."

"That will be good, Harry, but not too much sadness and grief—Joanie was a very happy person."

During the next few days, Harry assembled a group of people who had known Joan well and all enthusiastically supported having a party in her honor. They were an interesting group, and all were long-term friends of Joan.

Harry opened the dinner with a special grace wherein he thanked the Lord for giving each of them the privilege of having known Joan Stanton during her golden years and being able to share with one another the memories of her life at Bay Watch. It set the right tone. Wine flowed generously, and Harry's fish were beautifully complemented by a light hollandaise sauce, along with the stories involving Joan, her love of bridge, her wonderful wit, and her geriatric romance with Harry. The stories about Harry and Joan came at the end after several glasses of wine had been consumed and were slightly over the top. It left Harry a little flustered. He had liked Joan a lot; they flirted occasionally, but he had thought of her more as a sister than a potential lover.

It was a very successful party and left Harry feeling good about himself. After the guests left at about nine thirty and the caterers were cleaning up, Harry checked his voice mail and found a message from Vera that her flight would be arriving at 5:30 p.m. in three days. Harry felt himself getting a little excited; his thoughts about Vera were very definitely not brotherly.

Three days later, Harry arrived at the BWI pickup area at about six o'clock and found Vera sitting on one of her suitcases, waiting. He put her cases in the back of his wagon and gave Vera a big hug.

"Here's one guy who really wants you to stay with him!" he exclaimed.

"Oh, Harry! I'm glad someone wants me," she said.

On the way to Salisbury, she told him of the tensions that had built up within her family during her stay at her daughter's home.

"I just feel so humiliated," she said. "These are my children; I love them with all my heart, and they were glad to see me go!" She began to weep silently. "John is gone, and my family doesn't want anything to do with me." Vera was visibly upset, and Harry could sympathize with her. Getting along with your children after you lost your spouse was not easy. Emotions were very intense, and it was easy to feel deserted and hurt.

"I don't know any of your family, Vera," said Harry, "but I think they love you and want to help, but they feel frustrated, too. As I see the picture, they are trying to make a decent living in the big city, and they are doing okay, but not great. They want to take care of you, but it's all they can do to take care of their children. My hunch is that your daughter, Nancy, is shedding a few tears right now, just as you are. For now you have to be the visiting grandma and let things work out."

"But your family is so different. You say they want you to live with them, and even if you don't, doesn't it make you feel good that they want you?"

Harry laughed. "My family isn't much different. They say they want me because they know I will not move in with any of them. If I did, there would be a hell of a ruckus, and I would be out of there in less than two months. We must live on our own and earn their respect."

They stopped for dinner at the Bay Bridge in Annapolis and had a big bowl of oyster stew and a crab-cake sandwich at Chesapeake Crab House, and by the time they reached Salisbury, Vera had calmed down and was discussing her teaching position at Salisbury State.

"The dean gave me a leave of absence for this term," she said, "and he assured me that I could have my position back for the spring term, beginning in January, if I wanted it."

"See, Vera," Harry exclaimed, "this is where you belong! People around here need you … including me and my picture!"

He helped her unload her suitcases and put them in her condo and, as he bent down to kiss her good night, he was overcome by emotion and pulled her into a tight embrace.

She gently pushed him away. "Oh, Harry," she whispered softly. "You are a dear man, but I'm not ready for anything like a romance now. Let's just continue to be friends for a while, and you bring me that picture tomorrow."

"I'm sorry, Vera," he said. "I know you need time and space. It was a year before I had any interest in women after Mary Ellen died. Take your time; I'll be around here for a while. And I will bring that picture over in the morning."

Chapter 13:
THE UNVEILING

AFTER HARRY LEFT, Vera unpacked slowly and went out on her balcony with a cup of tea. So much had happened in the last six weeks; she was a widow now, one of many at her age. It seemed strange that women routinely outlived their husbands in this generation. Not so long ago, it had been the men who outlived their wives and often had several families with different partners. She thought about her vigorous, stalwart husband, who had seemed so invincible for so many years only to be suddenly stricken by a massive stroke and reduced to a helpless invalid for the last two years. What was ahead now? Should she sell her condominium here and move to the West Coast and try to start a new life there? She wasn't sure her family really wanted her to do that. Harry was probably right: her family did love and respect her, but they could scarcely make ends meet as it was, without the added responsibility of an aging mother.

Staying in Salisbury seemed to be the best option for now. She had a comfortable and affordable place to live; an interesting job teaching art history at Salisbury State; and a part-time job at the local art gallery. The income wasn't much, but with social security and John's life-insurance benefits, it was enough. And then there was Harry—what a rock he had been. She was aware that he was interested in her; he had tried to kiss her when he brought her home, and she had stopped him. Instead of being angry or hurt, he had understood her feelings perfectly. She liked Harry more now than when they were in school, but she was spent emotionally and needed to get her life back together before she would be ready to see what would happen with Harry.

She spent a restless night with her mind jumping from one subject to another so that it was impossible to relax. She finally fell asleep at dawn and was awakened by the telephone. She answered it and heard Harry's cheerful voice.

"I bet I woke you up, Vera. Are you still on Pacific time?"

"You did, and I am," she answered sleepily. "What time is it?"

"Ten thirty," said Harry, "and that's seven thirty Oakland time. Go back to sleep, and I will stop for you at twelve thirty. We'll get some lunch, and I will show you my picture. How's that?"

"Fine, Harry. I'll try to struggle up."

When Harry arrived at Vera's condo, Vera met him looking somewhat subdued and worn.

"Hello, Harry," she said. "Thanks for driving me home last night. You are a really good friend."

"That I am," announced Harry, "and I am looking forward to being a better friend. Now let's get you some lunch—you look a little forlorn right now."

"I guess I am," admitted Vera. "I've lost my husband, and there seems to be no room for me around the family I have loved and cherished for so long. My life is over."

"Now, now, Antonelli," said Harry, giving her a little squeeze, "stop being sorry for yourself and get a grip on your new life. If it makes you feel better, I went through a similar stage after Mary Ellen died. It still hurts, and I guess it always will, but I have discovered that it's not so bad being old and single and living alone. You are going back to your job with Salisbury State, aren't you?"

"Yes, I am, if they are willing to take on an old woman like me. The dean said he would give me a leave of absence this term, and I will see him as soon as I can get an appointment." She sighed heavily. "You know, Harry, you are a good influence on me. You are a very kind, compassionate man."

"That surprise you?" he asked.

"Yes!" said Vera emphatically. "Back in our school days, the only thing you were interested in was getting into bed with me."

"Some things never change," he said with a broad smile. "Let's go over to the Riviera and have a nice lunch, and then I'll take you over to Bay Watch, and you can see where I live and look at my crummy old picture."

Vera brightened up and took Harry's arm. "Let's go," she said.

They had a leisurely lunch at a table overlooking the Wicomico River. It was a lovely early fall day, and the trees along the riverbank were beginning to show a little color.

Harry noticed that Vera was staring intently at the river. "Does that artist's eye of yours see something that I don't?" he asked.

Vera smiled. "I guess so," she said. "It is a beautiful scene here by the river, with the blue sky and those puffy little pillows floating around up there, and there is a hint of autumn in the trees. But I am seeing too much man-made rubble around here, like that old piece of concrete sticking out of the water and the brown stains on the rocks along the bank, which look like oil stains."

"Can't you just sit back, relax, and enjoy a pretty day by the river?" asked Harry. "It must be very depressing to keep seeing only the bad side of nature."

"Oh, Harry," she said, "I'm not a pessimist, and I do love the little rivers and creeks we have down here, but I am a dedicated environmentalist, and I see my talent as an artist as a way of influencing public awareness of the need to clean up our natural resources and treat them with more respect. One of my more ambitious projects is to get a sponsor for a series of environmental paintings like the one I did of our park."

"Where do these sponsors come from?" he asked.

"A lot of different organizations make grants for environmental projects," she answered. "There is a book listing their names and contacts. If I could get one of them to sponsor me, it would give me credibility, exhibit space, and publicity."

"Have you contacted any of those people?"

"Yes, and there seems to be zero interest in an elderly painter whom nobody has ever heard of."

"Could I sponsor you?" he asked.

"That is such a nice offer, Harry, but that's not the way it works. If you were a well-known philanthropist or patron of the arts, it would be wonderful, but I am afraid nobody in the art or environmental fields knows anything about you, either. A well-known charitable trust, like the Wallace Foundation or the Abel Foundation, would have the clout I need. They are wealthy and highly respected, and I could get publicity and arrange exhibit space in Washington or New York or even Annapolis, where people would write about my art and its message. But I am afraid that's not going to happen."

"Well, don't give up," he said. "There is still a lot of fire under that old gray head of yours. I think you will succeed. In the meantime, let's look at my painting, and you can tell me how much you will charge to fix it up."

"I'm expensive!" she said, giving his arm a little squeeze.

Harry drove her to Bay Watch and gave her a tour of the facilities ending at his villa. Vera was impressed.

"This is lovely!" she exclaimed. "Such a nice, roomy house, and your garden is impressive."

"Gardening is about all I can do these days," remarked Harry. "I had to quit tennis years ago, and my golf game is pathetic."

"It must be very comforting to your children to know you are in a place like this."

"Yes," agreed Harry. "They were worried about me after Mary Ellen died and even thought I was drinking too much whisky."

"Do you?" she asked.

"At times," he answered. "But let's not delve too deeply into my many sins; it might scare you off. I'll bring in the picture."

He went into his bedroom, brought the painting to Vera, and unwrapped it. She could see that it was in bad shape; the glass was cracked, and it was very dusty, and the painting itself seemed to be stained in a few places.

"This seems to be an old painting, and it will take a lot of work to clean it up. You said it reminded you of someplace in Virginia. Why is it so special?"

"Because I know this place," he said. "I remember this old beech tree in this bean field; I hunted there with some of my best friends about forty years ago and with my best bird dog, Junior."

"I think this picture was painted before the Second World War; are you sure it's the same place?"

Harry hesitated and spoke slowly. "When we hunted that field, we saw an old abandoned farmhouse, some decaying storage bins, and an old barn. I remember we went in there to rest and have lunch before going after the singles in the woods. So it must have been a working farm at some time, but that field and that beech tree look awfully familiar."

"I'll take it with me and see if I can get someone in the art department to help me. This will need some restoring work, and it will probably cost a couple of hundred dollars to get it looking decent. Do you think it's worth it?"

"See what you can do, Vera," he said. "I really like that picture; it brings back some memories of very happy times."

When Vera returned to her condo, she studied the painting carefully and removed the cracked glass and the frame. She could see that the artist was skilled in watercolor techniques. The use of complementary colors emphasized the size and shape of the beech tree, which was the focal point of the painting. And she could see evidence of some sophisticated brushwork in the patterns of the leaves and branches. The paper on which the watercolor was painted seemed unusually thin, and yet the painting itself seemed pretty heavy.

She turned it over, removed the cardboard backing, and stared at it for a full two minutes.

She then picked up the telephone and called Howard Cohen, head of the art department at Salisbury State. "Howard, this is Vera calling. I'm back."

"Welcome back, Vera!" exclaimed Howard. "I hope you will be with us for the spring term."

"I hope so, too," answered Vera. "I'm going to call the dean's office and see if they really want an old lady like me on the faculty and whether the budget has room for me."

"Don't worry about that; my budget has already been approved, and you are in it."

"Wonderful!" she exclaimed. "I really need to get back to work, but I called you this evening because I want you to look at an old watercolor a friend bought. It needs some restoration, but there is something strange about it."

"What's strange?" he asked.

"It's a watercolor on thin paper, but the back of it is canvas on a stretcher."

"Now that is odd," agreed Howard. "Can you get to my office tomorrow morning around seven thirty? We'll look at it before my first class."

The next morning, Howard and Vera studied the watercolor together.

"The artist seems to be well trained," observed Howard. "The tree is quite well done, but the rest of the picture looks very sketchy and incomplete."

"Like maybe the artist was in a hurry?" asked Vera.

"Exactly—and that would be understandable if this watercolor were painted to cover up the oil painting that I think is under it."

"But if we took this watercolor off, wouldn't it be damaged?" Vera asked.

"Yes, I think it would be destroyed. I suggest you get an infrared image that will show what's under there. I have a friend at the Philips Gallery in Washington, and they have infrared equipment. I'll call him and arrange an appointment."

When Vera got home, she called Harry and told him what she had discovered about his painting.

"What happens to my picture if you try to find out what is under it?" he asked.

"If we found something interesting, I'm afraid your picture would be destroyed when we took it off," she answered.

She could sense that Harry was distressed; he had paid $200 for the painting, and now she was telling him that she wanted to destroy it, not restore it.

"It isn't a very good painting, Harry, and what's underneath may be a valuable piece of art. Aren't you curious about what's there and why it was concealed?"

"I guess so," he answered.

"Here's what I'll do," she said. "I will photograph this painting, and if we have to destroy it, I will paint it for you just as you remember it, with the old barn and with your old bird dog, if you have a picture of him somewhere." That seemed to satisfy Harry, and he consented to having the watercolor painting taken off if she deemed it necessary.

Howard Cohen called and confirmed her appointment with Dr. Jennings at the Philips Gallery. Vera made arrangements to stay with an old friend, Sarah Burns, who had done some high-level restoration work for the Mellon Gallery . Sarah was nearly eighty, but still active, and she was very interested in the picture.

"You say your friend bought this painting in southeastern Maine?" she asked.

"Yes, the receipt shows that the dealer purchased it from an auction company at an estate sale. The painting belonged to an old woman who died in 2003, and the painting was evidently stored in her garage."

"This is an old painting," Sarah observed, "and Maine is where Winslow Homer spent the last thirty years of his life. You might keep that in mind when you're looking at what's under there."

"Homer?" Vera was surprised. "I never thought about him. My friend says this looks like a place in southwestern Virginia, and I was thinking Civil War dates and a Virginia artist."

"You are probably right," conceded Sarah. "There is just something about that tree that reminds me of Homer's work. He was a master watercolorist, you know."

The next morning, Vera walked over to the Philips Gallery with a rising sense of anticipation and excitement. Sarah's remark about Homer had raised her expectations. What if this turned out to be a long-lost masterpiece? Why was it covered up? Had it been stolen? She felt nervous and a little giddy as she showed the picture to Dr. Jennings in his office. He examined it closely.

"There is very definitely something under here," he said, looking around the edges with a magnifying glass. "You say Sarah was thinking Homer?"

"That's what she said."

"Homer didn't do this picture," he said. "The tree is well done, but the rest of the picture is just a sketch. His work may have seemed sketchy to some of his critics, but it wasn't. He was a master at watercolor."

"I think she meant it looked like his technique around the tree, but I think she was speculating about what's underneath," Vera amended.

"Well, let's put it under the scope and see what it is."

Dr. Jennings took several shots and displayed the images on a backlit panel, similar to x-ray equipment. The result was startling. The images clearly showed a portrait of a young woman reclining in a chair, and at the right-hand corner appeared an inset with unintelligible initials and what appeared to be a date, partially obscured.

"Ah," said Dr. Jennings softly. "As usual, Sarah was on to something. You want to take this watercolor off, don't you?"

"Yes," replied Vera. "I have permission from the owner."

"All right, then. Call Sarah and see if she can get over here and tell us what she recommends."

Vera dialed Sarah's number and said, "Sarah! You've got to see this. Can you come over right away?"

"I'll be there in ten minutes," she replied.

Sarah came in the room a few minutes later and looked the images without speaking. Finally she looked up.

"This looks like a portrait, and the initials suggest Homer. But Homer didn't do many portraits—only a few that we know of. So if this is authentic, it is something very unique, Vera."

"Can you get that watercolor off?" asked Vera.

"Yes," she answered. "It is pretty old, and I will have to be careful; that cracked glass has let in some moisture, and the paper will probably adhere to the oil in some places, but leave it with me for a week, and I'll get it done."

"What will your fee be for this restoration?" asked Vera. "This may be a tough job, and the stakes might be pretty high."

"Very high," said Sarah. "You are an old friend, and I want to do this, so I will charge $1,000. Can your friend afford it?"

"Yes, he can," replied Vera. "I'll call you in a week."

"And call us, Vera," said Dr. Jennings. "We can help with authentication."

"I will, Dr. Jennings," said Vera, "and thanks so much for your help."

"We are honored to be a part of what we hope is a major art discovery," he replied. "If it is what we think it is, we would like to be considered as the exhibitor. It will cause quite a commotion among the art community."

When Vera returned to Salisbury, she called Harry. She was so excited she could barely get the words out about their discovery.

"So you see, Harry," she said breathlessly, "this painting Sarah is restoring may be a Homer and worth hundreds of thousands of dollars."

Harry was silent for a moment. Then he said slowly, "Vera, there is no such thing as a free lunch, and there is no way I will ever be lucky enough to pay two hundred bucks for an old picture and have it turn out to be worth thousands of dollars."

"But these people are experts!" she exclaimed. "They believe it is a rare Winslow Homer painting."

"Let's see what they say next week. In the meantime, have dinner with me tonight, and tell me when you are going to start work on my picture of that beech tree and the bean field with Junior in it, pointing a covey of quail."

At dinner, Vera explained to Harry why Homer was considered to be such a great artist. He was considered to be a completely American artist. Although he studied briefly in England and spent some time in France, his work was uniquely American, and his subject matters were creative and compelling. He had no formal training as an artist and started his career as an illustrator for weekly magazines. He was sent to cover the Civil War with the Union army and did some wonderful scenes, telling a story of the war and the soldiers that was more eloquent than any story filed by a journalist. During the war, Homer matured as an artist, and some of his oil paintings, such a "Prisoners at the Front" and "The Sharpshooter," are considered masterpieces.

"But why would one of his pictures show up in Maine?" he asked.

"The shop where you bought the painting in Maine was close to a place called Prouts Neck, where Homer lived for the last thirty years of his life."

"If he was such a famous artist, why hole up in Maine for most of his life?"

"Not much is known of Homer's personal life," said Vera. "He never married, and his brother was his only heir. After the Civil War, he painted many pictures of contemporary social life with lots of attractive women in them. He painted one portrait of a young woman, Helena DeKay, who was supposedly a girlfriend. It such a somber-looking portrait, I can't believe he had much of a romantic interest in her. But there was another woman who appeared in some of his brighter, livelier-looking paintings. She had red hair and was dressed in various fashionable poses. She was quite attractive, and there is some speculation about her and Homer. She is sometimes referred to as the Mystery Woman."

"So did Homer have a little romp in the hay with this Mystery Woman?" Harry asked.

"We don't know," replied Vera. "About a year after the paintings of the Mystery Woman appeared, Homer stopped painting pictures with attractive women in them. He went to England and then settled in Maine as a confirmed old bachelor and became something of a recluse."

"I think you think this woman dumped him, don't you?"

"I do," answered Vera. "From sources I have read, Homer was a sensitive, generous man—quite shy, but warm and outgoing, and he had many friends. Something happened that changed his whole personality."

"And I suppose you think this oil painting under my picture is a portrait of the Mystery Woman."

"I really think so, but who painted the watercolor and why the oil was covered up is another mystery."

The next few days were very busy for Vera. She had a conference with the dean of the faculty at Salisbury State, who was happy to have her back; she was popular with the students and other faculty members, and he had no problem at all with her age. Later she met with Howard to discuss the course she would be offering in the spring term. At the end of the week, she called Sarah.

"How's it coming?" she asked.

"I was about to call you," Sarah replied. "It's done. There were a few spots where the pigments came off the oil when I took the watercolor off. I called Jennings and showed him where they were and then I took care of them. He is having some experts examine it. Can you come up next Tuesday? He said to get there about ten."

"I wouldn't miss it!" Vera said. "And I will bring the owner."

Immediately after talking to Sarah, Vera called Harry. "You must come," she urged, "and there may be questions about where you got it, so bring the receipt."

"Okay, I'll come," he said, "but I can't believe it will be worth anything. Is this appraisal or whatever you call it going to cost me anything?"

"Oh, I forgot," she said. "You owe Sarah $1,000 for the restoration work, and I don't know whether there will be a fee for the authentication."

"What!" choked Harry. "I already owe a thousand dollars? What have you gotten me into, Antonelli?"

"A half-million-dollar windfall is what I've gotten you into," said Vera heatedly. "Just shut up and come to Washington with me next Monday."

"Shall I book us a room at the Dupont Plaza?" asked Harry coyly.

"You stay at your club, and I will be staying with Sarah," said Vera firmly, "and we will meet at the gallery at ten on Tuesday morning."

"I'll come," said Harry, "but I have a strong feeling this will turn out to be a fake, and I am going to be out a lot of money."

Driving up to Washington on Monday afternoon, Harry could not suppress a rising feeling of anticipation. He tried to keep a level head; he didn't believe in the tooth fairy, and the idea of accidentally buying a painting worth thousands of dollars wasn't realistic. It was too good to be true. Yet a nagging and persistent fact kept coming back to him: Sarah, a genuine expert, had told Vera there was no doubt in her mind that this was the real thing.

"Stuff like this doesn't happen to people like me," he complained.

"I can hardly wait," said Vera. "Discovery of an important work of art is such a special and exciting event."

They made the trip in just under three hours, and Harry dropped Vera off at Sarah's apartment and then checked in at the Metropolitan Club. Sarah and Vera had a dinner date with some artist friends, so Harry dined alone at the club and watched a TV movie after dinner. He met Sarah and Vera at the gallery a few minutes before ten. Vera introduced them, and Sarah shook his hand warmly.

"You are one lucky man, Harry," she said.

"So they say," he said, looking a little dazed. "But I still can't believe it."

At ten o'clock, Dr. Jennings came out and ushered them into his office.

"There she is," he said, pointing to the painting hanging on the display wall. It had been fitted with a temporary frame and was hung where the soft ceiling wall wash highlighted the colors of the painting.

The woman in the picture was reclining in a dark-green robe. She had shoulder-length, dark-red hair and large, expressive, greenish-brown eyes that seemed to be looking directly at the audience no matter where they stood. The woman was seated under what appeared to be an arbor of grapevines, and the light and shadows from the sun created a breathtaking image of a strong, beautiful woman. In the lower right-hand corner of the painting was a three-inch inset of a manor house overlooking a river with the battle flags of the Confederate and Union armies at either side. The effect was spellbinding, and no one spoke for a long minute.

Harry finally broke the spell. "That is one drop-dead gorgeous woman," he said hoarsely.

"Yes," said Sarah, "and it has very definite romantic overtones in it. She is properly covered up—nothing lewd—but there is just enough skin showing to put your imagination into overdrive."

"Who is she?" he asked.

"That, Harry," said Vera with conviction, "is the Mystery Woman."

"Is it really Homer's work?" he asked, still unable to believe his good fortune.

"No doubt about it. We all agree," said Dr. Jennings, indicating the three men who were standing on the other side of the room.

"How can you be so sure?" asked Harry skeptically.

"We have equipment that allows us to estimate the age of this painting accurately," said one of the experts. "And we have analyzed the pigments, and they match ones used by Homer in his other works. The paper is also the same as was used for watercolors in the 1860s."

"There really isn't any doubt about it, Mr. Walker," said Dr. Jennings.

"My God," said Harry softly.

Chapter 14:
LAURA ASHTON

I. Yorktown, 1862

THE UNION ARMY, commanded by General George McClelland, was slowly working its way toward Richmond on the peninsula between the York and James Rivers. Not a bold commander, McClelland was very reluctant to commit his troops to battle unless they had a significant advantage. The army stalled a little short of the historic village of Yorktown, the site of the decisive battle of the Revolutionary War. The Union army discovered that the Confederate forces had fortified positions across the Warwick River, and the general waited for heavy siege guns to arrive at the front lines before attacking.

In the meantime, it was necessary to equip and feed the enormous army McClelland had assembled. In addition to supplies brought in by ship to Newport News and Hampton Roads, the Union army relied on foraging parties to confiscate food and equipment from the local farms and communities. On that warm spring day in April, a foraging party was working its way up the James River, concentrating on some of the large plantations that had sizable stores of grain and livestock.

Among the soldiers in the party was a young man assigned by Harper's Weekly Magazine to cover the peninsula campaign. He was small in stature with pleasant features and dark brown hair and beard. He wore a Union field jacket without insignia and carried no arms. The party stopped at a plantation manor house identified by a sign over the entrance as Ashvale. The soldiers went up to the house and ordered two slaves and a young girl, all of whom were working in a garden where numerous vegetables and berries were growing, to go into the house. The slaves immediately complied with the order, but the young girl stood her ground.

"I don't take orders from Yankees," she stated matter-of-factly.

"Get in there, or by God, I'll take this whip to you!" roared the sergeant, shaking his riding whip.

"Go ahead! I'm not moving."

The sergeant dismounted and advanced toward the girl in a threatening manner. Abruptly the young man addressed the angry sergeant. "A picture of a Union soldier whipping a young girl wouldn't look very good back home, would it?" He spoke softly, yet with some force and asperity. "Why don't you go and do your duty, and let me talk to her."

The sergeant turned and stared angrily at the young man. "You are a royal pain in the arse, Homer," he said gruffly. "Stay out of my way." He turned back to the young girl, who glared back at him with defiant, angry eyes that showed no sign of fear. Finally he turned away and muttered, "All right, you talk to her, but if she gets in the way she'll get hurt" He mounted and rode back to join his men, who were already loading the wagons with supplies from the plantation's storage buildings.

Homer dismounted, tethered his horse, and looked at the girl. He judged she was around twelve, tall, and well proportioned, with lovely red hair.

"What's your name, young lady?" he asked.

"I don't talk to Yankee soldiers," she said sullenly.

"But I am not a soldier," he replied as he sat down on the stone fence next to the garden. "I am an artist ... or at least I hope to be an artist." As he spoke, he opened his knapsack and took out a sketch pad. "So you don't have to hate me. I try to make pictures that show what this war is like in Virginia, so people up north can see what is happening here."

"Why don't all of you go back up north and leave us alone?" she exclaimed emotionally. "We just want to live as we always have lived."

Homer looked at the girl carefully and began sketching. She was a beautiful child with very unusual brownish-green eyes. "Do you know the name of that little village on the York River near Williamsburg?" He continued sketching while he talked.

"That's Yorktown. What about it?"

"About eighty years ago, a very famous Virginian named George Washington commanded an army composed of Virginians and other Southerners, along with men from Massachusetts, New York, and other places up north. They defeated the British army at Yorktown, and our country was born. Other great men from Virginia, like Jefferson, Madison, and Monroe, nursed our country through its infancy, and now we have a great union of many states ... so why would you want to tear apart something your forefathers worked so hard to create?"

She looked a little disconcerted. "We don't want to tear anything apart. We just want you to go back where you came from."

"You didn't tell me your name. I am Winslow Homer, and I was born in Cambridge, Massachusetts. Will you tell me your name?" he asked gently.

"Laura Ashton," she said reluctantly. "And Ashvale is my family's home."

"Do you hate me?" he asked.

The question startled her, and she hesitated, her eyes brimming with tears. "You Yankees killed my daddy, and you are stealing all of our food, so we'll probably starve," she said, choking back the urge to cry. "That's why I hate all of you."

"Would you like to see what I have done on my sketch pad?" he asked, handing it to her.

She gasped as she looked at the picture of herself standing in the garden with the graceful old manor house behind her and the Union soldiers loading wagons from the barns in the distance. "I didn't know anyone could draw like that."

"Not many can," he replied with satisfaction. "Would you mind if

I came back to visit in a few days? I will try to finish this picture, and I want to give it to you."

He could see she was getting confused; her manner was less belligerent and defiant, and her voice was softer and even a little friendly.

"Well, I don't see how we can stop you if you want to come." She hesitated and then said, "I better go inside now."

Three days later, Mrs. Lucy Ashton observed a lone rider coming up the road to her house. He was dressed in a Union field jacket but carried no arms.

"Laura, is that the man you were talking to the day those Yankees raided our farm?"

"Looks to be," answered Laura.

"What on earth do they want now?" she said with a worried frown. "They took everything we had."

"Maybe he's bringing us something, Mother," said Laura. "His saddlebags are pretty full."

"I don't want you to have anything to do with him," Lucy said sternly. "You are a young girl, but those Yankee soldiers don't care who they attack and ravish. Stay away from him!"

"Yes'm." Laura smiled at her mother. "But he's different."

Homer dismounted and knocked on the door. He doffed his hat when Lucy opened it a little way and stood eyeing him defiantly.

"Good afternoon, madam," he said. "I hope I am welcome; your daughter and I had a most interesting discussion a few days ago."

"You have stolen everything we have, and you Yankees killed my husband at Manassas. Why on earth should you be welcome?" Lucy's face blazed with anger and indignation.

"Yes, the war," he said mildly. "Both sides have suffered severe losses and now hate each other, but we are individuals, madam, and we don't have to hate each other. I am an artist, and I have worked hard to produce this painting of your lovely daughter and your beautiful home. What do you think of it?" he asked, handing her the picture.

In spite of her anger, Lucy was overcome by the scene. The focal point was her daughter with her beautiful hair, looking down at the raiding party of Union soldiers with dignity and defiance. "Oh, my, "she said. "Laura looks so … so … kind of majestic. She's just a little girl; she's not that way at all."

"That's the way she looks to me," he said with a smile. "She has courage, integrity, and dignity, and that's what I painted. She represents what is good about the South—and there is much good in the South, madam, especially in Virginia, where the great men of this state fought and worked so hard to establish our country."

"Well, come in, then," said Lucy, shaking her head. "You do have a way about you, sir."

"Let me bring in my saddlebags," he said. "And perhaps Laura can help me; they are quite heavy." Homer took the bags into the kitchen; they were loaded with bread, potatoes, vegetables, and several large hams.

"Where did you get all this?" Lucy asked suspiciously.

"I thought our troops were too hard on you, and I asked one of the quartermasters if I might return some things to you so that you would not go hungry."

"And they agreed?"

"No," he said. "So I stole them."

"What!" exclaimed Laura "Won't you get in trouble if you are caught giving them to us?"

"Most assuredly," answered Homer coolly. "I would certainly be sent home in disgrace, and I might even get shot."

Laura was distressed. "How terrible!" she cried. "You have been so kind to us, and it would be awful if you got shot for helping us."

Homer laughed. "Don't worry too much about me," he said. "I'm not a soldier, and the troops try to stay on my good side. They want me to send pictures back home showing that they are good fellows doing good deeds. I told them I was taking some of the food back to you, and no one objected."

"Then why did you lie about it and tell us you might be shot?" asked Laura indignantly.

"Because I wanted to impress you, little lady," he said with a broad smile. "I wanted you to think I was noble and brave."

Laura retreated to stand beside her mother, looking confused and a little pleased. Lucy chuckled and wagged her finger at Homer. "You are a very strange Yankee," she said. "I think I might even come to like you someday ... but don't you go flirting with my daughter. She's only a child."

"And will become a beautiful and strong woman whom I hope to meet when this is over. But right now I must be getting back to our base camp."

"So, Mr. Homer," she said as he was preparing to mount his horse, "will we see you again soon?"

He shook his head. "There seems to be a big buildup of troops just outside of Yorktown, and I fear there will be another battle at that historic place. But I assure you, Mrs. Ashton, that I will come back someday, and I hope to find both of you in good health."

They said their farewells and, as Homer rode away, Lucy turned to her daughter.

"That's a very unusual man," she said. "Do you like the picture he did of you?"

"Yes. Mother, I think it is wonderful!"

"So do I," she said. "I think I will hang it in the dining room, where it will get the afternoon light."

II. Ashvale, 1876

Fourteen years had passed since Homer last visited Ashvale. He remembered Laura vividly and wondered how she had fared during the war and its aftermath. There was much despair here; the old way of life was disappearing but not without a struggle. The newly emancipated slaves still did the same hard menial labor but had no one to take care of them, and it was apparent that the gap between black and white was as strong as ever.

Homer had matured as an artist, and his genius was recognized by many critics in America and abroad. He had come to Virginia on a commission from some of his agents to paint scenes of the Reconstruction, and he had accepted partly because of the prestige such an assignment carried and partly because of his desire to see Laura. He drove his rented horse and buggy up the lane to Ashvale and turned in the gate; he would soon find out how she looked as a young woman. He wondered if she was married. As he stopped in the shade and tethered his horse, he gazed critically at the old manor house. It was in good repair, but the paint was peeling around the windows, and the grounds were overgrown and full of weeds. The ravages of war and the difficult Reconstruction had taken their toll on the great James River plantations, and Ashvale was no exception.

"Looks like we have company," observed Lucy Ashton. "Can't say as I recognize him."

Laura stared intently at the man driving the buggy. He was small and conservatively dressed in a fashionable suit, and was looking over the house and grounds carefully. There was something familiar about the way he looked at the house. When he walked up to the door and knocked, Laura greeted him.

"It is so nice to see you again, Mr. Homer," she said with a warm smile. "Please come in."

Homer was astonished. "You recognized me?"

"It's that artist's look you have," she replied. "You looked over our house the same way you looked at me when you did that picture. And do you recognize me?"

"You have changed in many ways," he answered. "But you are exactly as I imagined when I was driving out here. You are a beautiful woman."

"Thank you, sir," she said, looking very pleased as she led him into the parlor.

He went up to Lucy and bowed. "It is nice to see you again, madam, and to see you are in good health."

"What brings you here?" she asked, looking at him with open hostility.

He hesitated, aware that she was not pleased to have him in her home. "I have at long last established myself as an artist, madam. I am no longer employed by magazines that dictate to me what I shall paint and how I shall do it. So I am free, much like your former slaves down here … and, like them, I am finding that freedom isn't altogether free; it carries some heavy burdens."

"Such as?" asked Lucy.

"Making a living," answered Homer. "I am obliged to sell my work to collectors, dealers, museums, and the like. So really, you see, I am not free at all. I must cater to the whims of my customers, or I will not eat."

"Am I hearing a tale of the poor starving artist?" Laura asked with her eyes dancing. "I seem to remember a story about a brave, noble gentleman who risked getting shot to bring us food."

Homer threw up his hands and laughed heartily. "What a memory you have!" he marveled. "The difference is that I am trying to impress a beautiful woman instead of a delightful twelve-year-old child."

They talked for a while about their lives since the war. He learned that Laura was running a small drayage business with some local men, and Lucy was trying to earn money growing and selling tobacco. Keeping up the plantation was difficult, but they were getting by. He also learned, to his great satisfaction, that Laura was not married nor engaged. She showed him the painting he had done fourteen years earlier.

"Not bad for an amateur painter," he remarked.

"It is beautiful!" she exclaimed. "I will keep it forever."

As Homer prepared to leave, Laura asked him where he was staying. He told her that he had been asked to leave the rooms where he had been staying by the landlord, who had accused him of being sympathetic with the former slaves who had been the subjects of several of his paintings.

"Well, are you?" demanded Lucy harshly.

"I suppose so," he said softly. "I am here on commission from several art dealers in Chicago who want me to do a series of paintings on the

Reconstruction. The plight of the Negroes seems tragic to me, and I must paint what I see; it's my nature."

"And what is it you see down here?" Lucy asked bitterly. "How do you see the results of this reconstruction on us?"

"I see a desperate struggle against poverty and despair; a culture dependent on slave labor trying to change; and slaves who are no longer slaves, but are doing the same work and are perhaps are worse off because they have no one to care for them. It is very depressing to me, madam, and not at all like I thought it would be."

"You must stay here, Mr. Homer," Laura said firmly, "at least until you find suitable lodging. Tend to your horse; there is hay in the barn, and I will get the spare room ready for you."

He hesitated; he could feel Lucy's hostility, and he understood her bitterness, but he also sensed that Laura was the dominant person in the household, and she seemed to really want him to stay. His desire to get to know this remarkable woman overcame his natural shyness, so he accepted.

He stayed at Ashland for nearly a week, doing many sketches of life along the peninsula. He could see the awkwardness when Lucy visited the old slave quarters. She no longer was the mistress, and they no longer were forced to obey her orders, but both sides still needed each other, and there seemed to be a wary understanding between them that led to an accommodation that satisfied neither of them, but resulted in a workable arrangement on the plantation.

One evening, a tall, impressive-looking man came to visit. Homer learned he was a former Confederate cavalry officer, and his name was Robert Stuart—a cousin of General Jeb Stuart, one of Lee's most trusted officers. Robert was an ardent suitor of Laura.

He was courteous but reserved, and when he left, he looked Homer squarely in the eye and said with a decidedly dangerous tone, "I think you should know, Mr. Homer, I intend to take Miss Ashton as my wife."

After Robert left, Homer asked Laura whether she and Robert were engaged to be married. She shook her head.

"Robbie is a dear man, and he is pretty possessive sometimes, but I have no plans to marry anytime soon. There is so much turmoil here that I can't bear to think of settling down and raising a family."

Homer was so relieved, he blurted out impulsively, "Oh, Laura, I love and admire you so much! I am doing pretty well as an artist, and I have a lovely place on the New Jersey shore. Would you consider marrying me?"

He seemed so sincere and agitated and so small. At five feet, eight inches, she stood a good three inches taller than Homer. And he was so shy; he hadn't even tried to kiss her. But he was honest and sincere and so talented, and she felt strongly attracted to him. She took his hand, pulled him close to her, and embraced him. He could feel her full breasts against his chest and felt her tongue in his mouth as she kissed him passionately. When they broke apart, Homer was breathing heavily.

"Laura," he said in a voice that quivered with emotion, "I have never been kissed like that before. Does that mean you have accepted my proposal?"

"My dear Winslow," she said softly. "The brave, talented artist who was so kind to us will always have a place in my heart, but you must know it is quite impossible for me to leave my home and live in the North after all we have been through."

"Well, think about it, Laura. The war has been over for a long time now, and we will eventually get back together."

"I will, Winslow," she said kissing his cheek, "but I think you know how difficult it would be."

In spite of Laura's misgivings, Homer was ecstatic. He had never been attractive to women; his natural shyness and small unimpressive physique was not appealing to most young women he knew, and Laura's warm response had been far beyond anything he had hoped for. For the next few days, he was with her constantly, sketching her in a variety of poses and costumes. He wanted to do a portrait of her, and after some coaxing, he persuaded her to pose in the garden wearing a dark-green robe that was very becoming to her.

His time with Laura was the happiest time of his life, and he was reluctant to leave at the end of the week, but his patrons were anxious to see some results from his Reconstruction commission, so he boarded the train to New Jersey after assuring Laura that he would return and persuade her to change her mind about living in the North as his wife.

After returning to New Jersey, he worked diligently on his paintings of the Reconstruction, telling the story of the newly freed slaves and the changes occurring in the lifestyle of the South. He also did some watercolors using his sketches of Laura in some of his paintings of contemporary social life and finally finished her portrait, which he hoped to give to her when she came to visit. But he did not hear from Laura in spite of numerous letters he sent her, and in the summer of 1878, he again visited her at Ashvale.

He found her in good health but looking a little worn from the constant struggle to keep the plantation operating. She listened to his ardent pleas and told him how much she admired and respected him. When he left, he felt confused and depressed; he knew she was attracted to him and admired him, but she refused to talk of marriage.

At last, on a bright winter day in 1879, he received the long-awaited letter from Virginia. "My dear artist friend," it began. "I had hoped that you would forget me in time and give your attentions to some other woman who is worthy of you, but after our last visit, I decided you deserved to hear my decision directly from me. I cannot marry you, much as I admire and respect you. My mother passed away last month, and there is nothing to keep me here any longer, so I have accepted Col. Robert Stuart's proposal. It is increasingly difficult to maintain Ashvale, and the conditions here are very stressful. After we are married, I will sell Ashvale, and we will move to a community west of Richmond that is more conducive to the way of life we formerly enjoyed. I shall never forget you, and I shall follow your distinguished career with great interest and pride."

And with that letter, the flame went out in Homer's heart, never to be rekindled again.

Chapter 15:
THE SEARCH BEGINS

AFTER HARRY RECOVERED from the shock of learning he was the owner of a painting potentially worth hundreds of thousands of dollars, he asked Dr. Jennings and Sarah if they could give him some idea of what the painting might bring if he decided to sell it. Sarah estimated that it probably would bring close to a million dollars if sold through one of the large auction houses, but Dr. Jennings raised some disturbing questions regarding provenance.

"What do you mean by provenance?" Harry asked.

"Provenance means chain of title," explained Dr. Jennings. "The circumstances of the discovery of this Homer suggest that it was stolen, and the watercolor was intended to cover up the identity of the painting so that it could be removed unnoticed."

"You mean there is some question whether Mrs. Perkins was the legitimate owner?"

"That's right," Jennings answered. "What you bought was a watercolor of no particular value. How Mrs. Perkins came to possess it is unknown. She probably was unaware of the oil painting underneath; otherwise she would have uncovered it and sold it."

"So we have to prove Mrs. Perkins was legitimately in possession of the Homer even though she didn't know she had it?"

"I'm afraid that's it. Art theft has increased significantly in recent years. Part of the increase is due to the high prices paid for works of art, and part of it is due to the ease of stealing and transporting stolen art. There was a notorious heist of old masters from the Isabella Stewart Gardner Museum in Boston, estimated to be worth over one hundred million dollars at today's prices. It happened over forty years ago and is still unsolved—and still very much front-page news today whenever the subject of art theft is raised. You must develop a good and plausible story about how and why this Homer was concealed, and your story better be backed up with solid documentary evidence. And if you can't do that, I am pretty certain the price you can get for the painting will be significantly reduced."

"By how much?"

"It's hard to say," replied Jennings. "Probably some dealers would be willing to pay twenty or twenty-five thousand for it and take a chance on facing an adverse claim, but you would never get close to a million, in my opinion."

Harry looked at Vera. "What do you think, Vera? Should I try to find out how old Mrs. Perkins got this thing, or should I just unload it for the best price I can get?"

"Oh, let's try, Harry. I want to study this painting a little more. That inset scene of the manor house by the river is intriguing. There must have been some reason for inserting it, and it might give us a clue as to who the Mystery Woman is."

"What will we do with it while we are looking?" he asked. "I don't want to insure it, and if I just put it in my closet at home, it might get stolen."

"Let me take it and put it in a secure lockbox at the university," said Vera.

"All right then," Harry agreed, "we'll take it with us. Before we go, I think I have some obligations to settle. Sarah, here is my check for $1,000 for your restoration work—and what do I owe you, Dr. Jennings, for the authentication?"

"Just promise me, Mr. Walker, that you will talk to us before you sell the painting. We might like to make a bid for it."

"It's a deal," Harry replied. "You own the right of first refusal."

On the way home, Vera explained why she thought the painting was so exceptional. The colors were so vivid, and the use of light and shadows highlighted the beauty and the strength of the woman.

"Many contemporaries of Homer studied abroad at the Beaux-Arts studio in Paris," explained Vera. "They believed this would bring them more prestige as painters and thus were influenced by the French Impressionists. But Homer never had any formal art training; he visited England and France, but his style was purely American. This is a big country full of opportunity and optimism. Whereas the European style was more subtle, relying of deft brush strokes, the American style was bolder and more direct, and you can see that in the portrait of the Mystery Woman. Her face shows lines of worry and hardship—the war, reconstruction, grief—but there is an overarching sparkle of optimism that gives the painting such a glamorous effect. Brilliant use of light and shadows on her dark red hair and the green robe open just enough to be seductive. You can almost feel Homer's desire for her."

"Horny old coot, was he?"

"No, decidedly not," said Vera emphatically. "She probably was his only true love. As a young man, he was friendly and liked to be around young women, but he wasn't a ladies' man. He was physically small and somewhat shy, so you can see how losing a woman like this would be a tragic blow to him."

Vera asked Harry to drop her off at the university. She wanted to show the painting to Howard Cohen and then store it in a safe place. They agreed to meet the next morning and discuss how they should proceed.

Harry returned to his villa feeling both exhausted and exhilarated. He poured himself a generous portion of MacAllan fifteen-year-old single malt and sat down on his patio. *What a day! What a dilemma.*

His natural conservative instinct told him to get the best price he could and get rid of the painting. But he was curious. What was this watercolor of a Virginia landscape doing up in a Maine garage, and why had it been put on top of the portrait? Obviously Mrs. Perkins didn't know she had a valuable painting, so how had it come to be in her garage? And what about Vera? If it hadn't been for her, he probably wouldn't know the Homer painting was under the watercolor. She certainly was entitled to some share in the windfall that seemed to have come his way. Furthermore, he needed her; she was the art historian and the artist, and he would have to rely heavily on her knowledge if he were to unravel this mystery.

As the scotch took hold, Harry could feel himself relax, and a rosy glow spread over his consciousness. He not only needed Vera, he wanted her; he liked having her with him, and this project was a good way to keep them together. It might take a lot of work to find the answers to this riddle, but such efforts also represented an opportunity to get reacquainted with Vera.

The next morning, Vera invited him over for lunch, and while they were eating, she told Harry about Howard's reaction to the painting and what she had done with it upon her arrival at the university. "He was stunned, Harry. He said he had never seen such a beautiful and unique portrait. I told him we were working on establishing provenance and we needed to keep it in a safe place, and he agreed to store it in a lockbox and not tell anyone about it until we find out how Mrs. Perkins got it. I hope that's all right with you, Harry. It's your painting, and I don't want to do anything with it unless you approve."

He hesitated a moment before speaking. "Before we go any further, Vera, we need to get your part in this project settled. I bought a crummy old watercolor, which is gone; you discovered a valuable painting, which we now have. We are partners in this endeavor; if we can establish provenance, we will share equally in the proceeds when we sell the painting. That fair?"

"But … but … Harry!" Vera was nearly speechless. "That's almost like giving me a half million dollars! Your family would be horrified."

"I doubt it," grunted Harry. "And anyway, I'm not going to ask them. I will draft a letter setting forth our arrangement and put it with my will, so if anything happens to me, my daughter Pat, who is my executor, will find it, and she will honor it." He paused while he thought about Pat. "Now that I think of it, I believe I will call her now and tell her about this. She's a pretty good lawyer, and she might give us some insights on what kind of documentation we need to produce in order to establish title, and she will understand the importance of your contribution."

"Oh, Harry," Vera said softly. "I just don't know what to say!"

"Then don't say anything," he said, patting her hand. "Now let's try to figure out what to do next. I think you said Homer never married and never had children—that right?"

"That's right. He was close to his brother, Charles, who gave him financial help several times and became sort of a caretaker when Homer became ill at the end of his life."

"So probably Charles inherited his estate."

"I think so. I can look it up if you think it's important."

"I don't know," he said. "It's probably not necessary, except it's nice to know where these adverse claims might be coming from."

"Maybe there aren't any living heirs," she said hopefully. "Maybe no one will make an adverse claim."

"From what Jennings told us, as soon as word gets around about this picture and how we discovered it, we can expect all kinds of heirs to come crawling out of the woodwork. They don't need to be legitimate to make a claim, and the lack of a solid chain of title will scare away the legitimate buyers because nobody wants to buy into a lawsuit that might cost as much as the painting is worth."

"But, Harry, we don't have to tell anyone how we found it, do we? Can't we say we bought it and when we restored it, we found out it was a Homer?"

"It's not a secret," said Harry, shaking his head. "Lots of people know how we discovered it: Howard Cohen, Sarah, and Dr. Jennings and his panel of experts. Word will get around, so we better get busy, before the buzzards start circling."

"So what's the next step?" she asked.

"Do some more research on Homer's life—particularly toward the end, when you say he was ill—and I'll talk to Pat about the legal issues.

Then I suppose we go to Maine and see what we can learn about old Mrs. Perkins."

"I'll go over to the library this afternoon, *partner!*" she said, leaning over and giving him a firm kiss on the cheek.

Harry was delighted. "Don't get too cute with me, Antonelli; remember, I'm the big, bad wolf."

Vera giggled. "You don't scare me," she said, ruffling up his hair.

Harry was in a very optimistic mood when he called Pat and left a message for her to get back to him as soon as possible. Vera was starting to flirt a little, which made him feel good about himself. He was under no illusion about his looks—he was old, and he looked it—but Vera's interest in him gave him more confidence and made him feel younger. Having a girlfriend at his age was ridiculous; sensible people getting close to eighty put all those emotions behind them. But Vera's affection for him was very flattering, and he supposed it would do no harm to dream a little.

While waiting for Pat to return his call, he decided to make a list of the things they knew and what they needed to find out.

The known facts were
1. The watercolor was a landscape of southwestern Virginia.
2. The watercolor resembled Homer's techniques.
3. The watercolor was not done by Homer.
4. The oil painting was done by Homer
5. It was in possession of Mrs. Perkins at the time of her death.
6. It was sold at auction to the dealer in Maine from whom Harry bought it.

The things they needed to know were
1. How did Mrs. Perkins acquire the painting?
2. Why was the portrait by Homer covered up?
3. Who painted the watercolor?
4. Who was the Mystery Woman in the portrait?

Later in the afternoon, Pat called, and Harry reported to her what they had discovered about the old painting he had bought in Maine last August, explaining the concern Dr. Jennings had expressed over provenance. They agreed to meet for lunch at the Metropolitan Club on Friday. He drove up to Washington on Thursday afternoon and met Pat on Friday at twelve thirty.

Pat listened carefully as Harry outlined the facts they believed were true and the unknowns that would have to established. When he finished, she asked him, "How does Vera fit in? It's your painting, but she seems deeply involved in establishing the ownership chain."

Harry produced the letter he had drafted setting forth the arrangement with Vera and gave it to Pat. After reading it, Pat looked intently at Harry. "Dad, are you emotionally involved with this woman?'

"I like her," he admitted. "We were in school together, and we both lost our long-term spouses in a difficult manner, and I ... I ... well, you see, we just sort of like to be together," he said lamely.

"Well, that's a pretty generous offer you have made to her, and it very much resembles a gift, although I suppose you could say her work in identifying and uncovering the portrait is adequate consideration for making her a partner."

"And the work she is now doing to help establish provenance," he said. "She has access to experts in the field that I never even heard of."

"That's good enough for me, Dad," Pat said. "I can see you are very fond of this woman, and I don't know where you are going with it, but I do hope to meet her sometime soon.

"Now to the legal issues: some complexities here may cause difficulty down the road. If the Homer was stolen, the owner is entitled to get it back. That's why buyers of valuable items are so concerned about the chain of title. So your first job is to establish that it wasn't stolen. But even if you are able to do that, you aren't entirely out of the woods. There remains the issue of what was sold. The executor of Mrs. Perkins's estate may take the position that he sold a watercolor to the dealer, not the Homer. The beneficiaries of her estate could make a reasonable case for its return to them. That said, I am inclined to believe that their remedy is against the executor, who has a fiduciary duty to the beneficiaries to get the best price for the assets of the estate."

"What about the dealer?" asked Harry. "Could he make the same kind of case for its return to him?"

"I doubt it," she answered. "As a dealer, he would be considered as an expert who should have made a thorough examination of the picture. If he sold something and didn't realize its value, I would say it's his bad luck. He doesn't stand in as good a position as the beneficiaries of the Perkins estate, but if word gets back to him that the watercolor he sold had a valuable Homer under it, there is a very good chance he would try to get it back."

"So what's the bottom line?" he asked.

"If you can show that Mrs. Perkins came into possession of that picture legitimately, I think you will be able to get a good price for it. The way it was discovered works both ways; it raises serious questions about title, but it also adds glamour to the painting, and if you can also find out who this so-called Mystery Woman is, it would really attract some serious money."

"Thanks, Pat—you helped me a lot. So how much do I owe you for all this high-powered legal advice?"

"How about a nice hug?"

"Done!" said Harry, giving her a big bear hug.

"Good luck, Dad," Pat called out as she was leaving, "and remember I want to meet Vera and see this painting before you sell it."

Later that evening, at dinner, Harry summarized Pat's legal analysis for Vera, and Vera gave Harry the results of her research. Homer had two brothers but was especially close to Charles, who really was Homer's caretaker over the last five years of his life. He began suffering a series of stomach ailments beginning in 1903 that significantly curtailed his artistic work, and he had a serious stroke in 1908. His last really great painting was done after his stroke. The title was *Right, Left* and showed a hunter in the background firing at two goldeneye ducks; one had been hit and was dying, and the other was frantically trying to escape. The focus was on the ducks, not the hunter, and the painting conveyed vividly the terror felt by the birds and the cruelty associated with the sport of hunting. The painting had been an immediate sensation and had sold for $6,000 in 1908. Creating a work like that while handicapped by the effects from the stroke was a remarkable achievement.

That evening Harry called Spiro, Nick's brother, and asked him what he knew about Mrs. Perkins. Spiro said that she had been a widow for about ten years, and all of her children were now deceased. However, there was a granddaughter living in the old home who was single, and Spiro thought she would be willing to talk to them about the picture Harry had bought. Spiro said he would talk to her and see when they could have a visit.

Spiro called back the next day and said Agnes, the granddaughter, would be delighted to meet with them on Wednesday, November 8, and suggested they come to her house at ten for coffee. Spiro said he would reserve rooms for them at the local motel for Tuesday and Wednesday night.

During the past several weeks, Harry had been dropping in on Vera in the morning for coffee and a light breakfast. At first he called before coming over, but lately he had just appeared, and it seemed to suit Vera just fine. She always had a place set for him, and they had plenty of time to talk. After Spiro's call, Harry asked her if she wanted to join him on the trip to Maine. It would be a quick trip, and they would have to get up early to drive to Baltimore to catch the morning flight to Portland.

"I don't care how early I have to get up," she said. "I wouldn't miss that interview even if I had to stay up all night."

"There's just one little obstacle," said Harry, trying unsuccessfully to look serious.

"Oh, yeah? What is that?" she said with her eyes sparkling and her eyebrows arched.

"There is only one vacancy at the motel, and it has a double bed."

"Well, Harry, I hope you enjoy sleeping on the floor," she said, shaking her head. "You are such an old curmudgeon!" She got up and came over to Harry and suddenly sat down on his lap.

"Oof!" he said.

"Oof! Such an unromantic thing to say!" She put her arms around Harry's neck and kissed him in a way he hadn't experienced in quite a number of years.

"My God, Antonelli," he said hoarsely, "you haven't lost your old touch." He reached around her waist, pulled her in close to him, and began to fondle her breasts.

"Last summer, you said you didn't like my bazooms," she murmured and kissed him again passionately.

"I never said that," he protested. "I just said they look different, but I sure do like them—better than ever!" He started to reach under her sweater, but Vera slapped his hands and stood up.

"Now, now, we are still a little too early in our relationship to play games. I just wanted to show you that maybe you are the one who might not be safe if we room together."

When Harry got back to his villa later that morning, he poured himself a heavy jigger of single malt. Vera was a piece of work. Here he was at the age of seventy-seven, acting like a green teenager savoring his first kiss—and what a kiss it had been. She seemed to still have a strong sexual drive at the age of seventy-five, and it was thrilling to think that she was attracted to him. At the same time, he felt vaguely apprehensive as he contemplated what it would be like to sleep with her. His wife had contracted her terminal illness over two years before, and he had not felt any sexual stimulation since then—well, until he had met Vera. And really, for several years before that, sex had not played much of a part in his life. Early in their marriage, he and Mary Ellen had been ardent lovers, and that had morphed into a very comfortable relationship. Sex was still an important part in their domestic life in those wonderful middle years, but love had come to mean more than just sex. Then, as they drifted into the eighth decade of their lives, companionship and mutual respect dominated their relationship. Harry couldn't remember how long it had been since he had experienced sex—probably around three years—and he was a little uneasy about how well he could perform. But the whisky was having its desired effect, and his doubts and worries began to fade away. He smiled as he thought about the Maine expedition next week. This provenance project might be like chasing a rainbow, but it would be very interesting.

Chapter 16:
MAINE

VERA SAT AT her desk, enjoying the autumn sun streaming through her window and taking the morning chill out of her office. This was a lovely time of year on Maryland's eastern shore; the nights were chilly, but the days were warm, and the trees were now showing their colors vividly.

Vera was working with a slide projector, going over the images of paintings she would use in her art-history lectures. The spring term began on January 12 and ran for seventeen weeks, finishing up on May 9. She had two classes per week, so she would have a busy two months getting ready for the term. Since she was already involved with her research on Homer, she decided to focus her class on mid nineteenth-century American painters, which included Homer, Mary Casset, Sargent, Eakins, and Prendergast, and the extent to which they had been influenced by the French Impressionism movement, with its emphasis on light. Some of Homer's contemporaries had studied in Paris, and the French influence was discernible, but they all had a distinctly American style.

As she worked, Vera thought about the painting she and Harry had discovered. The striking scene of the woman in the garden, with sunlight streaming through the grape arbor, casting shadows along her robe and highlighting the strength and animation in the woman's face, conveying the suggestion of past hardships and an indomitable optimism for the future, was Homer at his best. It was too bad she couldn't show a slide of the Mystery Woman, but she understood Harry's concern about making some progress on provenance before word got around about their discovery.

And then there was Harry to think about. What would she do with him? She had come a long way since John's death, and Harry was a very big reason for her quick emotional recovery. Her husband's death and the subsequent awkward relationship with her family on the West Coast had left her shaken and unsure of herself. Harry had taken care of that; he had her deeply involved—first in the discovery of a beautiful, important work of art, and now in the establishment of provenance that, if successful, would substantially increase her net worth. He had proved to be a loyal and generous friend, and she owed him a lot.

She had been a little startled at her own reaction when she kissed him. She only meant to give him a nice warm, friendly kiss showing that she appreciated his kindness and generosity, but it ended up as something substantially different. She smiled when she thought about his reaction; he really was shocked and excited, and when he had begun to fondle her breasts, she had gotten aroused. What was the attraction at this age? The urge to reproduce that brought a man and a woman together was very strong in young people and led to long-term relationships. But starting a new relationship at seventy-five? That didn't make sense; there was no urge to mate now. She liked Harry; he was old but still had some of that alpha-male personality she had found overbearing in high school. Now, however, he was more laid-back; he wasn't trying to impress anybody, and she sensed he was comfortable with who he was, and this made him more attractive to her. Moreover, she knew he liked her; she could see it in the way his eyes lit up when they were together, and it was very flattering.

So where was this going? She didn't want to get married again, but she didn't want him to go away, either. Vera had always liked men and had had many male friends during her life. She and Harry were good friends; they were comfortable with each other. But that kiss the other morning had been a little too high-voltage for people who were just friends.

For the first time in many years, she thought about getting her hair colored and set. They were going up to Maine in a few days, and she wanted to give Harry a new look. She called the beauty shop and made an appointment and then went shopping for a new dress.

It was dark when Harry picked her up at 5:00 a.m. on Tuesday for the two-hour ride up to BWI airport. She promptly went to sleep and didn't wake up until they were crossing the Bay Bridge. Harry offered some coffee from his thermos, which helped get her awake, but they spoke very little until they got to the terminal. After they got their boarding passes, Harry turned to speak to her, and his reaction was almost comical.

"My God, Antonelli, what have you done to yourself?"

Vera laughed. "I wondered when you were going to look at me. I just had my hair cut and put on a dress and jacket. I want to look nice for our interview."

And indeed she did look nice. Gone were the jeans and baggy sweaters; her hair had been subtly darkened, cut, and set in a fashionable way. She had applied eye makeup that emphasized her unusual and beautiful eyes, and she had really splurged on the light wool dress and jacket. She only faintly resembled the old lady artist he had met last August in the park.

Harry looked at her with open admiration. "I was just getting used to you, Vera," he said, shaking his head, "and now you have gone and changed yourself, so I'll have to get used to you all over again."

"I'm the same old woman," she sighed. "I just put on a coat of paint and a new costume, but underneath, I'm just the same."

"Good!" he said. "I was really getting to like that old lady."

When they arrived in Portland, Harry rented a car and drove to the little village where Spiro lived.

Vera was delighted with Harry's reaction to her new outfit. She had purchased a foundation garment and an uplift bra that had transformed her overweight and somewhat spreading figure into something suggesting a slightly overripe voluptuousness. She still got mad when she thought about those rude remarks Harry had made last summer about her ass and her bazooms. She was enjoying giving him an eyeful when she stretched and crossed her legs. It certainly was nice to look and feel attractive again.

When they arrived at the village, Harry called Spiro and found he was out fishing and would be in at about three in the afternoon. He made an appointment for four thirty, and after lunch, he and Vera took a drive to locate Prouts Neck, where Homer had spent the last thirty years of his life. They were surprised to learn that it was only about ten miles from the village. Vera had thought Prouts Neck was a remote outpost on the barren shores of Maine, far from any metropolitan area, which would be an ideal place for an irascible old recluse, as Homer was described in his later years. Perhaps that had been true in 1883, when Homer first settled there, but now it was close to the metropolitan area of Portland, Maine's largest city, and was an upscale resort town with lovely beaches and a high-quality inn. There was something different in the quality of the air and light in this seaside town that was identifiable from some of his later paintings.

They stopped at the museum in Portland and studied the collection of original oils and watercolors exhibited there. Vera was captivated by some of his early work during the Civil War, especially the sharpshooter in the tree, looking very prosaic with a foot dangling off the tree limb, but at the same time so deadly, looking down his sights in search of a soldier to kill. What was Homer's message here? Perhaps it was that war was a deadly game, but it was waged by ordinary citizens with loved ones who knitted those very unmilitary socks.

At four thirty, they stopped by Spiro's home, and he greeted them warmly and insisted that they join him for a cocktail.

"Can you tell us a little about the granddaughter?" asked Harry.

"Not much to tell. Agnes is in her middle forties," he said. "She used to teach in the local elementary school, but when it closed, she didn't want to take a position over in Springfield at the new school, so she is working part time at the hospital. Works the afternoon shift from one to seven, which is why she invited you to come over in the morning. What do you want to talk to her about?" He looked at them quizzically.

Harry started to speak, but Vera cut him off. "I am an artist, Mr. Loukakis," she said, "and I am working on restoring the painting Harry bought up here last summer. The work is that of a well-trained and talented artist, and I want to know who he was and whether there were other works by this artist up here. I thought Miss Perkins might have some information and some other paintings by the same person."

Spiro looked closely at Vera. "So you are an artist, eh? I wondered how Harry got a good-looking lady like you to come up here with him." He turned to Harry. "Now I see why you bought that old picture."

Harry laughed. "You got it, Spiro. I'm not as dumb as I look. So now you know why we are here and want to talk to Agnes. What's she like? Does she hate strangers, like a lot of you old Yankees do? We want her to open up; the picture I bought came out of her garage, and maybe she has some others like it."

"Oh, she's very friendly, and we old Yankees don't hate anybody— we're just reserved and suspicious of old goats who run around with nice-looking artists. As for Agnes, she is right good to look at and had some boyfriends early on, but I guess it didn't take, because she never married."

Harry got directions to the Perkins home and was putting on his jacket when Vera turned to Spiro and said, "Is it true that you were able to get only one room for us? Harry said you got the last one, and it has a double bed."

Spiro roared with laughter. "You sly old fox!" he exclaimed. "I told you I got two rooms. If I had known you were such a randy old geezer, I would have gotten them on separate floors. You call me, Vera, if he bothers you. The chief of police is a friend of mine, and if Harry starts to get fresh, we'll lock him up until he cools off."

Driving back to the hotel, Harry scowled at Vera. "You like to get me in trouble, don't you, Antonelli?"

"Why, Harry," she said innocently, "I just wondered whether you were telling me the truth."

"Yeah, right!" snorted Harry. "Spiro will call his brother, Nick, who is married to my daughter, Gwen, and tell him all about my little joke, and he will tell Gwen, and the next thing you know, all of my kids will descend on me and wonder who their senile old father has picked up."

Vera smiled like a big cat. "Do you think they will like me?"

Harry parked their rental car, and they walked up one flight of stairs to Vera's room. After she unlocked the door, she paused and looked at Harry intently.

"You know," she murmured, "I almost wish we really could only get one room." She lifted her face to be kissed, and Harry swept her into his arms. She felt herself pressing her lower body into him eagerly. He was kissing her passionately, and they stumbled into the room and fell on the bed. She opened her legs slightly and felt his hard erection pressing into her stomach. He put his hand under her skirt and pulled it up to her waist and then struggled to pull down her panties.

"God damn it, Antonelli," he panted hoarsely. "What have you got on down here, a coat of armor?"

"It's my foundation garment, Harry," she groaned, her voice heavy with passion. "It's supposed to make me look more alluring." She began unhooking her bra and unbuckling her stockings.

"I can't get it off," he grunted. "Doesn't it have a hole in it somewhere? I'm on fire, and I want to get inside of you now." She could feel his throbbing erection against her bare thighs, and she was close to climaxing. She arched her back as she pulled off her bra, and as Harry bent down to kiss her hard, erect nipples, he exploded all over her thighs and stockings. He shuddered and called out her name and then collapsed on top of her.

"My God, Vera," he muttered. "Look what I've done! I just couldn't get that thing off you in time. I'm so sorry."

Vera gazed at him with an expression full of love and a little amusement.

"It was wonderful for me, Harry," she said. "I haven't had sex in so long, I wasn't quite ready for you. I will get rid of that foundation garment, so you won't have to work so hard to ravish me next time."

Harry looked miserable. "I really made a mess of it, didn't I? What'll we do now?"

"I think you better go back to your room and take a shower, and I will clean myself up."

The next morning, they got their emotions under control during a leisurely breakfast. Harry was quiet and subdued but brightened up when Vera told him that the night before had been one of the most exciting experiences she had ever had.

"It was so spontaneous, Harry, and I am afraid my Mediterranean ancestors took control. I must have seemed like an aggressive nymphomaniac, but that's what you do to me. You are a sexy old man."

After breakfast they went over to see Agnes at the old Perkins house, and Harry explained to her why he had purchased a painting in such bad condition. Agnes was a handsome, robust, gregarious woman, and she was enjoying talking to Harry.

While they were engaged in their animated conversation, Vera looked around the parlor. It was an old-fashioned, comfortable room. The furniture was nice but nothing exceptional; there were no original antiques that she could see, which surprised her a little, since the house was well over a hundred years old. The one exception was a beautiful Oriental rug that she judged to be over one hundred years old and had probably come from Turkey.

Vera tuned into the conversation just as Harry was inquiring about the location of the landscape he purchased.

"So you see, Agnes, I was surprised to see a picture up here, in Maine, of a place in Virginia where I used to hunt quail."

"Well, Harry, I have never been to Virginia, and I don't think Mom or Dad ever went there, either, but I'm not sure about Gran. My father was the executor of her estate; there wasn't much in it except this house and the furnishings. He had the probate papers in his closet, but I haven't looked at them since he died last year. I'll get the file and see what's in it."

While Agnes was out of the room, Vera pointed to three watercolors hanging together on one of the walls. "I think those paintings were done by the same artist who painted your beech tree."

Agnes returned with a large pocket file, which she opened and spread out on the dining-room table.

"I see your grandmother's middle name was Turner," said Harry, holding a copy of the will. "Could that be her maiden name?"

"I think so, yes," she said. "Here's the inventory of assets. You can see there's not much, except the house, furnishings, and the junk in the garage, which my father sold."

"Do you know the origin of this rug?" asked Vera, indicating the lovely Oriental they were standing on. "It looks like a valuable antique Turkish rug. Those things are very expensive these days, and it is exceptional."

"Yes, it is," agreed Agnes. "We never had it appraised, so we don't know its worth, and the probate judge accepted the inventory as just household furnishings. We're pretty informal up here. But where it came from? I think Gran said it was a wedding present … but from whom, I don't know."

"Did your mother and father always live here with your grandparents?" asked Vera.

"No, they moved in with Gran after Granddad died in 1991—she was pretty shook up when he died, and they didn't want her to be alone. He was a bit older than Gran; I think he was born in 1902, and Gran was born in 1910."

"Here's a certificate of marriage," said Vera, holding up a tattered piece of paper. "They were married in 1929, when Eliza was only nineteen, so that indicates that she must have been local to get to know your grandfather at such a young age."

"I don't think so," replied Agnes, looking through the pile of documents on the table. "I'm looking for the obituary, which my father wrote. Ah, here it is."

She picked out a newspaper article taped onto a piece of paper and began to read:

Eliza Turner Perkins, 93, died Tuesday morning, July 18, of congestive heart failure. Eliza and her father, a professor at Hampden-Sydney College, were frequent visitors to the Perkins family home during a period from about 1915 to 1930. Ben Perkins, a few years older than Eliza, was captivated by her charm and natural beauty. Raised in Virginia, Eliza never lost her soft Southern accent and gracious manner. They were married in 1929 and had three children: James, of the home address; George, of Portland, Maine; and Grace Robinson, of Boston.

"So there you are," said Agnes. "She was born and raised in Virginia."

"Well, well," mused Harry. "So my picture of the Virginia landscape is beginning to make sense."

"Tell us about those pictures on the wall in your parlor," said Vera.

Agnes shrugged. "They have been there for as long as I can remember."

Vera studied them for a few minutes. "The colors are faded in a few places," she said, "but I think a good restorer could bring them back, and they would look stunning."

"But wouldn't that cost a lot of money?" asked Agnes.

"Yes," said Vera thoughtfully, "but you might consider it. Those are very fine watercolors, and they are skillfully done—especially the one showing a snowfall over autumn leaves. Lots of color and clever work with shadows on the snow."

"So you really think these are good?" asked Agnes.

"I do," replied Vera. "They might well be worth restoring, if I can find out who the artist is."

"Do you have anyone in your family with the initials of R. S.?" asked Harry, indicating the initials at the bottom right corner of the paintings.

"Not to my knowledge," she replied.

"Your grandmother must have known some artist friend up here," insisted Vera. "These pictures weren't done by amateurs."

"Well, for heaven's sake!" exclaimed Agnes. Her interest in the old pictures had increased exponentially now that they might have some value. "I'll look around here and see what I can find out. I haven't heard of any artist around here except Mr. Homer at Prouts Neck, and I think he died before Gran was born."

"These weren't done by Homer," said Vera, "but they were certainly done by someone who studied his techniques pretty carefully."

As Harry and Vera were saying their good-byes to Agnes and thanking her for the coffee and biscuits, Vera advised her to hang onto those paintings and to let them know if she had any ideas as to who the artist might be.

Agnes was very much caught up in the hunt by now. "Mercy!" she said, her eyes sparkling. "This is like a detective story. I'll get over to the library and go over our old newspaper files to see if there were any artists around here. How far back should I go?"

Vera thought for a moment. "I think you should go back to the turn of the century, if you can. This work may be by one of Homer's protégés, although the literature indicates he was a loner."

After returning to Salisbury, Vera and Harry had a late dinner and discussed the results of their trip.

"I guess our relationship has changed, hasn't it, Vera?" Harry spoke softly and looked intently at Vera.

"Yes, it has," she replied thoughtfully. "There is no sense kidding ourselves trying to be friends and flirting a little. It seems strange to have a boyfriend at my age."

Harry smiled broadly and looked at Vera eagerly. "We'll have a geriatric fling. Next time I get you in bed, we'll do it right."

"Don't be in such a hurry, Harry," she said. "I need to think about where we are going with this."

"Just let nature take over," said Harry, looking very pleased with himself. "Now, getting back to our project: what do you think, Vera?" he asked. "Do you think we made some progress?"

"Oh yes, Harry," she said. "Get your pad and pencil out tomorrow, and let's review what we now know and what we need to know."

"That I will," said Harry. "But one thing sticks in my craw: who the hell is R. S.?"

Chapter 17:
ROSALEE STUART

I. Farmville, Virginia, 1905

IT WAS DUSK in the village of Farmville, located in the heartland of Virginia, not far from Appomattox Courthouse, where General Lee had surrendered in 1865, ending the bloodiest war in the history of the United States. Laura Stuart was lighting the candles in the hallway and turning up the gas lights that had recently been installed in the small but comfortable home that she and her husband, Robert, had built shortly after they came here from Yorktown.

Many of the veterans of the Confederate army had settled in the area after the surrender and helped provide the labor and energy that made Farmville into a small, but thriving, community at the turn of the century. Tobacco was the cash agricultural crop, and Hampden-Sydney, one of the oldest colleges in the country, was an attraction for people with education and vision.

Laura was still a handsome woman at fifty-five, although years of hard work and childbirth had left her with chronic pain in her back and knees, and her once slim, erect figure had thickened and settled with age. Her husband had purchased 120 acres of farmland in 1879, and they had added 200 acres more over the years, so they now owned half a section. Approximately half of the farm was under cultivation with tobacco, corn, and other crops, and the other half was in timber.

Robert, eight years her senior, had had to give up active management of the farm, which was now handled by their son, James, age twenty-three, and his wife, who lived a short distance away. Robert had opened a farm equipment distributorship recently, and his business was progressing nicely.

Robert walked in the house at about five thirty and greeted Laura warmly. He was still an impressive-looking man, with clear, blue eyes and full head of iron-gray hair, but the erect military carriage had gone, and he walked with a slight limp and found it difficult to stand for any length of time. He noted a letter in Laura's hand and a quizzical look in her eye.

"Looks as if you have an interesting message there, Laura—anyone send you some money?"

"Nothing like that, dear," she said with a little smile, "although we sure could use it. No, this is about Rosalee; we have talked quite a bit about her lately."

"Yes, we have," said Robert. "Seems she's going through a restless spell out here lately, but she'll get over it."

"You know, Robert, she has become quite an accomplished artist," remarked Laura.

"You have said that before, but how do you know?"

"She has been studying drawing and design with a young instructor over at Hampden-Sydney who seems to be knowledgeable about artistic things, and he told me she is already beyond him in her techniques, particularly in watercolor. He thinks she should study with someone more skilled than he is."

Robert raised his eyebrows. "So?" he asked, looking at the letter.

Laura looked at him with a broad smile. "Do you remember Mr. Homer?" she inquired softly.

Robert answered with a hearty laugh. "So that's what you're up to," he said. "I sure do remember him; I thought I was going to have to murder him to keep you from running off with him. What did he say?"

"I wrote to him last month, and I just got a reply from the office of

Mr. Charles Homer—apparently his brother—telling me Mr. Homer is in Florida for the winter and is expected back around the first of April."

"That's two weeks away," observed Robert. "What did you say in your letter?"

"I asked him if he would consent to work with Rosalee this summer to help her with her watercolor studies. I have heard he has become one of America's most prominent painters, and watercolor is his great passion."

Robert looked very pleased. Rosalee was his great joy these days. Lively and beautiful, with a keen intellect and a zest for living, and she was so much like Laura that it took his breath away.

"What an opportunity for her," he said.

"I hope so," said Laura. "The articles I have read about him are troubling, though. It seems he has become a recluse and is very difficult to approach. He doesn't like strangers, and I wonder if he will remember who I am."

"He will, Laura. Yes, he will," said Robert gently. "When we met, he was deeply in love with a very beautiful and unusual woman. You will hear from him."

Spring began to make its presence felt in the Virginia heartland. The frosty nights gave way to warm spring rains, and the buds on the trees were swelling and bursting with renewed life. Birds were calling and nesting, and the agricultural community was coming to life with a restless energy after the long winter's rest.

Rosalee was talking to her mother about going to Richmond to look for more challenging and stimulating work than existed in Farmville. "There's nothing for me here, Mother," she explained. "Richmond has become a big rail center and is attracting a lot of wealthy people. I know I could find work as a fashion designer or interior decorator. It would be so much more interesting than staying here."

"What about your art ambitions?" asked Laura.

"I do love it, Mother," she replied, "but it is so frustrating these days. I think I am pretty good at drawing and making sketches, but working in watercolor is very difficult for me. Too often my colors blur together in a way I don't intend. The shadows get distorted, and the light source ambivalent. It's all so unmanageable at times, so I think it is better for me to use my artistic talents in a way that will earn me some money."

"Have you ever heard of Winslow Homer?" Laura asked.

Rosalee gave a little bark of laughter. "Who hasn't!" she exclaimed. "But what on earth would he have to do with me?"

Laura led her over to the small oil painting hanging on the dining-room wall. "Do you know who this is?" she asked, indicating the young, redheaded girl.

"That's you," said Rosalee proudly. "At least that's what you told me."

"Do you know who painted it?"

"You said it was done by some Union army illustrator."

"That's right," said Laura, "and his name was Winslow Homer."

"What!" Rosalee looked shocked and stunned. "You never told me that! I would have been thrilled to know he painted you. Why didn't you tell me?"

"Mr. Homer wanted me to marry him and move up north. I refused him and married your father instead. It seemed best not to discuss my little dalliance with a famous artist."

"Have you ever heard from him since you married Daddy?"

"No, but I have written to him and asked him to take you as a student this summer, and I am hoping for a reply in a few days."

Rosalee shook her head in wonder. "The articles I have read say he is very difficult—pretty much a recluse. I am just a young Southern girl with no artistic background. Why should he want me as a student?" She hesitated and then asked, "Do you think there is a chance he will consent?"

"I don't know," admitted Laura, "but when I look at that little painting over there and remember how he was in those days, somehow I think he will take you. Anyway, delay your plans for Richmond for a few weeks, and we will see what happens."

On April 12, Laura picked up a letter addressed to her at the Farmville post office.

"My dear Laura," it began,

Of course I remember you. One could hardly forget that courageous young girl standing up to an angry, brutal sergeant during those dark days of the war. I am glad you still have that painting, and I wish I could see it again myself.

For the last year or so, I have not been well, so I must conserve my energy as best I can, but I would be delighted to give whatever help I can to further your daughter's artistic career. Please contact my brother, Charles, at the address below, and he will make suitable arrangements for her accommodations for the summer up here in Maine.

At dinner that evening, Laura read the letter to Robert and Rosalee. There followed a long period of silence, finally broken by Robert.

"Rosalee, are you serious about pursuing an artistic career?" he asked in his deep baritone voice. "Because if you are, you must go; you are unlikely to ever again have an opportunity like this."

"Oh, I do so much want to go, Daddy," she said softly, "but I'm scared! What if he tells me I have no talent and sends me away?"

"That is a possibility," said Laura firmly, "but if you don't go, you will never know whether you really have a spark of genius in you; you must not be afraid to fail."

"But if he rejected me, Mother, it would be so humiliating. I don't know if I could stand it."

"You may not have the talent we think you have, but we believe in you, and I think deep down, you believe in yourself." Laura paused and cocked her head to one side. "And I don't believe the man I knew would ever humiliate you."

And so it came to pass that in the spring of 1905, Rosalee Stuart, daughter of Laura Ashton Stuart (formerly of Ashvale plantation and now of Farmville, Virginia), prepared to leave Virginia for the first time in her life for a long journey to Maine to study with a famous artist who had first come into her mother's life forty-two years earlier.

She packed her trunk carefully, enclosing some samples of her best work to show to Mr. Homer. Charles Homer made meticulous arrangements for her to stay with a family named Perkins, who lived close to Prouts Neck, where Homer's studio was located. She would study with Winslow from two to five in the afternoon, four days per week. Transportation would be arranged through Charles's office.

As the time for departure grew near, Rosalee's excitement was boundless. She hardly slept at all on the night before her departure, and the trip north was arduous. She was obliged to change trains in Washington, New York, and Boston, and arrived, after sitting up all night on a crowded coach, in Portland, Maine, in the early afternoon. There she was met by a tall, courteous gentleman with an authoritative manner and a distinctive New England twang that she would learn to enjoy.

"Miss Stuart," he said, raising his hat. "I am Charles Homer, Winslow's brother, and I am very happy to meet you. Winslow has told me about his acquaintance with your mother during the war, when she was a child. She certainly made an impression on him."

"Thank you for meeting me, sir. I do appreciate all you have done for me. It is my first time away from home, and I am so thankful to have a gentleman such as you taking care of me."

"It is my pleasure," said Charles gallantly. He took her bag and signaled a porter to bring her trunk from the baggage car.

"Let me take you to your lodgings and introduce you to Mrs. Perkins," he said, helping her into a waiting taxi.

The trip to Fairhaven took about thirty minutes, and Rosalee was carefully briefed on Homer's health problems and his need for rest and regular light exercise. There was no doubt that Charles was committed to taking care of Winslow and preserving the artistic work his brother produced. Charles emphasized that nothing could be taken from the studio without his consent.

They arrived at a small frame house not far from the sea coast and were greeted by an austere woman with gray hair and sharp, shrewd eyes.

"Mrs. Perkins, allow me to introduce Miss Stuart, who will be studying with my brother this summer. I hope you will make her feel at home."

"Pleased to meet you," murmured Eliza Perkins.

Charles tipped his hat and left in the waiting taxi while the two women surveyed one another.

"I'll show you to your room." Eliza led the way upstairs to a small, but comfortable, room with a southwestern exposure overlooking a small vegetable garden that was just beginning to show signs of growth.

"Dinner will be served at six," she said and left. Rosalee was a little taken back by the frosty reception from Mrs. Perkins. She smiled a little; this would be her first test, getting to know Mrs. Perkins and thawing her out. She changed into a work housedress and went down to the kitchen, where Eliza was preparing the evening meal.

"How can I help, Mrs. Perkins?" she asked cheerfully.

Eliza eyed her with suspicion. "You are a guest here, Miss Stuart," she said primly. "There is no need for you to work here."

Rosalee laughed lightly. "Ever since I was born, I have worked. I help in the kitchen; I work in the fields at planting time; I help harvest and cure the tobacco in the fall; and I am very good in a vegetable garden. Here, let me peel these potatoes," she said, taking the bowl of potatoes and the peeler from Eliza. "And if you have some flour and buttermilk, I'll make you some really nice Southern biscuits." Rosalee bustled around the kitchen with such energy and good humor that Eliza couldn't help but respond.

"I declare," she finally said. "You don't seem to be at all like I expected."

Rosalee was delighted with that comment. "I could tell!" she exclaimed. "You think of us Southern girls as pampered, sheltered, delicate little things, taken care of by servants and not able to boil an egg! Isn't that right?"

"Well," admitted Eliza, "that does seem close to what came to mind."

"Mrs. Perkins," said Rosalee earnestly, "I am a long ways from home; I have never been outside of Virginia. I want you to like me and for us to be friends. I need friends now, and I want to be of help, so that I can feel like I belong here. Life in Virginia has been very difficult for my parents and their generation; my beautiful mother suffers terribly from pain caused by the hard work she has been doing for twenty-five years, and my father is all bent over from a lifetime of hard work, along with raising a family. I know how to work, and I hope you will let me help you. I was born long after the war ended, and I don't have any ill feelings toward the people up north. I want to get to know you, because you all seem like first-rate people to me."

"For heaven's sake!" exclaimed Eliza.

Mr. Perkins came home at about five in the evening from the local hardware store that he owned, and the three of them had dinner in the small dining room. The conversation was awkward at first, and Rosalee was aware of hostility from Mr. Perkins, but her personal charm and good humor were hard to resist. She brought him a slice of apple pie for dessert and a steaming mug of hot coffee and inquired about his family. She found he had served with the Union army at the end of the war but had not been under fire. She told how her grandfather had been killed at Manassas and of her father's service under General Stuart in the cavalry. It seemed to serve as an icebreaker; everyone shared old family stories, and the Perkins' became very interested in her upcoming work with Winslow Homer.

"Can't say as he's real friendly," observed Ben Perkins. "But then I don't think he met anyone like you."

"Oh, yes, he met my mother when she was about twelve and saved her from being beaten by an angry soldier. He painted a picture of her in front of the old plantation where she was born and we still have it—it's beautiful!"

"My stars!" exclaimed Eliza. "I just know you will get along with him."

"Just be yourself," said Ben, grinning, "and you will do fine."

For several days, Rosalee had lived on practically no sleep, driven by adrenaline-charged nervous energy. As she got into bed that night, her mind jumped back and forth between home and family; her new friends, the Perkins', in Maine; and what awaited her the next afternoon, when she would meet the famous artist. She was tense, excited, and scared: Would she be able to sleep? Would she look tired and haggard? Would he like the art samples she brought? Would she like him? Somewhere among all of these diverse thoughts, nature took control, and she fell into a deep and dreamless sleep.

At breakfast the next morning, she found that Eliza and Ben had thawed out considerably, and they had a leisurely, relaxed conversation about Homer and his brother, Charles. She found out that Homer loved the wilderness and excelled at hunting and fishing in the Adirondack Mountains and in the semitropical jungles of Florida.

"Why did he become such a recluse up here in Maine?" Rosalee wondered.

"Don't really know," replied Ben. "I think he just got old and crotchety."

"Some woman jilted him," said Eliza grimly. "You can see it in his eyes. He was not a big, handsome, strapping man, and he fell for some tart, and she had no time for him."

"Really?" asked Rosalee, her eyes big as saucers.

"That's what I think," replied Eliza.

My mother, thought Rosalee. *She turned down his proposal.* Was it she who had broken Homer's heart and turned him into a recluse? But his letter had been so cordial. She knew she looked very much like her mother and wondered what his reaction would be when they met.

After lunch a carriage came for her and drove her to the nearby town of Prouts Neck. Homer's studio was a simple structure with large windows and a balcony overlooking the sea. Charles greeted her at the door and ushered her in.

"This is Rosalee Stuart, Winslow," he said. "As you know, the tentative arrangement is for her to come to you from two to five o'clock, four afternoons a week. If you find it is too tiring, let me know, and we will modify the schedule."

The small man hunched over a drafting table looked up from the well-worn, thick book he had been intently studying. She saw he was old and looked very frail, except for his eyes, which were sharp and penetrating. He looked at her for a long moment and then broke into a wonderful, warm smile.

"Laura!" he said softly. Charles looked puzzled.

"No, Winslow, her name is Rosalee Stuart."

Rosalee put her hand on Charles's arm and turned to Homer.

"Thank you, sir," she said with a dazzling smile. "That is such a wonderful compliment for me. You see," she said, turning to Charles, "my mother's name is Laura, and Mr. Homer knew her when she was young and beautiful. I am told I do resemble her, and I find that very flattering."

"Well, yes, I see," said Charles, looking a little uncomfortable. "I'll leave you to get acquainted, and I will send a carriage for you at five."

Homer went over to a small coffee table and sat down. "Come sit beside me over here and tell me about your family." Rosalee sat down on the chair next to Homer and described her home in Farmville and her parents.

"It has not been an easy time for my parents," she said. "They have worked very hard establishing a home and taking care of us. There were no servants out there, and there was no money to hire anyone to help, so we all worked, but the burden fell on them. None of us children ever experienced the culture where most of the hard work was done by slaves and the plantation owners lived like ladies and gentlemen.

It was hard for them to adjust, but for us children, working in the fields and around the home was what we did."

Homer nodded sympathetically. "Ah, yes," he said. "I could see the pain and despair the Reconstruction was causing in the South, not only for the landed gentry but for the freed slaves as well. It has been a long and bitter period in our history, but seeing you here gives me hope that the worst is over."

"I think so, Mr. Homer," Rosalee said earnestly.

"Good!" he exclaimed with a smile. "Now: have you brought me some samples of your work that I can look at?"

"Oh dear," she sighed. "I'm afraid you will find me frightfully backward. These seem so … kind of primitive." She opened her case and took out four small watercolors. Homer inspected them carefully and nodded.

"Good, good! You have approached your subjects in the traditional manner, using opaque pigments and using the same techniques as you would with oil paints. I can see most of these were painted indoors. Did you have a skylight in your studio?"

Rosalee frowned and shook her head. "I didn't have a studio; most of these were painted in a classroom at Hampden-Sydney College. Jim Turner was my instructor, and he doesn't know much about color or painting."

Homer picked up the fourth painting and examined it closely. "Now, I must insist this one was painted outside. The light is coming down on your subject from above—and look, your colors are different: more natural, spontaneous."

Rosalee looked at the painting closely; it was a scene at the farm in early autumn, focusing on the tobacco-curing shed and nearby red barn.

"You are right," she said. "I remember that was such a beautiful day, with the sunlight on the barn and the color beginning to show in the trees. But how could you tell?"

"My dear young lady, it is the colors. Did you know that light has colors, and the colors are different depending on the time of day and where the light is coming from? You have an eye for color and your brushstrokes are quite sophisticated, which is remarkable, since you have had so little training." He paused, and his eyes lit up. "You are like me!" he exclaimed.

"I am?" asked Rosalee, looking startled.

"Yes," he answered. "Like you, I never had a real lesson in painting—or even drawing, for that matter. What I have learned is from my own experience, with a lot of encouragement from my mother. Now, tomorrow, bring your sketch pad. We will go out together and sketch a scene we want to paint, and we will explore the use of transparent pigments and washes to produce light that comes from the inside of our picture as well as reflected light. It is a new technique—more expressive, with a layering of the brushstrokes. You have a nuanced hand, and you will have no trouble picking up the technique. This will be an interesting summer, and we will learn much from each other."

When the carriage came for her at five o'clock, Rosalee was bursting with energy and enthusiasm. *Some curmudgeon!* Homer Winslow couldn't have been more charming and encouraging, and his restless energy and enthusiasm was contagious.

Homer had insisted that she return the next morning. He wanted her to be with him while he sketched an old church close to the sea, so she could see the difference in colors when the sun was coming off the sea and when it was coming off the land in the afternoon.

When Charles heard about the change in plans, he objected. It was much too long a day, he said. Winslow must rest and conserve his strength. But Homer was adamant; he had never had the opportunity to work with such a young, talented artist as Rosalee Stuart. Rosalee had assured Charles that she would fix him a nice lunch and see that he rested two hours before going out in the afternoon.

When she arrived the next morning, he was ready with two sketch pads and a case filled with brushes and paints. He gave one of the pads to her and set out on a narrow path close to the sea.

"An old church is not far from here and is a good subject for watercolor. It is made of stone, which reflects light in many different tones, so we will make several sketches from different places of observation."

Rosalee was amazed at how swiftly he worked. He made about a dozen sketches and put on layers of tinted transparent pigments. After working steadily for about two hours, Homer had produced six rough sketches from different angles, all featuring the vivid, bold colors of the church. The church's contrast with the deep shadows on its western side startling. The little cemetery was in deep shade; the gray granite headstones and the dark-hued green grass covering the graves bore the colors of death and sadness, while the church itself seemed to shine with an inner luminosity. These were the colors of hope and optimism.

Rosalee looked at her sketches; the pen and ink drawings were not bad, but her application of colors had produced nothing like what Homer had created.

"We are trying to reproduce what we see," explained Homer. "As artists, we see things a little differently, and we want others to see what we see." Pointing to the church, he said, "This church is very modest, not at all like the grand cathedrals of England and France. But it is a symbol of hope in a small rural community. I see it shining and inspiring, and that is how I paint it. And that little cemetery on the western side? I see in it the inescapable tragedy of life; we all must die, and death causes sadness and grief. The dark shades caused by the shadows reflect sorrow and grief."

Rosalee gazed intently at her own sketches. They were a good likeness of the church and the yard around it, and she showed them to Homer. He inspected them carefully.

"These are good representations of the church as you see it: drab and uninteresting. And the cemetery is not a gloomy place, as is mine; it seems … well … almost like a happy place. You have not been exposed to death and grief yet, have you?"

"No, I guess not," replied Rosalee. "All of my family are alive and well, and the people in our community who have died were very old and seemed ready to go."

"Are you a religious person?" he asked.

"I'm a good Christian," she replied. "I go to church every Sunday, but the rest of the time, I don't spend much time praying or thinking about God or the Bible."

"Perhaps this is not a good subject for you," he said thoughtfully. "You are skillful in your drawing and your application of paint. I need to teach you more of the techniques of layering and the use of the transparent pigments, but you show no passion here—not like the talented, enthusiastic person you are."

"Maybe I just don't have the talent to become an artist," she said softly.

Homer shook his head. "You are very talented," he said with conviction. "You are also very young. We will try again this afternoon, when the sun comes from the west. Maybe your sketches will show more life, and mine will be dull and uninteresting!"

After a nice lunch and a two-hour nap for Homer, they went again to the little church. The low sun in the west cast long shadows on the church and illuminated the cemetery and the grave markers. Homer worked hard on the shadows and contrasting shades of green on the grass and shrubbery. He brought out with consummate skill the subtle changes in the color of the church structure as the sun reflected on the contours of the stone walls. The result was a beautiful painting of a small-town church, but the passion of the morning rendition was not there.

Homer looked at Rosalee's sketches carefully They were done in warm colors of green and white for the grass and headstones in the cemetery and the complementary reddish and brown tones of the church structure. There were no stark contrasts of vivid colors and shadows. The result was a peaceful, lovely landscape, with the church as the focal point.

"This looks like a happy place," he said. "What were you thinking about when you did this?"

"I was thinking of people gathering in front of the church after services, children playing in the yard, weddings, things like that."

"Good!" he exclaimed. "These sketches reflect those thoughts; they are more spirited and lively. Tomorrow, let's take our sketches in the studio and see if we can make one of them into a finished painting. I can show you how to make the sun seem warmer in your painting and emphasize the wildflowers in the yard to give it more color and make it seem like a natural play area. And I will make my painting show more of the mist that comes off the sea in the morning and try to emphasize the latent power of the sea, out of which the sun is rising." He paused and then smiled. "This has been a wonderful day, and I am looking forward to many more like it."

What a day, thought Rosalee as she rode back to her boardinghouse. She could hardly wait to tell Eliza and Ben about her day working out in the field with Winslow Homer! Hearing him talk about expressing his thoughts in a work of art and then seeing it come alive before her eyes was a fantastic experience. Yes, Homer was frail and old, but the furnace of creativity still burned brightly in his soul.

II. Farmville, 1906

Laura Stuart sat in the morning sunlight on her veranda, which overlooked a small pond they had constructed the previous winter. In the hot days of late summer, the creeks and waterways generally dried up, and it was hard to get water for the farm animals; Laura and Robert hoped the pond would provide enough water to get through the dry spells.

It was mid-June, and she was reading a letter from Rosalee, who was back in Maine for her second year of study with Homer. As usual, the letter was filled with enthusiasm and pride. Rosalee was beginning to understand her mentor's techniques and his philosophy of color, and he had been very impressed with the painting she had done last November of the first snowfall. Laura remembered how hard Rosalee had worked, standing out in the cold wind, trying to catch the late-afternoon lights and shadows on the snow and the colorful leaves beneath. Working with Homer was such a wonderful experience for her daughter.

The last paragraph of the letter made her catch her breath in surprise.

> Mother, he has a painting of you that he said was done at Ashvale just after the war. It is you, all right, in a beautiful green robe, sitting in a garden under what looks like a grape arbor, with the sun streaming down on your face. It is the most beautiful portrait I have ever seen. He said he was going to give it to you as an engagement present, but then you married Daddy, and he put it away in his storeroom and

tried to forget about it, but now he wants me to give it to you. Charles doesn't know it exists, and Winslow doesn't want him to know about it. We are trying to think how to get it out of the studio without a confrontation with Charles. He is so good to Winslow, and he is so protective, so we have a little conspiracy to get it to you without offending Charles. We are getting to know each other so well, and I do like and admire him. I just know you will love this painting. You look simply gorgeous, and it will be so interesting to compare it with the one he did of you as a little girl.

Laura felt her cheeks flush. She remembered posing in that robe with very little on underneath. It had been a pretty daring thing to do, and she had never told Robert about it. But she was pleased and flattered and very anxious to see it.

But now Laura had a decision to make. Robert was seriously ill with pneumonia. It had started as a hard spring cold but had hung on and gone into his chest, eventually developing into pneumonia in both lungs. They kept a steam kettle in his bedroom to ease his breathing, and he was bravely trying to cough up the heavy, sticky mucus that was gradually filling up his lungs. Laura had heard him calling out Rosalee's name several times the last few nights, and the doctor had warned her that the end may be near.

Reluctantly, she went into Farmville the next day and sent a telegram to Prouts Neck informing Rosalee of Robert's illness, requesting her to return home immediately.

The news of Robert's illness hit Rosalee like an earthquake. She showed the telegram to Homer, who agreed she must return home immediately.

"You must do all you can for your father," he said.

The next day, as Rosalee was preparing to leave, she said to Homer, "I do hope I get home in time to see Daddy, and I do thank you so much, Mr. Homer, for being so patient and encouraging. I feel ever so much more confident in my work, and I want to keep learning. If Daddy recovers, will you take me back?"

"Of course, my dear," he said. "You have made remarkable advances as an artist, and I think these"—he indicated the array of paintings on the work table—"show the progress you have made. I would be very distressed if you did not return."

She went over to Homer and hugged him before turning to Charles. "And I thank you, sir, for your many kindnesses and your thoughtfulness in making my stay in Maine so enjoyable."

"It has been a pleasure to know you, Rosalee," said Charles. "I have a carriage outside waiting to take you to the Perkins home. I have a ticket for you on the afternoon train. There isn't much time, so the cab will wait for you and take you to the station. I suggest we move right along now."

"Yes, I must," she said, turning to go.

"Would you like to take these?" Charles asked, pointing to the paintings Homer had spoken of.

"Why, yes, I guess so," she said.

"I will pack them in this canvas bag and put them on the carriage for you." He picked up the paintings and carefully stacked them in a large canvas bag. Among them was an unfinished painting of a spectacularly large and colorful beech tree.

Rosalee gave a little gasp and looked over at Homer. He smiled, and his mustache twitched a little.

"Bon voyage, my dear," he said softly.

Rosalee packed hurriedly and said good-bye to Eliza and Ben Perkins. She had grown very fond of them and looked on them as part of her family—almost like another mother and father.

"You have been so good to me," Rosalee said, hugging Eliza. "I shall miss you terribly. You and Ben have done so much to make me feel a part of your family."

"And you, my dear," said Eliza, her cheeks wet with tears, "have been a bright ray of sunshine in our lives. I do love my children, but you have become another daughter and have brought me so much joy and happiness in my old age."

As she prepared to leave, Rosalee turned to Eliza and said, "I have packed some of my paintings in that canvas bag. I don't want to risk damaging them on the train without protecting them. Could you store them in your house until I can get back?"

"We'll take good care of them, Rosalee," said Ben, "and that will give you a good reason to come back."

And so, as Rosalee Stuart began her long journey home in the summer of 1906, some of her most advanced paintings and the magnificent gift from Homer to her mother were left behind in care of Eliza and Ben Perkins.

III. Farmville, 1910

Much had happened in the Stuart household since Rosalee's return from Prouts Neck four years earlier. Robert had rallied and responded to Rosalee's constant and efficient care and her unflagging, cheerful energy. By the end of June, he had been out of danger and beginning the slow process of regaining his strength and energy.

But the ordeal had drained her mother, who seemed so pale and exhausted. She complained of periods of dizziness and disorientation. One day in early July of 1906, Rosalee heard her give a little cry and found her slumped over the dining-room table. Two days later, she died from a massive stroke at the age of fifty-six.

Rosalee found herself the sole caregiver of her heartbroken father; her return to Prouts Neck was postponed indefinitely. In March of 1908, after a long courtship, Rosalee married Jim Turner, a professor of architecture at Hampden-Sydney College and her former art instructor. She continued to paint and progress as an artist and had several successful exhibitions in Richmond.

Rosalee's father, while still frail and despondent, had recovered sufficiently so that she revived her ambitions to resume her studies with Homer. Her husband, Jim, was very supportive and urged her to go. As she was preparing for the journey to Maine in the spring of 1909, she received word from Charles that Homer had suffered a debilitating stroke the year before and was unable to continue to work.

Now, in April of 1910, Jim Turner sat in a chair next to his wife in the Farmville hospital. Rosalee had just given birth to a lovely baby girl during the night. It had been a long and painful delivery, and she lay pale and exhausted on the bed. Jim was holding her hand.

"We have a beautiful baby girl, Jim," she whispered. "I'm so happy, but I feel so faint and weak."

"You are going to be fine, darling," he said, trying to sound confident and reassuring. "It was a long ordeal for you, and you need lots of rest. I'll stay with you until you go to sleep."

Jim sat there in silence for a few moments while Rosalee closed her eyes and seemed to drift off. The clasping of their hands calmed and comforted both of them.

Finally, Rosaleee opened her eyes and gazed steadily at her husband. "I want to name our baby Eliza Ashton. You have heard me talk of Mrs. Perkins, who was so good to me in Maine, and I want my mother's maiden name to be carried into our next generation. If something should happen to me, please call Eliza; I am so very fond of her."

A week later, on April 23, 1910, Rosalee Stuart Turner died of an infection she had sustained during childbirth. She was twenty-five years old.

On the morning of April 26, the telephone rang in the home of Eliza and Ben Perkins in the village of Fairhaven, Maine. Eliza answered and heard a low, masculine voice, obviously agitated and emotionally charged.

"Mrs. Perkins," he began. "I am Jim Turner, Rosalee Stuart's husband. She wanted me to call you." A long silence ensued, during which the caller tried to start to say something but couldn't quite get it out. So much anguish was audible in his voice that Eliza became alarmed.

"What is it, Mr. Turner?" she asked. "Are you all right? Is Rosalee all right?"

"She ... she died three days ago," he finally blurted out.

"How perfectly dreadful," Eliza whispered.

Gaining some control over his emotions, Jim explained, "She died after giving birth to a beautiful little girl. She named her Eliza, and she wanted you to know that. Rosalee was very fond of you, Mrs. Perkins."

When she hung up the telephone, Eliza put her head in her hands and wept.

Chapter 18:
CLOGGED PIPES

HARRY WOKE UP in the morning after returning from Maine and found he could not urinate. The urge was powerful, but nothing came out, and the increasing pressure was becoming very uncomfortable. At eight thirty, he called the health clinic at Bay Watch and was told to go to the emergency room at Salisbury General Hospital.

"I can't drive," muttered Harry. "I feel like I'm going to burst."

"We'll call an ambulance, Mr. Walker," replied the nurse in a clear, calm voice. "It will be at your house in ten minutes. Hang on."

A few minutes later, the ambulance arrived, and Harry was carried out on a stretcher. Concerned neighbors appeared in their doorways and asked about him.

"What's wrong, Harry? Where are they taking you?" asked Kate Summers, who lived across the street.

"I can't pee," said Harry between clenched teeth.

"Oh, you poor man," said Kate sympathetically.

When they put Harry in the ambulance, the paramedics talked into a radio, describing Harry's symptoms to the hospital. They were instructed to catheterize him immediately. When the tube was inserted, Harry felt instant relief from the pressure, but still felt some pain and was hot and flushed.

After a long session with the admissions office and another two hours of waiting in the emergency wing of the hospital, Harry was greeted by one of the staff urologists, who came in and introduced himself as Dr. Earnest. He was followed by an array of technicians, who removed the catheter, took his temperature, checked his blood pressure, collected a sample of his blood, and examined his prostate gland. Then they disappeared, and Harry felt the pressure rising in his bladder again. He rang for a nurse, who reinserted the catheter.

Several more hours passed, and Harry rang again and inquired whether he would be going home soon. The nurse informed him that they were preparing a room for him at the hospital and would keep him overnight, and he would see the doctor in the morning. Harry pointed out that he had not eaten all day and wondered if there might be some way he could get a sandwich and a soft drink. The nurse said she would inform the dietitian's office.

At last, at about six in the evening, some nine hours after arriving at the emergency room, he was taken to a room in the hospital, hooked up to a confusing array of monitors, and given an antibiotic pill.

An hour later, a tray arrived, and Harry noted it was labeled "low-sodium diet." It consisted of a gray, tasteless soup; a piece of rubbery chicken; and an evil-looking concoction that he assumed was a vegetable of unknown origin. It all tasted like cardboard, but it was filling, and he felt much better after dinner.

The night was long and certainly far from restful. Every hour or so, someone would come in and take his temperature and blood pressure, empty his urine bag, give him his medications, and do something with his chart. He was pretty groggy the next morning when Dr. Earnest came in.

"Good morning, Mr. Walker," Dr. Earnest said cheerfully. "The lab reports confirm that you have a bladder infection, which has caused you pain and is responsible for your fever. It also has irritated your prostate gland, causing it to swell up and shut off the passage from your bladder, which was the reason you were unable to urinate. We are going to clear up that infection with the antibiotics you're taking, and then we will bring you back here for a surgical procedure where we will clean out the bladder passage and remove the excess tissue causing the blockage."

"Huh!" said Harry suspiciously. "If the infection is cleared up, why won't my prostate shrink back to how it was before?"

"You have a greatly enlarged gland, Mr. Walker," said Dr. Earnest. "Your urethra is unlikely to open up enough to be comfortable. This procedure is very common among men of your age, and I strongly recommend that you consent to it. You will feel much better."

"What are the side effects?" asked Harry. "I know some men who had prostate surgery, and they are now impotent."

"There is always some risk of that, Mr. Walker, but not much in this type of procedure. All we are doing is enlarging the passage, so the urine can pass through freely, and all we take out is the tissue that caused the blockage."

"Sort of like using a plumber's snake in the toilet?"

"Something like that," agreed Dr. Earnest.

"And you're sure I can get a hard-on afterward?" asked Harry, looking very grim.

Ted Earnest looked over at Harry's anxious, almost agonized expression and had to suppress a smile. This was something they all worried about, especially the older men. "Mr. Walker, don't worry about that," he said. "At your age, I can't guarantee anything. You may not be able to have an erection, but I feel very confident that you will be just as good after the procedure as you are now."

Harry relaxed a little. "Can't you do better than that?" he asked with a little smile.

Dr. Earnest laughed heartily. "We'll do our best!" he said. "I'm going to discharge you from the hospital and send you back to assisted living at Bay Watch. They will check your condition to make sure the infection is gone, and we will tentatively schedule your surgery for November 22. How's that?"

"That's just a few days before Thanksgiving. I was going up to Baltimore to visit my daughter. Will I be able to go?"

"Not a good idea, Mr. Walker. We will want you to rest and stay quiet for at least a week to be sure it doesn't start bleeding."

"Do I have to keep this thing in?" asked Harry, referring to the catheter.

"Yes, we want to keep your bladder open and make sure it drains well and gets all the infection out. We'll fit you with a bottle; it won't cause you much inconvenience, and it will only be another three or four days."

"Christ!" muttered Harry.

After Harry checked into his room at the assisted-living quarters, he was pleasantly surprised at how clean and comfortable his room appeared. He picked up some messages from Vera at the front desk, the last being an imperious "Call me immediately" message. She was out when he called her back, and he left a message telling where he was and his telephone number. Later in the afternoon, she called.

"For heaven's sake, Harry," she said in an exasperated voice. "I have been trying reach you for two days. When I heard they took you to the hospital in an ambulance, I was worried sick. Why didn't you call?"

"I couldn't call, Vera. I was stuck in limbo for nine hours, and when I finally got into a room, I didn't feel like talking on the telephone."

"I called the hospital three times yesterday, and they said they had never heard of you, and then I called this morning, and they said you had just left. I was so mad I wanted to punch somebody. What's the matter with you?"

"Ah, Vera." He sighed. "You don't want to know."

"Why not?"

"It's just … it's personal," he said lamely.

Vera gave a soft snort, suppressing an urge to laugh. "I suppose you are having trouble with your prostate?"

"Yes, and I don't want any visitors, either. I've got this bag, and it's … it's just not pleasant."

"I'm coming over tomorrow whether you want visitors or not. I'm not going to have you lying around feeling sorry for yourself. And get out your pad and pencil—let's get back to work on our project and decide what we are going to do next."

Harry did his best to clean up before Vera arrived. The nurse's aide emptied his bottle, washed it out, and then sprayed deodorant around the room. He put on clean underpants and tried to arrange the bottle so it would be inconspicuous.

Vera came in looking very concerned and gave him a big hug and a kiss. "What are they going to do to you, Harry?" she asked. He outlined the procedure the doctor had recommended and the time frame of when he would be laid up.

"So, you see," he said sadly, "I'll be stuck here over Thanksgiving and into December. Then there is the Christmas season, and in January, you start teaching, and God knows when we can get back on the track to find out if we legally own this painting." He looked so miserable and tense that Vera was a little alarmed.

"Did the doctor tell you that you have cancer?" she inquired.

"No, it's not that."

"Are you worried the operation will leave you impotent?" she asked gently.

"Well … they say it might happen," he muttered.

"And you are worried that I will lose interest in you if that happens, right?"

Harry did not answer and looked down at the floor. "Let me tell you something, Harry. We have found each other very late in our lives after we both went through a difficult period. I don't know how our relationship is going to work out, but we need each other, and I am devoted to you. Whatever happens won't make any difference. I want to be with you. Okay?"

He stared at her for a long moment. It was now obvious to him that sex was an important part of their relationship. Even as he was approaching eighty, he could feel that his sex drive was still strong, and it appeared that the fires of romance were still burning brightly in Vera. Now she was telling him that she was devoted to him and wanted to be with him even if he were unable to perform. That was very important to Harry. He knew what he looked like; he was no model of a man who had grown old gracefully. She was aware of his shortcomings, and yet she still wanted him. Vera was no ordinary seventy-five-year-old woman; she was physically attractive and talented, and she possessed that certain unexplainable charm that attracted attention wherever she went. Vera would never be without admirers, and he was overwhelmed that he was the object of her affection.

He smiled and in a loud, clear voice said, "Okay!"

"Good," she said and reached into her handbag to pull out a notepad and a ballpoint pen. "Now let's play detective. Write down all the stuff we now know."

"All right," he said. "Let's start with what we learned in Maine."

1. Eliza Perkins was born in Virginia, and her maiden name was Turner.
2. The Turner family were frequent visitors of the Perkins family in Maine.
3. Eliza Turner and Ben Perkins were married in 1929.
4. Eliza was born in 1910, so she was nineteen when she married Ben.
5. Agnes Perkins is the granddaughter of Eliza Perkins and lives in the Perkinses' ancestral home.
6. Agnes owns some very good watercolors that suggest Homer's influence.
7. The paintings have the initials "R. S." in the lower right-hand corner.
8. At the time of Eliza Perkins's death, the Mystery Woman painting was in her garage, concealed under a painting of a beech tree.
9. The beech tree suggested Homer's influence but was not initialed.

"But," interjected Vera, "I can say with reasonable certainty that the beech-tree painting and the 'R. S.' paintings were done by the same artist, and Sarah will back me up. It was she who first called attention to Homer when she looked at the beech-tree painting."

"Okay," said Harry. "We have a couple of more things we don't know for sure but think we can prove."

10. The beech tree suggests a landscape in Virginia where I used to hunt quail.
11. It was probably done by R. S.
12. R. S. was probably a student of Homer's.

"That's a pretty imposing list of what we now know," observed Vera. "So what don't we know?"

"First, in my mind," said Harry, "is the connection between the Turners and the Perkinses. What is it?"

1. Why were the Turners frequent visitors to the Perkins family?
2. Who was R. S.?
3. Why did the artist conceal the Mystery Woman portrait?
4. Who owned the painting when it was concealed?
5. Why didn't R. S. come back and claim the painting he had concealed?
6. Who is the Mystery Woman?

"I think we are going to find out who R. S. is somewhere up in Maine," observed Vera. "If Homer had a student or a protégé, such a relationship was bound to have been noticed by someone. He died in 1910, so it had to have been earlier than that."

"And somehow there is a connection between Virginia, where the Turners came from, and Maine," added Harry.

"But where in Virginia?" asked Vera. "Virginia is a big state."

"If I ever get my plumbing straightened out," said Harry morosely, "we'll start with that place where I used to hunt. I have a strong feeling we will find that the Turners came from around there."

"And another thing," said Vera thoughtfully. "I'm wondering where that beautiful Oriental rug came from. Agnes said she thought it was a wedding gift, and if we find the Turner home, I have a hunch we'll find some other antique Orientals there. I think that rug was a wedding gift from Eliza Turner's parents."

After Vera's visit and their brainstorming session, Harry felt much better about himself. The doctor didn't think his sexual functions would be affected, and he wasn't going to worry about it anymore. He and Vera did have something going that was hard to define, but it was pretty wonderful, whatever it was, and she had made it very clear that she wanted and needed him regardless of the outcome of the surgery. It was a very comforting thought.

Harry's infection cleared up fairly quickly, and he was in an optimistic mood when he entered the hospital for surgery on November 22. The day after, he was pretty groggy from the sedation but was surprised at how little pain he felt. He was discharged in two days and went directly home instead of to assisted living.

He and Vera had a quiet Thanksgiving dinner at her condo, and he began his convalescence. It was a little depressing. *Holiday seasons should be spent with families*, Harry thought, *not sitting around in an institution for old people*. Vera gave him a learned tome on Homer and the art of watercolor, telling him he should learn a little about the artist who had painted his soon-to-be-famous picture.

Harry did find the book interesting. Homer had been an avid hunter and fisherman, and some of his paintings were charged with the excitement and emotions of the hunt. One thing stood out in Harry's mind, and that was the extent to which Homer focused on the prey: the deer that had just been shot or was about to be overtaken by hunting dogs, for example. He seemed to capture the terror and agony of the animal. And Homer's last great picture, *Right, Left*, showed the muzzle blast of a shotgun in the background, with one duck hit and dying and the other trying to work skyward, its face showing fear and panic. You could almost hear it crying "Help!" Harry loved to hunt ducks and didn't intend to give it up, but he wondered if he could ever kill another duck without thinking about that remarkable scene.

Two weeks after his operation, Harry was given a final examination and was cleared for normal activities. He felt pretty good, and no blood had shown up in his urine for over a week. His son, George, called and invited him to spend Christmas in New Jersey with his family, and one of Mary Ellen's oldest and dearest friends called and insisted he come to her annual post-Christmas cocktail party in Washington. At dinner with Vera that evening, he told her of his holiday plans to see family and old friends in Washington and asked her if she would feel comfortable going with him, so she could meet them.

"I am sure my family suspects that you and I are more than just friends," he said, "but they have never met you or seen you. You are sort of like the mystery woman to them."

Vera did not answer immediately while she digested what Harry had said. "Harry, are you thinking that we should get married?" she asked.

"I really hadn't gotten that far," he said. "I guess what I'm saying is that we have become pretty dependent on each other, and we are probably going to stay together in some fashion until one of us dies, so maybe our families should get to know us. But if you think we ought to get married, fine. I just don't want to lose you."

"No, Harry, I really don't want to get married again, at least right now," she said slowly. "But I don't want to lose you, either."

Harry's eyes brightened. "We'll just shack up, then. It's more fun if you're not married!"

"Yes, Harry," sighed Vera, looking a little disgusted. "And at our age, thinking about it is sometimes better than actually doing it. But seriously, I want to meet your family, and I want you to meet mine … but not this Christmas. My children have all insisted that I come out for a week. They even bought my ticket—business class. It's working out as you predicted. Now that they know I have a life here, they love me as a visiting grandma."

"And you will feel good about visiting," he said. "My kids and grandchildren just love to see me, because they know I won't stay long."

"It will be a good week," she agreed. "But what about our project? We seem to be derailed right now. Is there any danger if we take too long? We have made some progress, but we still don't know if this R. S. person stole the Homer."

"It worries me," said Harry. "I'm afraid someone is going to leak a story about an important work of art that has been concealed by a buyer who knew it was stolen and is trying to manufacture bogus evidence of title. Something is bound to break; we've got to get to Virginia and try to come up with some kind of a plausible theory, and we need to do it soon. I know your classes begin right after the new year, and you won't have time to travel until spring break in March, but I think that's too late."

"There is one possibility," said Vera thoughtfully. "My classes are Monday and Thursday; plus, I am required to have office hours two days a week for student conferences and faculty meetings. Martin Luther King Day is the third Monday in January. I could leave on the Friday before the holiday and wouldn't have to be back until the following Wednesday—provided Howard excuses me from office hours, which I think he will."

"That would give us about five days to look around," said Harry, "and I could stay longer, if necessary, but I sure want your eyes down there to look at artwork that we will surely find and I will not recognize."

"Let's go for it," said Vera. "I'll talk to Howard as soon as I can get him."

A week before Harry was scheduled to go up to New Jersey to visit George and his family, he received a note from Agnes Perkins enclosing a copy of an article from the Portland newspaper dated May 23, 1906. It read,

> Benjamin and Eliza Perkins of Fairhaven hosted a tea party for their houseguest, Miss Rosalee Stuart, who is studying with the prominent artist Mr. Winslow Homer, of Prouts Neck. Mr. and Mrs. Charles Homer attended, and Mr. Winslow Homer also made a rare public appearance.

Harry immediately called Agnes. "Where did you find this?" he asked.

"In the library," she answered. "The old newspaper articles are on discs and are indexed by subject matter. I opened the social section and started with 1900, and this turned up. And here is our mystery artist—with the right initials and all." Agnes was very pleased with herself.

"But the Eliza Perkins we know, your grandmother, wasn't born in 1906, so who are these people?"

"I'm trying to find out," said Agnes. "Apparently there was another set of Elizas and Bens. I'm going through old family records, but they are very confusing."

"Can I come up for a couple of days and look with you?" he asked. "I think you are onto something, Agnes."

"Sure, Harry, come on up. You can stay right here in the house, and I'll show you what I am looking at."

Harry smiled, recalling Agnes's buxom good looks and her down-to-earth Yankee good humor. "You sure about that, Agnes?" he asked. "You might not be safe!"

Agnes gave a loud guffaw. "I can handle you! Just come up as soon as you can."

"I'll try to get up there on December 19. I am due at my son's house for Christmas on December 22, so that will give us a couple of days to unravel your family history."

"Fine, Harry. Call me when you get into Portland, and I'll pick you up."

Harry called George and explained that he had to go to Portland for a few days before Christmas. He said he would drive to Newark, park his car, and fly to Portland on December 19. He would then fly back to Newark, pick up his car, and get to their house before dinner on December 22.

"Well, Dad," said George, "that works fine for us, but it's a lot for you to undertake. We would hate to see you get stuck in heavy traffic or stranded at the airport with your heart out of sync. Why do you have to go to Portland now?"

"All will be revealed when I get to your house," he said. "It's a weird story. In fact, if someone told this story to me, I wouldn't believe it."

Gorge laughed. "All right, Dad. We'll wait, but all of us are pretty nervous over your escapades. There's been lots of talk between us kids, and Gwen is positive you have a girlfriend."

"Ouch!" said Harry. "See you next week."

Traffic on the drive up to Newark was very heavy, and parking was an even greater chore. It involved following a confusing array of signs through a maze of parking lots and buildings and then getting on a bus to get back to the airport. Harry wondered if would ever find his car in that vast sea of automobiles that seemed to stretch out for miles in all directions. So when he arrived in Portland, he was pretty exhausted. Agnes picked him up and drove him to her house and gave him a big drink of scotch. She related with great relish how hard she had worked and how many articles she had read before running into that obscure note about Rosalee Stuart. Harry was impressed.

"You'd think there would have been a bigger splash in the newspaper over a story involving Homer and one of his students," Harry mused. "After all, he was a nationally known artist even back then."

"It does seem strange," agreed Agnes. "But then, Portland wasn't a big art center like New York, and Homer didn't like publicity, so I guess a little tea party in a small town like Fairhaven didn't seem like much."

"Well, you did find it, Agnes," said Harry, "and that was a great piece of work. And if your R. S. paintings are the work of one of Homer's students, they might be worth big, big bucks."

"I know." Agnes laughed nervously. "But I haven't any idea how to get them appraised or what to do with them if they are all that valuable."

"Leave that to Vera," said Harry. "She feels sure we will run into some more R. S. paintings in Virginia, where your grandmother came from."

Agnes looked very pleased and excited. "So what do you want to do up here?" she asked.

"I want to get some sense of who Eliza Perkins and Ben Perkins of 1906 were and how they relate to your grandmother and grandfather. Do you have some old family records we can look at?"

"Yes, but they are pretty confusing, and you look very tired. Let me show you to your room, and we can tackle the records in the morning, when you are fresh."

"I am tired," admitted Harry. "And my heart is jumping around a little, so I better take it easy for now."

Agnes was an excellent cook, and she enjoyed fixing a gourmet dinner for Harry. She started with a spinach and egg-drop soup with a big slab of butter in the middle. She followed this with lobster thermidor, long-grained rice, and asparagus. For dessert they had homemade apple pie with a scoop of vanilla ice cream. He ate every bit of it.

"That was an outstanding dinner, Agnes," Harry said enthusiastically. "How come a good-looking woman who can cook like this is still single?"

Agnes sighed. "Almost did it about fifteen years ago, but I never could see myself as a mousy little housewife taking care of a grown-up boy."

"Too bad," said Harry. "Do you have any special friends right now?"

Agnes laughed. "Nosy old geezer, aren't you?"

"Yes," he answered.

"Don't worry about me; I have plenty of men friends. Trouble is, the best ones are already married."

Harry slept soundly after dinner and woke up feeling much better. He and Agnes looked over some old photo albums and tried to decipher the sometimes cryptic entries in the old family Bible. It appeared that there was an Eliza Perkins who was sixty-one in 1906, having been born Eliza Philips in 1845. Ben Perkins of 1906 was the son of Caleb Perkins and had been born in 1841. They were married in 1868 and had two sons: Robert, born in 1871, and Seth, born in 1875.

"So how did Ben, who married your grandmother, get here?" asked Harry.

"This is where it gets confusing," said Agnes, referring to the old Bible. "It looks as if he was Robert's son, who I think married a Mary Coffin in 1897. Ben was one of their sons, and it looks as if he was born in 1901 or 1902. The entries are smeared, so it is hard to read."

"That confirms your memory that Ben was older than your grandmother, who was born in 1910. I remember you said your mother and father moved in with her after Ben died, because she was pretty despondent after his death."

"Yes, that's right," said Agnes.

"Now, we have Eliza at sixty-one in 1906, when Rosalee Stuart was a houseguest. When did that Eliza die?"

"She passed on in 1931 at the age of eighty-six."

"According to your grandmother's obituary, written by your father, the Turners were frequent visitors at the Perkins home, and one of the Turners was Eliza. One of the Perkins' was also Eliza," said Harry, looking very thoughtful. "Now, Eliza is not a common name, and you certainly will not find many by that name in Virginia. So I would bet serious money that Eliza Turner was named after Eliza Perkins."

"How about Rosalee Stuart?" asked Agnes. "How does she fit in?"

"I think she is the link between the Turners and the Perkins'," he answered.

The next day, Harry and Agnes tried to verify the accuracy of their findings. They went to the library and read old obituary notices. They also visited the Perkins family plot at the cemetery. Most of the dates checked out with only minor discrepancies. Harry called Vera and reported on what they had discovered about R. S. and the link between the Turners and the Perkins'.

"We're on the home stretch, Vera," he told her. "We've just got to get to Virginia next month. I'm sure we'll find the smoking gun down there."

"What's the smoking gun, Harry?" asked Vera.

"Something that tells us who owned that Homer when it was concealed and why it was concealed by R. S., who we now know is Rosalee Stuart."

"Nothing will stop me from making that trip!" exclaimed Vera. "I have clearance from Howard to skip the office days, and he will take my class on Thursday if I don't make it back on time. And tell Agnes to hang onto those paintings. When all of this is made public, she will have some pretty valuable paintings hanging on her walls."

"I already told her," said Harry. "Have fun in California with your family, and I'll see you next year."

At the airport, he said good-bye to Agnes. "You have been wonderful, Agnes," he said earnestly. "With your help, we are very close to a big discovery about this Homer fellow. We'll give you the full story as soon as we find out what it is."

Agnes impulsively pulled Harry over to her and gave him a big hug and a kiss. "You are something else, Harry," she said, her eyes bright with humor. "If you were twenty years younger, I'd give Vera some real competition."

"Agnes," said Harry, trying to sound sinister and dangerous. "If I were twenty years younger, your virtue would now be tarnished beyond repair."

Agnes gave a delighted snort. "Get out of here, you old goat, and you take good care of Vera, you hear?"

Harry laughed. "She is in good hands, Agnes, and thanks again for your good work and hospitality."

He boarded his flight to Newark and settled into his seat. He would have a very strange and unusual story to tell George and Jean, and it had all happened as a result of his decision to buy that old picture in Maine last summer for $200.

Chapter 19:

THE HOLIDAY SEASON

HARRY ARRIVED AT his son's house in Summit, New Jersey, at about five in the afternoon. With Christmas only three days away, traffic had been heavy, and the airport had been jammed. His flight was delayed for ninety minutes because the arrival gates at the Newark airport were full and slow to open.

Fortunately, Harry found his car and escaped from the airport without mishap. George left his office early to avoid the evening rush hour and was home to greet Harry when he drove up the driveway.

"Dad," he called out, "glad you made it! We were a little worried about your flight. The radio reported air traffic is very heavy and there were lots of delays."

"It was a zoo out there," he replied wearily. "I sure need some R&R, and you can start with a big shot of scotch on the rocks."

"Coming up," said George. "Do you have any baggage in the car?"

"Just my suitcase and a bag of gifts; leave the presents in the car for now, and give me a hand with this suitcase."

"I'll bring them in, Granddad," said Patrick eagerly.

Harry was given the basement bedroom and bath just off the recreation room, which was very comfortable and quiet. He changed into a warm, informal sweater and slacks and came up to greet the family. The Christmas tree was up and decorated, and lots of brightly colored packages were arranged around and under it. Harry noted with amusement that his bag of gifts had already been set out by Patrick, and the long, tubular package wrapped in brown paper with a bright ribbon stuck on it was displayed in a prominent place. This obviously was the custom-made fly rod Harry had ordered for Patrick. It had been hand made by the proprietor of a small tackle shop in the Pennsylvania Pocono Mountains. Patrick couldn't take his eyes off of the gift and clearly couldn't wait to open it.

When the family had all gathered around the tree and Harry had had his first sip of scotch, they insisted he tell them immediately what he had been doing in Maine.

"What on earth have you been up to, Harry?" demanded Jean. "Everyone has been talking about you, and there are all sorts of rumors flying around … including that you have a new girlfriend!"

"A girlfriend!" exclaimed Harry. "What a preposterous idea!"

"Come on, Dad," said George. "Stop being coy, and tell us what's going on."

Harry took another long sip of his drink and looked at the family, sitting there with mixed expressions of curiosity and apprehension. They were a little worried about what he had gotten into, and what he was about to tell them would cause lots of commotion.

"It all started with that old painting of the beech tree I bought last summer in Maine. You were there, Jean, and questioned my sanity when I paid $200 for that beat-up old picture."

"I still don't know why you bought it," said Jean. "I think you said it reminded you of some hunting expedition you went on in Virginia."

"That's what I said," agreed Harry. "But we might as well get this out in the open: I really bought it because I had met a woman I went to high school with long ago, and she is an artist. I wanted to get her interested in restoring that old painting as a means of getting her interested in me."

George looked delighted. "Good for you, Dad! Did it work?"

Harry laughed. "Yes, indeed, it worked. And so I really do have a girlfriend."

"So, Aunt Gwen was right!" burst out Kathy, George's teenage daughter.

Jean looked a little startled. "Are you planning on marrying this woman?" she asked.

Harry shook his head. "We aren't thinking that far ahead. A romance at our age is about companionship and shared interests, and it also involves whatever it is that attracts a certain man and a certain woman to each other. We enjoy being together, and we are enjoying working together on this project."

"So what is this project, Dad?" asked George. "Is that old picture something really valuable?"

"I know you have talked to Pat," Harry said. "How much did she tell you?"

"Only that the picture turned out to be very unusual and that the background is very complex. She was pretty vague and said she really didn't know very much."

"I guess she was treating me as a client. We had a long discussion about where I stood legally, and I guess she thought any disclosures were confidential."

"So she knows," said George with some asperity. "I don't see why she should keep family secrets from me. After all, you are my father, too, and we are very concerned about your activities."

"I am going to tell you the whole story," said Harry, "but at the time I talked to Pat, it was essential that I keep a lid on publicity about that old picture."

"For heaven's sake, Harry!" Jean exclaimed. "Don't tell me that old painting was some kind of masterpiece. I'm not an artist, but I love art, and there was nothing special about that old painting."

"That old beech tree painting was destroyed," replied Harry, "and under it was a magnificent oil painting done by Winslow Homer that has been authenticated by the Philips Gallery in Washington and is estimated to be worth about one million dollars."

That stunning piece of news left George and his family speechless for a long time.

George finally broke the silence. "Dad, you're not kidding, are you?"

"No, I am not kidding," he answered. "That's why I was so anxious to keep this quiet until I could find out if I really am the legitimate owner."

"And I suppose the discoverer of this oil painting was your new girlfriend?" asked Jean.

"That's right," he answered. "Now let me tell you the whole story and what I just found out in Maine."

For the next half hour, Harry recounted the details of his and Vera's discovery of the painting, the removal of the beech-tree watercolor, and the problems he faced in establishing provenance because of the inference of theft arising out of the concealment of the Homer painting.

At dinner that evening, his son and grandchildren bombarded him with questions about the painting and what he needed to do to establish that he was the legitimate owner. There were even more questions about Vera.

"Aunt Gwen says she is beautiful," said Kathy, her eyes sparkling with excitement. "And she says you are having an affair with her."

Harry laughed loudly. "Your aunt Gwen has never seen her. Nick's brother, Spiro, is the only one who has seen her, and she did get herself all gussied up for that trip we made to Maine, so she looked pretty good. She is two years younger than me, so she is an old lady. She is overweight, with gray hair and lots of wrinkles. She also has a great sense of humor and lots of pizzazz. She is fun to be around, and we enjoy each other. But beautiful? No!"

"So what is your next move?" asked George.

"Vera teaches art history at Salisbury State University, but she has about a week off over Martin Luther King's holiday. We are going to Virginia, where I think we will find out who owned the Homer when Rosalee Stuart concealed it and why it was concealed. And while we are there, I think we will also find out the identity of that gorgeous woman in the portrait."

Over the next two days, the surprise and excitement created by Harry's disclosures about the painting subsided, and the spirit of Christmas took over. The family participated in a community caroling session on the evening of December 23, and on Christmas Eve, they were all invited to a lavish, family-oriented cocktail buffet given by a wealthy Wall Street investment banker who lived in a beautiful home a block away. Amid lots of singing, the wine and liquor flowed copiously, but Harry was very careful to restrain himself. His addiction to alcohol was still very strong, and the urge to overindulge was difficult to control in this kind of a festive setting. He helped himself to a generous plate of food from the sumptuous buffet and found a seat where he could rest and watch the crowd. He did not know any of the guests, except George and his family, but he was glad for a chance to be by himself and reflect on how Christmas had evolved during his lifetime.

It was a Christian holiday and had a strong religious theme as the supposed date on which Jesus was born. When Harry was growing up, the country had been trying to recover from the Great Depression amid periods of shortages and rationing caused by World War II. No one held elaborate parties in those days—at least none that Harry was aware of—and his family always attended church services on Christmas Eve. But even then, Christmas had been a magical day for children. The Christmas tree, the lights, the decorations, and the packages were all there. The feeling of mystery and the almost metaphysical excitement he had felt as a small child coming down to see the tree and open the presents was something he would never forget.

Later, when his children were small, he shared in their joy and felt their excitement while they opened their packages on Christmas morning. Still later he and Mary Ellen loved watching the antics of their grandchildren as they tore open packages and emitted loud shrieks of joy when a special toy was uncovered. There was nothing like it; Christmas was, and always would be, a very special day for children. And it was also a very unique time for adults. Christmas occurred at the end of the year, and the festivities were a time to enjoy the fruits of a year of hard work. A feeling of friendship and goodwill pervaded the atmosphere during the Christmas season. Worries about jobs, health, and the general malaise of the world in general were put on the back burner, not to be thought about until after New Year's Day.

This was Harry's second Christmas without Mary Ellen. Last year he had been so immersed in negotiating the sale of his home and moving from the Washington area where he had lived all his life that he hadn't gotten into the spirit of Christmas, and it had passed him by like a momentary bright spot on an almost nightmarish period of his life. But this year, he was really into it. Many people he didn't know stopped to talk to him and wish him a merry Christmas. He couldn't remember their names or even what they talked about, but such recollection wasn't necessary; the greetings were a part of the Christmas theme, and Harry enjoyed them thoroughly.

Christmas morning was again a magical time, although more restrained, since the children were older. It was still a time of goodwill and of giving. *It really is better to give than receive*, thought Harry as he watched Patrick's eyes glow as he put together the beautiful, handcrafted fly rod and take it out in the backyard to try it out.

Calls came in from Pat and Gwen. Pat expressed relief now that Harry's story of the painting was out in the open. After she heard of the latest episode from Harry, she asked to speak to George.

"I wanted to tell you about what was happening, George," she said. "But Dad was very worried that the press would get word that he had a valuable painting that appeared to be stolen, and he would have a lot of explaining to do."

"But is he any better off now?" asked George. "He still doesn't know who owned the Homer painting when it was covered up or why it was covered up."

"He now knows a lot more," she answered. "He knows who concealed the painting and knows that she was a student of Homer and a great friend of the Perkins family in Maine. The circumstantial evidence suggests something other than theft."

Gwen's call was mainly about Vera. After talking to Harry, she spent a lot of time talking with Jean.

"I am not pleased that Dad seems so obsessed with this woman," Gwen said. "He is very lonely and vulnerable now that Mom has gone, and it would be very easy for some young, good-looking woman to take advantage of him."

"I understand your concern, Gwen," said Jean, "but Harry says she isn't young and isn't beautiful. He says they were in high school together, and he bought the painting to attract her attention."

"So where do you think this is going, Jean?" asked Gwen.

"I wish I knew," said Jean earnestly. "He seems to know what he is doing, and I think he is very fond of this woman, but I don't think he will do anything until we all have a chance to meet her."

"I hope you are right," said Gwen ominously.

On Friday, December 27, Harry said good-bye to George and his family. "I had a wonderful time here," he said.

"You behave yourself, Harry," said Jean, giving him a big hug. "I don't want to hear about you running off with some bohemian artist until we get a chance to meet her."

Harry laughed heartily. "There seems to be a lot more interest in Vera than my million-dollar painting. But don't worry; you will meet her. I tried to get her to come with me this time to meet my family, but her family insisted that she visit them over Christmas on the West Coast."

"Keep us informed, Dad," said George. "I know some pretty influential art dealers in New York, so when you get ready to sell that painting, let me know. They might be helpful to you in establishing a price."

After a four-hour drive to Washington, Harry checked in at the Metropolitan Club and reviewed his calendar for the next few days. The annual Christmas cocktail party given by Claudia Simmons was on December 28 at the country club. He wasn't sure why Claudia had invited him. He had left the club scene in such disgrace the year before that he was surprised to get her invitation and even more surprised that he accepted it. At times he did miss the club. For many years, he had been an active participant in club activities, both sporting and social. Mary Ellen had been a great favorite at the club, and he fitted in easily as her husband. He also had many pleasant memories of golf games with some of the most talented members of the club. They were spirited competitors and accepted Harry more warmly than other members he met during social events.

After accepting Claudia's invitation, Harry called Ed McKee to see if he wanted to get together for lunch with some of their old golfing group. Ed promptly invited him to a small New Year's Eve party that most of the old golfers were also attending. Harry was pleased that Ed had greeted him so warmly after his disgraceful conduct at the senior tournament last year. He still shuddered when he thought about it.

So he had a full social calendar for the post-Christmas holidays, and he was looking forward to seeing some of his old club friends. He wondered how they would react to him. He had also invited Pat's family to join him for brunch at the club on Sunday. Peter and Pat accepted, but the children were busily engaged in activities with their college-age friends and declined. On Monday afternoon, Harry had a date to meet with Dr. Jennings at the Philips Gallery to report on the results of his investigations. And then on Tuesday, he would be at the McKeeses' for New Year's Eve.

Harry had been on the road since December 19, when he had left for Maine, and had been going nonstop ever since. He was pretty tired and was not very enthusiastic about going to Claudia's cocktail party. He decided to go early and leave early, making a mental promise not to overindulge.

When he got to the party at about six fifteen, some of his old crowd was already there. The early arrivals were mostly around his age and greeted Harry with some surprise and a little confusion. Some seemed to barely recognize him. These were people he and Mary Ellen had known for nearly thirty years, but for the most part, their reaction to seeing Harry was decidedly tepid. A few friends were genuinely glad to see him and were interested in how he was getting along at Bay Watch, but he was a little surprised at how few good friends he really had. He talked briefly with some of the notorious party animals who worked the crowd, hoping to find some socially important people. Harriet Shea came up to him, looking dazzling and sporting her latest face-lift.

"Harry!" she gushed. "You are looking so well and so handsome! I have just met the most divine couple, and you must get acquainted with them. He is a retired foreign-service officer and has lived all over the world." Harriet was speaking to Harry but was looking past him into the crowd.

"I would love to meet them," said Harry enthusiastically. "And from what you tell me, I think he would fit in well with the Redskins' new coaching staff."

"Yes, I'm sure," she said vaguely. "Oh, there is Megan Ingram; I must speak with her. Now, don't go away, Harry; I'll be right back. I want to hear all about what you are doing at your new home." She hurried away and quickly got into an animated conversation with a younger couple he didn't know.

Harry had always been intrigued with Harriet. She was a friendly, good-hearted person, but at affairs like this, she never listened to anything he said, and he enjoyed making off-the-wall comments to her. He wondered if she ever listened to anyone at these cocktail parties.

He wandered over to the bar, got another drink, and stopped to talk with a group of people standing a little way off from the main group of guests. He recognized them as the Barcroft Academy group. Most of them resided in Chevy Chase, Maryland, and were third- or fourth-generation members of the country club. All of them had either gone to Barcroft or had children who were students at the school. For many, the high point of their careers was the time they had spent at their prep school. Harry had played golf with some of them and found them to be very pleasant. They were well mannered and generally conservative in their political and social views. They were cordial to Harry, but as a product of the public school system, he would never be accepted as an equal.

By the time he was on his fourth drink, Harry was getting a little dizzy and decided it was time to leave. He helped himself at the club's buffet. Claudia always had lavish food, and the staff presented the dishes beautifully. He ate a dozen oysters from the raw bar, knocked back a shot of ice-cold vodka with a lemon peel, and had a crab custard dish in a pastry shell and a thick slice of roast beef with horseradish sauce. Many other salads, fish, and desserts remained to be tasted in the array before him, but he was tired and somewhat fuzzy from the alcohol. He was aware that it wasn't safe for him to drive home, so he thanked Claudia for the party and called a taxi. He would pick up his car on Sunday, after the brunch with Pat and Peter.

The brunch on Sunday was relaxed and pleasant. The food was very good and the atmosphere subdued in contrast with the tense mood of forced gaiety at the cocktail party the night before. Harry talked a while with Pat about what he should do after he finished his investigation. Pat volunteered to be the custodian of all the documentary evidence they had collected. She would take the sales receipt from the Maine dealer, the estate-sale auctioneer's receipt, the news item from the 1906 Portland newspaper, any affidavits from Sarah and Vera, the Eliza Perkins obituary, and whatever else Harry found in Virginia. She would make copies and arrange them in chronological order and have them ready to present to the Philips Gallery committee. She also suggested that Harry should discuss with Dr. Jennings how they should proceed with their presentation if the gallery were interested in pursuing their option of first refusal.

"Find out from Jennings what he wants from you and when he will be in a position to evaluate your claim," Pat advised. "You don't want them to stall you and prevent you from marketing the painting through other channels."

"I'll go through my file and send all the documents I have," said Harry, "and I will ask Agnes to make copies of the estate file for her grandmother and send them to you. There may be some clues there that will help us. And I'll talk to Jennings tomorrow and see whether he is interested and what he wants from us."

The meeting with Dr. Jennings on Monday afternoon was cordial and informative. Jennings listened carefully while Harry reported on the information he had obtained, and the former was particularly interested in Harry's conclusion that the watercolor that had concealed the Homer had been painted by Rosalee Stuart.

"I don't suppose we can prove that she did that beech tree, since the painting was destroyed," Jennings said.

"But we can get affidavits from Vera and Sarah that the R. S. paintings in the Perkins home and the beech tree were done by the same artist," said Harry.

"Does Vera have a financial interest in the painting?"

"Yes," admitted Harry. "But Sarah doesn't have any interest in it. Would that satisfy you?"

"I think if you can get such a statement from Sarah, it will pretty much resolve that issue."

They discussed timing, and Jennings thought his art committee would be interested in hearing their evidence of provenance and that he could get them together on thirty days' notice.

"When you are ready to make your presentation, let us know, and we can have a meeting within a month. Then the committee's recommendations will have to be reviewed by the board, and they will have to approve it and approve the acquisition price ... so we are looking at another two months, at least."

"Well," said Harry. "I hadn't thought there would be that much of a delay. That would be a big problem for me if you decided not to take it."

"Mr. Walker, I don't suggest you have to wait all that time before exploring other avenues for marketing your painting. All I can ask is that you give us a chance to bid for the picture before you sell it. If we aren't ready to make an offer when you have other people interested, we will just have to pass."

"Fair enough," replied Harry.

New Year's Eve marked a pleasant end to Harry's hectic holiday season. In anticipation of a long evening of drinks, he took a cab to Ed McKee's home, which was close to where Harry and Mary Ellen had lived in McLean. Jack Barlow was also at the party, and Harry knew that Jack and Ed would be watching him closely that night. The other guests included men who, at one time, had been very good golfers who loved the game and played by the rules.

Jack Barlow was a former club champion and had also been captain of the Harvard golf team. Ed McKee was also a former club champion and captain of the Princeton golf team. In June of 1941, the year both men were leaders of their golf teams, the Harvard-Princeton match had been played at the country club. Harry enjoyed getting them to talk about the match. Both agreed it had been a wonderful match and both teams had played well. Jack was very positive that Harvard had been the winner, and Ed was equally positive Princeton won. After a few rounds of drinks, the conversation became hilarious, and Harry was never sure who actually was the winner.

At ten o'clock, Ed reset the clock in the family room to twelve, proclaimed that the new year had arrived, and proposed a toast. After singing "Auld Lang Syne" a few times and kissing the ladies, they all went home. Not a word was spoken about Harry's binge the September of the year before.

It had been a wonderful, exhilarating, and exhausting two weeks for Harry. His stay with George had been delightful, and he had enjoyed visiting with Pat and Peter. He loved being the center of attention while he told his story of the painting and of his geriatric romance with Vera. He also enjoyed seeing some of his old friends in Washington. It had been an interesting experience.

The holidays were a time for celebrations and parties, and also a time when liquor and wine flowed freely. But Harry had controlled his drinking pretty well. The only time he had overindulged was at Claudia's party, and he had the good sense to recognize his condition and take a taxi to the Metropolitan Club. There was no doubt that his addiction to alcohol had diminished since he had met Vera. Harry was no ladies' man, but he had spent more than half his life with Mary Ellen, and he needed the companionship of a woman. In his mind, the visit to the country club confirmed that his decision to leave Washington had been the correct choice. Without Mary Ellen, he felt out of touch with the social scene in Washington. The people he really enjoyed were his old golfing friends, like Ed McKee and Jack Barlow, but they were well into their eighties, and their contemporaries were passing away rapidly. *That's another problem with old age*, Harry thought. *Seeing old friends die and knowing you will be next.* He would be glad to get back to Bay Watch with Vera and return to their project.

Chapter 20:
THE STUARTS OF VIRGINIA

VERA HAD JUST finished her first week of the spring term at Salisbury State and was telling Harry about the artists she was covering in her art-history class, along with their respective works.

"All of them were fascinated with light and its effect on color. The time of day, and even the season of the year, makes the image look different. Monet, one of the French Impressionists, once painted a cathedral half a dozen times at different times of the day, and the differences were remarkable. The pictures ranged from yellow to a dark, bluish gray; it was difficult to believe it was the same structure."

"So were these artists influenced by the French Impressionists?" asked Harry.

"Oh yes," she answered. "In fact Homer was called an American Impressionist. But he and his American contemporaries had their own style; where the French were very deft with their brushstrokes, American artists were inclined to be bolder in their use of color. Homer's paintings are bold and creative, and he understood the theory of color probably as well, or better, than any of his contemporaries. He was an ardent student of *Chevruel on Colors*, perhaps the most comprehensive work ever done on color and light."

"I would like to learn something about these artists," Harry said.

"I think they are offering some art courses in the senior education program."

"I wish you would enroll in some of them, Harry," she said earnestly. "I love art and love to talk about it, and it would be so much more fun if you were interested, too. We could look at exhibitions together and take art trips to view some of the great European artists, and it would be so gratifying to do it together."

They were sitting in front of Vera's gas fireplace after dinner and were in a relaxed, contented mood. They had shared their stories about the holidays with their respective families and, while they had both enjoyed their respective visits with loved ones, they were glad to be back together.

"Harry," said Vera, looking at him affectionately, "I am so glad you got interested in my painting in the park last summer. You have been a big help to me, and you are a very good, interesting man."

Harry leaned back in his chair and tried to look thoughtful and serious.

"Yes," he said, "I know I am. And you know, Antonelli, I can't figure out why you let me get away."

Vera's eyebrows shot up. "What was that?" she inquired sharply.

"Well, back in high school, there I was: a big-shot senior, star athlete, member of the student council, great dancer, and you were just a little sophomore ... but I was willing to take you on as a girlfriend, and you just blew it."

"Maybe I didn't think you were such a big wheel," she said airily. "I didn't think you were such a star football player. I watched you play a few times, and you didn't do anything except stand around shoving people."

"Hey!" said Harry. "That's called blocking, and I was good at it."

"Charlie Radcliff was the really good player on your team. He ran all over the place and scored all those touchdowns." Vera was enjoying Harry's reaction.

Harry was getting a little irritated. "He wouldn't have run anyplace if I and the other linemen hadn't opened holes big enough to drive a truck through. I was the all-league tackle, and Charlie was second team. I was also second team all-metropolitan."

"I don't see how you remember those silly details after all these years," she said, looking down her nose at him.

"They aren't silly!" he exclaimed hotly. "Football is the ultimate team sport, and learning teamwork helps you in everything you do. You just don't understand football."

"That's right," she said as she got up and walked over to Harry. "But I know how to get under your skin, don't I?" She smiled at him and sat down on his lap. "If you say 'oof' again, I'll smack you." She leaned down and kissed him gently but very passionately. They sat together for over ten minutes, enjoying the feeling of intimacy and affection for each other. Reluctantly, Vera got up and pulled down her sweater and rearranged her clothes.

"I don't know what you do to me, Vera, but whatever it is, don't stop doing it," he said, his voice shaking with emotion.

"It is exciting, and I do love being with you, Harry," she said softly, "and I think we will have many intimate times together. But let's not rush it. I don't have much of an idea how this will turn out, and right now, I feel a little strange getting involved with a man at my age, especially after all those years with John."

"I think I know how you feel," he said. "Do you ever feel a little guilty, like maybe you are being unfaithful to John?"

"Sometimes," she answered. "How about you? I know you were deeply in love with Mary Ellen. "

"Yes, sometimes I do," he admitted. "I think I will feel better about it when the family meets you, and I can see their reaction to someone they might consider a rival to their mother."

"That will help," she agreed. "And in the meantime, we both need our space while we try to figure out where we want to go with this relationship."

"Okay," he said with a smile. "I can take a hint, and I'll go home. I think Martin Luther King Day is January 20, so you can leave after class on Thursday, January 16. We have to be back here on Wednesday evening, January 22, which gives us about five days to look around. I'll do some research and book us at a place near where that beech tree is." He hesitated a moment. "And I promise I'll get separate rooms."

Vera smiled broadly. "No comment," she said.

Harry got on the Internet and checked some places to stay near Farmville. He was pleased to see the Sportsmen's Lodge, where he had stayed during his hunting trips, was still operating. He called and made a reservation for two rooms for January 16–21.

"Will you be hunting on this trip, sir?" asked the clerk, who sounded like a pleasant young woman.

Harry was a little surprised. "I didn't know the season was still open this late," he said. "I used to hunt down here in the fall thirty-five or forty years ago. We brought our own dogs and had some fabulous quail hunting."

"That would be back when we had wild-bird shooting," she said. "My father was running the lodge then, but now it is almost entirely preserve shooting, and we like to get our birds out a week or ten days before the hunters come down. It makes them a little wilder and sportier to shoot."

"We're coming down on business this trip," he replied, "but while I am there, I'll check out your program to see if it isn't too strenuous for an old geezer like me."

"We look forward to your visit, sir."

On Wednesday evening, Vera loaded her suitcase into Harry's car, so she would be ready to leave when her class was over at noon. It was about a 250-mile drive to Farmville, and only the Norfolk-to-Richmond leg was on an interstate. The rest was slow going, so they were anticipating a five-and-a-half-hour drive, which would get them there at about dusk.

"You said the lodge used to be very rustic, but they do have indoor plumbing ... don't they?" inquired Vera.

Harry laughed. "It's not as bad as that. We had inside bathrooms forty years ago, and I imagine it's been spruced up and modernized now that the hunting is all preserve shooting."

They chatted a while about Vera's classes, and she told him she had begun to work on the beech-tree painting she had promised to do for him when the original had been destroyed in the uncovering of the Homer painting.

"I brought my camera and want to take some shots of the area where you hunted. I hope that old tree is still standing. It was pretty big back in 1906, and that was a hundred years ago."

"It was still going strong in the sixties, when we hunted there," replied Harry. "But that was forty years ago. I don't know how long they last; oaks sometimes live over two hundred years, but I'm not so sure about beech trees."

They arrived a little after five thirty and were assigned to a modern unit consisting of two bedrooms with a connecting living room with a wet bar and a coffeemaker. After unpacking they went into the lounge for a before-dinner drink. Harry ordered a scotch on the rocks and was surprised to hear Vera order gin on the rocks with a lemon twist.

"I thought you were just a white-wine lady," he said. "I didn't know you went in for the hard stuff."

"When in Rome, do as the Romans do," she answered, indicating the rough masculine decor of the hunting lodge.

"It still does have a certain amount of rustic charm," he answered. "The restrooms are still identified by those dogs. Can you tell which one is yours?"

"Well," she answered, "I can sure tell which is yours. That old dog has his leg up, showing off what he's got in a typical egotistical male manner, so the other little dog squatting in the field must be mine. What kind of dogs are they?"

"My dog is a pointer, and yours is an English setter—very descriptive names, I think. You seem to fit right in here, and if I decide to try hunting down here again, I might take you with me."

"How exciting!" she replied, rolling her eyes.

When the bartender brought them their drinks, Harry asked him if he was part of the family that ran the lodge.

"My wife is the reservations clerk, the receptionist, and the bookkeeper; I am the bartender in the evening and the maintenance man in the daytime; my brother-in-law runs the business end, and his wife runs the kitchen. So it's family owned and family run and has been that way for a long time."

"We're looking for information about an artist named Rosalee Stuart Turner who lived down here about a hundred years ago," Vera told him. "Ever hear of her?"

"Before my time, and I'm not much into art," he answered. "You might inquire over at the information center in Farmville; they have quite a bit of historical information."

"Thanks," she said. "We'll try that in the morning."

The next morning, they spent about an hour talking with the director of the information center. They found that about sixty Stuarts lived in the area and about the same number of Turners, but no information about Rosalee Stuart Turner could be found. The obituary in Agnes Perkins's file indicated Turner might have had a connection with Hampden-Sydney College, so they tried the development office at the college. The college did have a record of Jim Turner, who was a former professor.

Jim Turner had died in 1943, but there was no reference to any children or collateral heirs. After a day and a half of making cold phone calls to various Stuarts and Turners and not turning up any leads, Harry and Vera were becoming very frustrated, and time was running out.

"This is a lot more difficult than I imagined," remarked Harry as they sat in the lounge, sipping a drink, on Saturday evening. "I thought Rosalee would be some kind of celebrity around here, but we haven't come up with anything."

The bartender caught Harry's eye and nodded toward a weather beaten, grizzled old man in a wool shirt. "That's Ray Tapley over there; he was running this place when you used to hunt and wants to meet you."

Harry and Vera walked over and introduced themselves.

"I understand you were in charge here when I used to hunt wild birds about forty years ago. There were four of us, and we brought our dogs and had some fabulous hunting."

"I remember you guys," he said with a warm smile. "You came down for quite a few years, and one of you had a big white pointer. Was that you?"

Harry was delighted. "That was Junior, the best bird dog I ever saw."

"I was doing a lot of guiding back then, and we could see him on point a quarter of a mile away. He stuck his rear up in the air and when we could see that big tail stuck up like a flagpole, we knew there were birds over there, and we would go over to see if you left any for us."

"I'm surprised you remember Junior so well," said Harry. "You must have had hundreds of dogs down here in those days."

"Don't you remember that dog fight?" Ray asked.

Harry shook his head. "Junior got into so many fights, I can't remember any specific one. He was a mean old bastard."

"I had a big, mean pointer named Buck, and he jumped Junior during feeding time. Junior like to have killed him until you came over, grabbed him by the collar, and knocked him down with a big stick. After that, I never had any more trouble with Buck fighting."

They traded dog stories and recounted memorable hunting trips for a while until Vera broke in.

"One of the things I am interested in is locating a field with a huge beech tree in it where Harry said he found the biggest flock of quail he had ever seen." She hesitated and then added, "I am an artist, and a rather prominent artist from around here painted that tree a long time ago. Do you know where it might be?"

"Oh, yeah, I know that place," he answered. "It was a great place to hunt. It was part of the old Stuart farm. Jim Stuart farmed it for a long time but usually left plenty of feed and cover in some fields and leased out the hunting rights. He died about the time you were coming down here, and his daughter, Julie Harris, now owns the farm."

"Do you think she would talk to us?" asked Harry.

"Sure," said Ray. "She's well into her eighties now and a little despondent since her husband died last year. But she's still pretty spry, and she likes people to visit with her. Call her up; she lives out on Lee Road, near the Appomattox River. She'll be glad to talk to you."

"We'll do that," said Harry, "and before we go, let's talk about whether there is any kind of hunting a gimpy old guy like me can do around here."

"Come on down anytime," said Ray. "We take you old hunters out with a guide and an ATV vehicle. The birds aren't tame, but they aren't wild, either; you'll be able to hit some of them."

"I'll give you a call," he said.

Harry got Julie Harris's number from information and made an appointment for Sunday afternoon. She told him how to get to the beech-tree field and assured him the tree was still standing.

"This is a real breakthrough," said Vera. "I wonder if the home she lives in is the same place where Rosalee was raised and where Eliza Perkins was born."

"From what Ray was saying, I think it must be the old ancestral home."

The next morning, after breakfast, they drove over to the river and located Julie's home and then drove around until they found the field with the beech tree in it. Vera marveled at its size; it was nearly a hundred feet tall and had limbs that spread out from the trunk thirty feet or more. The field around it looked as if it had not been cultivated for a few years and was covered with brambles and broom sage. Harry walked around the tree and saw signs of beech nuts having been eaten and bird scat in the underbrush; he heard some birds calling with that old familiar "Bob White" sound.

"This is the place," he said, looking around. "Right over there at the edge of the tree, we flushed a huge covey; must have been over fifty birds in it. I think they were feeding on these beech nuts."

"I am getting some great shots here," said Vera. "But I want to come back in the fall and see it with leaves beginning to turn, as they were in your picture."

"Good," said Harry. "We'll come down in the fall, and I'll hunt, and you can paint. Maybe we can get a picture of a bird dog working the field, so you can see what it's like."

After a light lunch, they went over to Julie Harris's home and introduced themselves. Julie was quite elderly—well into her eighties—but still active and alert. She greeted them cordially and confirmed that this was the original farmhouse built by her grandparents when they moved from Yorktown.

"Of course, we have updated it and remodeled it from time to time, so we have air-conditioning and hot-air heat, and it's very comfortable. Dad farmed it for a while, and when he died, Charles and I moved in and tried to run the tobacco operation, but that was just a sideline. Charles was a country doctor, and that took up most of his time."

While Harry was explaining their interest in Rosalee Stuart, Vera took a quick look around the room. As she had expected, there were several beautiful antique Oriental rugs in the house and quite a collection of paintings on the walls of the living and family rooms. One in particular stood out.

"Vera," Harry called, "Rosalee was Julie's aunt, and Julie does remember that she was quite an artist around here."

"Wonderful!" Vera exclaimed. "We know Rosalee studied with Winslow Homer in Maine in 1906, but we haven't been able to find out what happened to her since then. Can you help us?"

Julie thought for a moment and then said, "Let's go over to the church cemetery and look at the Stuart plot, and I think that will give you a pretty good picture of what my family went through around that time."

It was a short drive to a small, Episcopal church with a large cemetery in back. The Stuart plot was plainly marked by an imposing granite headstone marked with the surname in all capital letters.

Julie led them over to the grave markers. "Here's the first one: Laura Ashton Stuart, born Ashvale, Virginia, 1850; died July 1906. That was Jim and Rosalee's mother. Next is Rosalee Stuart Turner, born 1885 in Farmville; died April 1910. She was married to Jim Turner by then. Next is Col. Robert Stuart, born Yorktown 1842; died in June of 1917. He was my grandfather. Then there is Jim Turner, who was born in 1879 and passed on in 1943; he was Rosalee's husband.

"That tells quite a story, doesn't it?" mused Harry. "Rosalee came back here to care for her mother, who was dying. Then she got married and died—I guess in childbirth, when her daughter Eliza was born in 1910. We know Homer had a stroke in 1908, and so she couldn't work with him, and I guess she went before she could get back to Maine and claim that painting. And Jim Turner never knew about it."

"Is this what you wanted to know?" asked Julie.

"Quite a bit, Julie," said Vera, "but was there any correspondence between Rosalee and her mother or father?"

Julie thought for a while. "Dad had some old boxes he got after Col. Robert Stuart's death, and I think there are some old memorabilia in them that you are welcome to look at."

"We'd like to look at them tomorrow morning, if we could," said Vera.

"Come over for coffee at about ten," she said. "I'll try to find those boxes up in the attic and get them out for you."

Julie greeted them warmly the next morning and offered them a mug of very good, hot coffee. "Just the thing to take the chill out of my old bones," said Harry. "It gets pretty cold this time of year, doesn't it?"

"It does get cold down here," agreed Julie. "We're not far from the Allegheny Mountains, and sometimes the west wind blows that cold air down here and brings us some ice and snow. What would you like to look at this morning?"

"I think we'd like to know if there was any correspondence between Rosalee and her parents while she was in Maine, studying under Homer. She was a talented young artist, but untutored, and we would like to see how she progressed under his direction."

Julie nodded. "Look in that box over there," she said. "It is a collection of Col. Stuart's papers, and he gave them to Dad before he died. There might be some letters in there."

They opened the box, which contained an impressive array of

documents about nine or ten inches thick. Most were Civil War commissions, citations, and letters from Robert's former commander, Jeb Stuart. Then there was an array of domestic documentation regarding his marriage to Laura, the birth of his two children, the purchase of land, and the dealings of his farm-equipment business. After several hours of tedious work, Vera came across a thin file marked "Correspondence." After reading through it for about ten minutes, Vera called over to Harry.

"You've got to listen to this, Harry!" she exclaimed.

"What is it?" he answered.

"It's a letter from Rosalee to her mother, dated June 6, 1906. Here's what it says:

> Mother, he has a painting of you that he said was done at Ashvale just after the war. It is you, all right, in a beautiful green robe, sitting in a garden under what looks like a grape arbor, with the sun streaming down on your face. It is the most beautiful portrait I have ever seen. He said he was going to give it to you as an engagement present, but then you married Daddy, and he put it away in his storeroom and tried to forget about it, but now he wants me to give it to you. Charles doesn't know it exists, and Winslow doesn't want him to know about it. We are trying to think how to get it out of the studio without a confrontation with Charles. He is so good to Winslow and so protective, so we have a little conspiracy to get it to you without offending Charles. We are getting to know each other so well, and I do like and admire him. I just know you will love this painting. You look simply gorgeous, and it will be interesting to compare it with the one he did of you as a little girl.

Harry was overwhelmed. "There it is," he said softly. "The smoking gun. Laura is the Mystery Woman; Homer owned that picture and gave it to Rosalee to give to her mother. The concealment was an effort to avoid a confrontation with his domineering older brother."

"That's right, Harry. I think we have it now, and I think we should tell Julie all about it, because one of those pictures she has in the dining room is a young girl with red hair in wartime, and I think that is the picture Rosalee referred to that she wanted to compare with the portrait."

They reported to Julie what they had found, and Vera told her the story of the Homer oil that had been underneath a rough sketch of the beech tree resembling the one in her field.

"Harry bought that picture in a Maine antique shop, because it reminded him of your field; he gave it to me to clean up and restore, and we found the picture of Laura underneath. We have been trying to find out who concealed the Homer and why ever since. This letter gives us the answer."

"And," interjected Harry, "what do you know about that little oil with the red-haired girl in it?" He pointed to the faded, rather dingy-looking painting of a red-haired girl, a mansion, and a Union troop detachment in the foreground.

"I remember Dad said that was a picture of grandmother when she was a young girl during the war," Julie said, "but I don't remember much else."

"From the contents of this letter," said Vera, "I am pretty sure this was done by Homer and represents his first introduction to your mother and the beginning of a one-sided love affair that lasted about seventeen years and ended sadly for him when Laura married your grandfather. You can see how this little picture is such a unique piece of art, not only for its artistic value, but also for its impact on art history and the subsequent development of Homer's work and his sudden conversion into something of a recluse at Prouts Neck."

"But it looks so dingy and kind of faded now," said Julie doubtfully.

"It does need cleaning, and the colors should be restored," Vera agreed, "but a good restorer would be able to make that into a beautiful and enchanting painting probably worth a lot of money."

Julie sat quietly for a while. "That's an amazing story, and my family is very much of a part of it. I'm not sure what I will do about that picture of my grandmother. I don't want to part with it, but I would like to see it restored, and I wonder if it wouldn't be best to let the gallery have it, so it could be displayed for the public to see. I'll just have to think about it, and I do thank you for telling me this."

"Could we take the original of this letter and leave you a copy?" asked Harry. "I think we will need the original to prove our painting isn't stolen when we present our case to the gallery."

"Yes, go ahead and take it, and I assume you will return it when you are finished."

"Yes, indeed," said Harry.

"And I just noticed this, Julie," said Vera, holding up a copy of a telegram dated June 17 from Farmdale to Prouts Neck, Maine, asking Rosalee to return because of Robert's illness with pneumonia.

"You can have that, too," Julie said.

As Harry and Vera prepared to leave, they thanked Julie profusely for her assistance and promised to send her a good photograph of the painting of her grandmother. After they left, they visited the cemetery again and took pictures of the gravestones in the Stuart plot. By Tuesday at noon, they were ready to leave a day early and said good-bye to the receptionist-bookkeeper.

"I think we'll be back in October," said Harry. "Vera has some artwork she wants to do over at that beech-tree field, and I might do some hunting, if I can find somebody to take me out."

"You do that," said the receptionist. "Daddy told me you might come down in the fall, and if you do, he'll go out with you.'

"That settles it," said Harry. "I'll be back."

On the way home, they discussed what they had learned in Virginia. "So, I guess what really happened," said Harry, "was that Rosalee was called home suddenly to take care of her father and left the picture with the Perkins'. But then her mother died instead, and she had her father to look after; and then she got married, and Homer had a stroke, I think you told me, and she couldn't get back."

"Yes, Homer had a serious stroke in 1908, and then poor Rosalee died giving birth to Eliza in 1910, and nobody knew anything about that painting by Homer until you bought that beat-up old picture in Maine."

"Strange, isn't it?" mused Harry. "I guess we're ready to take this to Pat now and see what she can make of it."

Chapter 21:
THE CASE FOR PROVENANCE

AFTER RETURNING HOME, Harry and Vera were almost euphoric. The quest to establish legitimacy, which had begun only a few months ago and had seemed almost hopeless at the time, had now been fulfilled beyond even their most optimistic expectations. They were confident that they had all they needed to establish that Harry was the legal and legitimate owner of the painting. They knew who the Mystery Woman was; knew Homer had owned it when he gave it to Rosalee Stuart; knew why it was concealed; and they also knew why it had languished in the Perkins garage for nearly one hundred years. The *I*s were all dotted and the *T*s all crossed.

Vera and Howard Cohen decided that the picture should be fitted with a proper frame and after much discussion settled on a subdued gold color with an orange tint to bring out the green colors in the robe and the grape arbor. It cost Harry $500.

Over the next week, Harry stayed busy collecting and copying the various documents to hand over to Pat. He called Agnes to make sure she had sent her file on her grandmother's estate to Pat. After calls to George and Gwen to share the good news, he called Pat and made an appointment to hand over the documents to her.

"Have you told your kids the good news?" he asked Vera.

"Yes, and they are very excited," she answered. "But they are a little confused about how I got to be a part owner. I'm sensing a vague sentiment that I am a kept woman, and we are doing immoral things. They haven't met you, and they are a little skeptical."

"Yeah," said Harry with a little frown. "I haven't told George or Gwen that we are equal partners here, and I don't know how that will go over. Pat is okay with it; she knows what you have brought to the table and thinks it's reasonable. We'll just have to let it come out and see how they take it."

"When are you going up to see Pat?" she inquired.

"Next Tuesday."

"Howard and I would like to make an announcement of an exhibit of nineteenth-century American painters and feature the Homer painting. It would be great publicity for the university and will get the art community buzzing."

"Wait until I talk with Pat," he said. "Jennings was so helpful to us; I don't want him to think I am reneging on my promise to give him the first shot at buying it."

"All right, we'll wait," she said, obviously disappointed.

On Tuesday at noon, Pat joined Harry for lunch at the Metropolitan Club in Washington, and he handed over the briefcase containing all of his documents.

"It's all there, Pat," he said smugly. "We have the smoking gun and can prove that I am the legitimate owner of the painting."

"Wonderful, Dad!" exclaimed Pat. "Tell me what you found."

He went into great detail about how he and Vera had located the Stuart homestead, the graveyard, the beech-tree field, and the collection of "R. S." paintings owned by Julie Harris, granddaughter of Laura Stuart, the Mystery Woman. He described the letter from Rosalee, which he characterized as the "smoking gun." He was very proud of himself.

"Vera wants to arrange an exhibit at Salisbury State—nothing big, but enough to attract the attention of some big art dealers and give the university some good publicity. Do you think that would violate my agreement with the gallery?" he asked.

Pat thought for a moment. "You have really done a remarkable job, Dad," she said. "You definitely have shown that the painting wasn't stolen, and that is a huge plus for you. But there are some rather troublesome legal issues that keep bobbing up in my head."

"Like what?" exclaimed Harry indignantly.

"Like this was a gift from Homer to Rosalee's mother, but it was never delivered. Does that void the gift?"

"I don't know," said Harry irritably. "You're the lawyer."

"I don't know, either," she said, "but I better find out before we go public with this. And if the gift was valid, it became Laura's property; it certainly wasn't given to Rosalee. She was legitimately in possession of it, but she was just the delivering agent. Another thing: you got this painting from the estate of Eliza Perkins, who was Rosalee's daughter … but was she Laura's heir?"

Harry was upset and worried. "For Christ's sake, you lawyers give me a pain in the ass; you are always finding something wrong! You mean to say we went to all this trouble, and we haven't proved we own it?" he asked belligerently.

Pat laughed softly and patted his arm. "What we lawyers try to do is anticipate potential land mines and figure out how to avoid them. I think we can establish a credible chain of title, but there is still work to do; we aren't ready yet."

"All right, Pat," he grumbled. "We'll wait, but you sure have given me an awful letdown."

"Let me examine these documents carefully and do a little research, and I'll get back to you in a week."

That evening, when Harry reported on his conversation with Pat, Vera was very disappointed. "It's so frustrating to have this beautiful painting right here in Salisbury and not be able to display it or tell about its history and discovery. It is such a unique and fascinating story."

"I know it," sighed Harry. "Pat sometimes really irritates me; she is so meticulous. Everyone told us our one big issue was to prove it wasn't stolen, and we've done that, so why shouldn't we take what we've got and see what the art dealers will pay? I'm liable to die of old age before Pat is satisfied."

"I don't know her," Vera said, "but I am looking forward to meeting her; she sounds like an extremely competent woman."

"She is," he said. "That's why I'm willing to wait."

During the next several weeks, Harry made an effort to introduce Vera to many of his close friends at Bay Watch. The pair had cocktails and dinner at the dining room several times with Harry's bridge club and attended some local concerts and exhibitions at the university with some of his other friends. Vera's personal charm and vitality overcame any feelings of friction on the part of some of the resident widows who had looked on Harry as a source of companionship. They were fast becoming a couple, and Harry spoke to Vera several times about selling her condo and moving in with him.

"It makes economic sense, Vera," he explained. "Why keep up two places when one is plenty big enough for both of us? I have talked to the management about it, and they are willing to accommodate us. There would be an additional fee, which would be my responsibility, but you could reimburse me and save yourself a lot of money."

Vera was not convinced. "I'm not ready to give up my independence," she said. "This is my condo, and if I get mad at you, which sometimes happens, I can come over here and sulk."

"You can sulk all you want across the hall in my house," he answered. "I won't bother you."

"Harry," she said decisively, "it's better to keep it like it is, at least for now. There's no need for you to feel lonely; you know where I am. You come over for breakfast most mornings, and we have dinner together frequently. It is a very good arrangement for both of us."

On March 2, more than two weeks after Harry's conference with her, Pat called. "Sorry to be so long getting to you, Dad," she said. "Stuff came up at the office that had to be attended to, and I didn't get to study your documents thoroughly until last week."

"So what's the answer?" he asked.

"The answer is that we aren't ready. First, I want you or Vera, or both, to take Sarah to Maine to study the R. S. paintings up there; then take her to Farmville to look at the other R. S. paintings and the one you think was done by Homer, and I want her to review the photograph Vera took of your beech-tree painting. When that is done, I will send a court reporter down to take her statement.

"Next, I am going to hire an investigator to check the records in and around Farmville to locate the wills of Laura and Robert Stuart, and also of Rosalee and her husband, James Turner. I'm almost sure we will find the Stuart wills, since real estate is involved, and testamentary dispositions are a very important part in establishing clear title to real estate. I'm not so sure about Rosalee, who apparently died during childbirth.

"Now this is going to cost you some money, Dad … probably three or four thousand for the investigator, and about the same for Sarah."

"Jesus!" Harry exploded. "I've already paid Sarah a thousand dollars, and I had to shell out another five hundred for a fancy frame. I'm beginning to wonder if I shouldn't just dump this picture."

He heard a low, dry chuckle at the other end of the line. "I know, Dad—these expenses are terrible! When this is over, your share of the net profits from this transaction might be as low as $495,000."

"All right, all right, go ahead. Vera will contact Sarah, and you hire the investigators. But remember, I haven't sold that painting yet … and I'm not made of money!"

Sarah was delighted to be included in the investigation. They set aside three days for the Maine visit and four days for Farmville. Vera was on spring break starting March 8, so they began their visits on March 10. Sarah, who was charmed by Agnes, examined her six "R. S." paintings carefully, taking copious notes. She and Vera engaged in a rapid-fire exchange of comments, most of which Harry did not understand, except that there seemed to be a difference in the quality of the paintings.

"I think you can tell that these two were done after she had studied with Homer for a while," Sarah said. "See how she handles the shadows and the different shades of color when the light source is from above, in contrast to the colors when the light hits the image from the side? Also look at the use of blotting here, and perhaps a little sandpaper to create the illusion of an atmospheric event; here it looks like a snow squall is about to hit."

The trip to Farmville was equally interesting. Julie was proud to exhibit her collection of "R. S." paintings, and Sarah was amazed at how Rosalee had progressed after her return to Virginia.

"She really became an artist with her own style down here," commented Sarah. "She has refined the techniques she learned in Maine, and they are more subtle and less obvious, but the luminosity of these paintings, where light seems to come from within the picture? That she learned from the old master. She really learned how to get the most out of the transparent pigments that Homer pioneered."

Then Sarah turned her attention to the oil painting of the young girl. "You say you think Homer did this?" she asked.

"Yes," answered Vera. "It was mentioned in Rosalee's letter to her mother and seems to have been done during the peninsula campaign early in the Civil War. You can see the Union army detachment taking food from the outbuildings in the distance and the beautiful manor house in the background. If you compare it with that three-inch inset in the portrait, you will see a close resemblance between the house here and the one in the inset. We think he met Laura as a young girl, and that started a romantic interest in her, which intensified when she posed for him some years later and then ended tragically for him when she rejected him. He never got over that disappointment."

"Wow!" exclaimed Sarah. "What a romantic story! And I think you may be right: this probably is a Homer and an early Homer. I'd like to compare it with some of his early war paintings up in Maine; he did quite a few oils during the Peninsula Campaign." She turned to Julie. "You should get this restored. It should be cleaned with an alcohol solution to remove the dust, and then we could analyze the pigments he used and restore them to their original colors. You will be amazed at the transformation. You have a little gem here."

"That would cost quite a lot, wouldn't it?"

"Yes, my fees are pretty high," Sarah admitted. "But it's possible one of the galleries in Washington might get interested in having it in an exhibition and would hire me to do it for them."

On Sarah's return to Washington, arrangements were made to take her statement and transcribe it in the form of an affidavit. Harry called and asked Pat how it sounded.

"Just as I expected," Pat reported. "Very articulate, very meticulous, and very, very positive. There can be no serious question that R. S. Maine, R. S. Virginia, and the painter of your beech tree was the same person and was clearly very much influenced by Homer."

"How about the investigators?"

"We have the Stuart wills, which are being copied and certified and will be in my hands in a week. Rosalee died intestate, and we have a copy of the letters of administration issued to James Turner after death. Turner's will left everything to his only daughter, Eliza. We're ready to go now, Dad. Call Jennings and set a date; we've got a good case."

"How much did Sarah cost me?"

"She charged $100 per hour for an eight-hour day, but for only six days, which is $4,800. And the investigators billed me for $3,200, so you owe me $8,000."

"God!" muttered Harry. "I'll send you a check. And I'll call Jennings."

In their subsequent conversation, Harry found Jennings a little vague about when his committee could meet and hear their presentation. Harry was a little irritated, and his patience was wearing thin.

"We've done all our homework," Harry said, "and we're going to make a public announcement now. We thought you would be interested in hearing our story first, but if your committee doesn't want to meet with us, we'll make our announcement and see what interest there may be in New York."

After a slight pause, Jennings said hastily, "I'll get back to you tomorrow."

Harry next called George in New York and told him they were

about to make a public announcement and to see if he could get a ballpark figure of a reasonable asking price for the Homer.

The next morning, Jennings called and set a date for his committee to meet with Harry in two weeks. Pat agreed to make the presentation and set aside the date. She wanted Harry to bring a recent picture of the beech-tree field with leaves on the tree, and she wanted Sarah present at the hearing.

At 9:45 on the morning of Wednesday, May 3, Vera and Harry walked into the gallery carrying the painting in a cardboard case. Pat was already there with Sarah. Pat was lovely in a conservative, but feminine, suit, and she had her lawyer face on. She exuded confidence, while Harry felt some large butterflies roaming around in his stomach. They were ushered into the boardroom, which was packed with over twenty-five people. Harry handed over the painting to Jennings, who hung it on the wall in plain view of the committee.

"This is one big committee," commented Harry, looking a little concerned.

"Your presentation has attracted a lot of interest, Mr. Walker," said Dr. Jennings, smiling indulgently. "Most of our board members wanted to sit in on it. I hope you won't find it intimidating."

Harry thought that intimidation might be exactly what they wanted to accomplish. "Let me introduce my attorney, Mrs. Johnson, who is also my daughter," he said. "She will conduct the presentation of our evidence, and I assure you she will not be intimidated."

Pat strode to the microphone and with a warm smile addressed the board members and the committee.

"Good morning," she said in a clear, well-modulated voice. "It is nice to see so many of you are interested in the painting my father bought. As you know, the circumstances of the discovery of this painting are unusual, so I will go into quite a bit of detail about the history of the painting and why it was concealed from the public for so many years. I'm going to present our evidence to you as if you are a jury. You are the fact finders, and my job is to convince you that our chain of title is legal and legitimate. We have quite a few documents to show you." She opened her briefcase and extracted an imposing pile of papers, all neatly bound and identified, and spread them out on the table.

"Before I begin, let me distribute a few copies of this printed booklet, which is a summary of what I am about to show you. We will distribute these to interested dealers and organizations when we make our public announcement next week. It will help you follow our submissions."

While Pat was distributing the summary, Harry observed that some of the board members looked concerned and that Dr. Jennings had a wary look on his face.

They didn't think we would be this organized, he thought, *and they are a little apprehensive.*

"I have a feeling that Pat is shaking them up some," he whispered to Vera. "I think the board is beginning to realize that they will have to make a substantial offer to get this picture."

"Why must we go through this process, which is beginning to look like a legal argument?" asked a distinguished-looking gentleman sitting at the head of the table. "Why don't you just tell us what you have, and if anyone wants to check your documents, they may do so."

"Fine!" said Pat cheerfully. She guessed he was the board chairman. "I'll just give you a quick summary. My father bought the painting from an antique dealer in Maine, and the dealer acquired it at an auction from the estate of Eliza Perkins.

"Your father did not purchase *this* painting," interrupted a sharp-faced woman with a definitely hostile attitude. "He bought an old watercolor, and this Homer was concealed under it. Isn't that true?'

"It is true that the Homer was concealed beneath a watercolor of a beech tree, but it is *not* true that he only purchased the watercolor. The sales receipt describes the purchase, and I quote," said Pat, holding up the receipt. "'Antique painting, part of lot six from the estate of Eliza Perkins, as is.' So whatever this part of lot six was, my father bought it, including the frame and whatever was underneath it. Now do you want to examine the auctioneer's receipt? I have it right here."

There followed a flurry of whispered conversations among the board members. "Do you wish to confer in private?" Pat asked. "We will be glad to leave the room."

"No, no," said the chairman. "Go ahead; we may ask a few questions from time to time."

"Thank you," said Pat. "In order to establish that we are the legal owners of this painting, we must show that the painting was owned by Mrs. Perkins and that her estate was entitled to sell it."

The sharp-faced woman again interrupted and began popping questions at Pat. "Isn't it obvious that Mrs. Perkins didn't know she had this Homer? It was concealed under the watercolor, so she couldn't have been aware of it, could she? How could she sell something she didn't know she had? If she didn't know it was there, how could she sell it? Isn't this an obvious case of theft? Shouldn't you be investigating who stole it?"

During this tirade, Pat strolled over to the table and took a long drink of water. *Well, well,* she thought. *So that's the game, is it. She's an attorney, and she's trying rattle me.*

When she returned to the lectern, she held up her hand to stop the questions. "Do you ladies and gentlemen want to hear our case for provenance or not?" Her voice was bland, but she allowed a definite edge to creep into it. "Let me remind you that we are here only because my father made an oral commitment to give the gallery the right of first refusal in return for the help Dr. Jennings gave in authenticating the painting. All we are required to do to honor that obligation is to notify you when we have a buyer and give you a chance to make a bid. We thought you would be interested in what we have discovered so that you can better evaluate the provenance issue before it goes on the market. But I don't intend to stand here and be badgered by you, madam," she said, looking at the sharp-faced woman. "Would you please tell me your name?"

After some hesitation, she replied, "Helen Clift."

"Ah," said Pat. "Mrs. Clift, a well-known New York attorney specializing in controversies over works of art, I believe?"

"Yes," said Helen, beginning to look uncomfortable.

"Are you a member of the board or the acquisition committee?"

"No," she answered.

"Why are you here?"

"I invited her," answered the board chairman. "I was concerned over the manner in which this Homer was discovered, and I thought Helen could give us some insights as to the validity of your claim of title."

"I am sure she can. Now do you want me to proceed, or shall we all go home?" Pat asked, looking the chairman directly in the eye.

"Yes, yes," he said hastily. "I'm sorry we got off track here. We do want you to proceed; we're here to listen."

"Good decision, because you are about to hear a riveting story about how this painting evolved, why it was concealed, and how it got in Eliza Perkins's garage. Let's start with Mrs. Perkins. Who was she? She was born in Farmville, Virginia, in 1910, the daughter of Rosalee and James Turner. Now, Rosalee is a major player in this account. She was born in Farmville in 1885, the daughter of Robert and Laura Stuart. I have copies of all the essential documents proving the accuracy of these dates. Would you care to look at them, Mrs. Clift?"

"Not necessary," the woman replied, looking angry and embarrassed.

"Rosalee was an artist and studied with Winslow Homer during 1905 and 1906. We have an item in the Portland newspaper dated in May of 1906 that a tea was given by Ben and Eliza Perkins in honor of their houseguest, Miss Rosalee Stuart, who was studying under Winslow Homer. We found a number of paintings in Maine in the Perkins home bearing the initials 'R. S.' The Ben and Eliza Perkins referred to in the 1906 article had a grandson named Ben, born in 1902, and he married Eliza Turner in 1919. Again, I have all of the documentation.

"What brought Eliza Turner of Virginia and Ben Perkins of Maine together?" Pat continued. "The link was Rosalee Stuart. She lived with the Perkins' for two summers while studying with Homer. In 1906, while in Maine, she wrote a letter to her mother, and we have the original letter right here. Let me read a portion to you." After Pat finished, she looked at the board members; they were stunned.

"So ..." said Pat, pausing for dramatic effect, "this strong, gorgeous woman in the portrait is Laura Ashton, mother of Rosalee Stuart Turner and grandmother of Eliza Turner Perkins. There is another portrait of Laura Ashton painted during the Civil War, when she was a young girl. This painting now hangs in the ancestral Stuart home, along with more paintings by Rosalee, which are now owned by Mrs. Julie Harris. So the romantic attachment to Laura probably lasted about fifteen years before it ended unhappily for Homer when she married Robert Stuart. This painting was concealed under an unfinished watercolor of a large beech tree, and Sarah Burns, an internationally known and respected expert on art restoration, has stated positively that it was done by Rosalee. As the letter discloses, the concealment was done so that Homer could get it out of his studio and give it to Rosalee to deliver to Laura without a confrontation with his domineering brother."

. "I doubt that letter could be given any weight in a court proceeding," broke in Helen Clift. "It was hearsay and self-serving. If Rosalee stole the picture, she certainly wouldn't admit it, would she?"

Pat smiled. "As you well know, Mrs. Clift, provenance often involves documentation after all the parties are dead. This letter qualifies as an ancient document exception to the hearsay rule. All parties are gone. It is the best and only evidence which exists, and the fact that the letter is between mother and daughter adds to its credibility."

Helen nodded but still looked skeptical.

"Shortly after she received Rosalee's letter, Laura sent this telegram to her" —Pat held up a copy of the wire— "urging Rosalee to come home immediately because of her father's serious illness. She was required to make a sudden and hasty departure from Maine, and she left the paintings she had done under the tutelage of Winslow Homer, including the beech-tree watercolor, with the Perkins', thinking she would return later and pick them up. Some of these paintings are hanging on the wall of the Perkins ancestral home, now owned by Agnes Perkins, granddaughter of Eliza Perkins. Others, including the beech-tree painting, were stored in the garage and sold at auction when Eliza died. They were, you will note, property belonging to Rosalee, except for the beech-tree painting that concealed this Homer, which was the property of Laura as the donee of Homer's gift.

"What followed after Rosalee's return to Farmville in 1906 was tragic," Pat continued. "In July her father recovered from his illness, but a month later, Laura, the lovely lady in this portrait, died suddenly from a stroke. She was only fifty-six. Rosalee was the main caregiver of her father and could not leave to go up to Maine in 1907. In 1908, Jim Turner and Rosalee were married, and in 1910, Rosalee gave birth to a baby girl, whom she named Eliza. Again, we have all of the supporting documents, which you are welcome to inspect. One week later, Rosalee died from complications during childbirth. She was only twenty-five. After the deaths of Laura and Rosalee, no one else knew about the paintings Rosalee had left with the Perkins' except Homer, and he died in 1910, shortly after Rosalee.

"As a single parent of a baby girl, Jim Turner turned to the Perkins family in Maine for comfort and support. They became close friends and, as stated in Mrs. Perkins's obituary, Eliza and her father were frequent visitors to the Perkins home. They became such good friends that, in 1919, Eliza Turner and Ben Perkins were married. We have documentation supporting our story, and we will make copies for you at your request.

"I have checked the probate records, and Eliza was the sole beneficiary of both Rosalee and Laura and thus was entitled to all of the artwork they owned. That wraps up our case."

The chairman stood up and shook Pat's hand. "That was a wonderful presentation, Mrs. Johnson, and we are all very much impressed with your thoroughness. But aren't there some places in this narrative that are not subject to documentation, and we just have to guess at what happened?"

Pat thought for a moment. "I have no written statement from Homer that he gave the portrait to Laura, nor anything from Rosalee admitting she covered up the painting with the beech-tree watercolor or that she left her paintings with the Perkins family, but we do have an affidavit from Sarah Burns that the beech-tree watercolor was done by Rosalee. So yes, there may be places where we must draw inferences and make assumptions suggested by the evidence, but this is the case we have, and I'll take it to court anywhere and win it every time."

The chairman's eyebrows rose. "Every time?" he queried.

"Yes!" shot back Pat with conviction. "Every time."

Helen Clift gave a little snort and looked over at the chairman. "You know, John, I think she would."

Pat had turned out a bravura performance, and as board members milled about, Harry hugged her tightly and introduced her to Vera.

"So we meet at last," said Pat, eyeing her carefully.

"And I am so glad," said Vera. "You are everything Harry said you were and more. I want to get to know you, and I do hope you will like me and that we will be friends."

"We'll have lots of time to talk and get acquainted," said Pat. "I've heard so much about you and your background with Dad in high school."

As they were talking, the board chairman came up with Helen Clift and introduced himself. "I am John Rawlings," he said. "Sorry to interrupt, but I do want to ask Mrs. Johnson a question about a collateral issue."

"Yes?" Pat said.

"If the gallery does have an exhibit featuring your Homer, it occurred to us the paintings of this Stuart woman would take on some importance, as she was the only known student of Winslow Homer. These paintings seem to be in the possession of two different branches of the family. How do you see the ownership of these paintings, and with whom should we deal?"

Helen Clift added, "I think the lady in Maine is the granddaughter of Eliza Perkins, and the lady in Virginia is the granddaughter of Laura Stuart, if I followed your presentation correctly. So I guess the lady in Maine is the owner of all of them. Is that right?"

Pat sighed audibly. "You have put your finger on the most difficult aspect of this case. Under Robert's will, and under the testamentary laws of Virginia, Agnes Perkins,

granddaughter of Eliza, owns all the paintings, including that Homer of Laura as a young girl, which has been in the Julie Stuart

Harris home for generations. Both women are very fine people and helped my father a great deal in his investigation. Eliza never made any claim for the paintings from Jim Stuart for all those years, so there is the question of adverse possession, but were those pictures held adversely? And then there's the equity question of whether Eliza lost her claim by not prosecuting it. These are tough issues, and it would be a shame if the family got into litigation over it. You need to get a good negotiator to work out a settlement."

"Would you be available, Mrs. Johnson?" asked John Rawlings.

"Well, yes, I suppose so," she answered. "This is what I do generally. I do quite a bit of pro bono work for my firm, and it often involves settling family disputes like this."

"Do you have a card, so that I may get in touch with you?" asked Mr. Rawlings.

Pat gave him her card, and as they left, Mr. Rawlings complimented her on an impressive presentation.

"A very unique and fascinating story," he said. "You will be hearing from us."

Harry beamed. "Looks like you might have snagged a nice new client," he said.

Pat looked very pleased. "Let's hope so," she said.

"So what do you think is next, Pat?" asked Harry.

"Send a bunch of these booklets summarizing the provenance claim up to George, and let's see how good a marketer he is."

"And let's get out the announcement of our exhibition at Salisbury State and send that to George next week," said Vera.

"I have a hunch that will get the pot boiling," said Harry with satisfaction. "I am worried, though, about Julie and Agnes. The little oil of Laura when she was a child has been in the Stuart home for years, and I would hate to see it taken away from Julie."

"Yes," said Pat. "They were both so helpful to us. If I am called on to negotiate a settlement, I have some ideas that might work."

"Good," replied Harry. "I think they might hire you. You really impressed that board."

Chapter 22:
MARKETING THE PAINTING

The announcement of the exhibition at Salisbury State featuring the first public showing of the newly discovered Homer did not create as much interest as Harry and Vera had hoped. George sent copies of the announcement, along with the summary of the provenance, to some of the art brokers in New York, and the response was skeptical.

One of the more influential dealers was Art Friedlander, owner of Friedland International Galleries, with galleries in New York, London, and Paris. George called Art and asked if he was interested in seeing the newly discovered Homer. Art was not impressed.

"What are you telling me, George?" he asked. "That your father ran across a priceless Homer oil painting while rummaging through a pile of junk in some Maine clip joint?"

"Yeah, that's about it, Art," said George mildly.

Art snorted derisively. "You can't expect me to waste my time on crap like that. If that were an authentic Homer, the exhibition would be up here in New York, not in some hick town. I'm not interested."

"Okay, Art," said George, "but just remember, I was the one who tipped you off about this painting before word got out to the competition."

There was a long pause, and George could almost hear the wheels turning in Art's brain.

"Where the hell is Salisbury?" he finally demanded.

"I'm sure you'll find it, Art. Just mount your GPS on your belly and follow directions."

"Very funny, George," he said and hung up.

George leaned back and laughed softly. Art was a New Yorker, born and bred. He was smart, aggressive, and abrasive, and he had an almost uncanny eye for beautiful and valuable works of art. He thought Art might be interested, in spite of what he had said.

Back in Salisbury, Vera and Howard Cohen were busy assembling a collection of works of nineteenth-century American painters. They had an interesting collection on loan from local private owners and from some galleries in Norfolk, Baltimore, and Philadelphia. It was a modest exhibition compared with those done by the Metropolitan Museum of Art in New York or the Mellon Gallery in Washington, but it had the advantage of being the first public exhibit of the newly discovered Homer oil painting, which Vera had named *The Mystery Woman.*

The event had attracted some local interest, and it was scheduled to open on June 27 and close on August 31. Vera agreed to conduct two tours of the exhibition each day, explaining the paintings and the significance of the artists and their works in the development of American art. Then she would describe the details of the discovery of "The Mystery Woman," the story behind the painting, and the importance of Homer's failed love affair with the Mystery Woman on the development of his later work. Howard was able to obtain a loan of several of Homer's most original watercolors and persuaded Agnes and Julie to loan him several of Rosalee Stuart's watercolors that showed the influence Homer's techniques had on her development as an artist. It was a small but interesting exhibition.

Marketing the painting was more difficult than Harry had anticipated. George told him the art community in New York was very skeptical. Any aggressive campaign to sell it would, in George's opinion, increase the skepticism. The conventional option would be to hire a broker. The broker's fee would depend on the price he got, so he would be motivated to get the highest price available. The other option would be to let the art dealers and auction houses discover the painting—get the story of Homer's love affair with the Mystery Woman out in the public and hope dealers and museums would come to them. In view of the current lack of interest in his painting, Harry chose the less aggressive option.

After the exhibition had been running for a while, the story of the Mystery Woman and Homer's long romantic attachment was picked up by feature writers of the *Washington Post* and the *New York Times*, which published stories about the bizarre way the painting had been discovered and the remarkable love story behind it. Visitors from New York and Boston began to come down to see the painting, and attendance at Vera's tours gradually increased.

Among the visitors attending Vera's tour was a pleasant, dapper Frenchman named Claude Raymond who presented his card to Vera and wondered if he might have a word with the owner. His card identified him as the director of the Musee d'Orsay, Paris, France.

Vera was a little startled. "Why, certainly, Monsieur Raymond," she said. "We are honored by your visit. Your museum is world famous for its art collection and for its creative presentations. But what brings you to our exhibition at our small community college?"

Raymond smiled pleasantly. "We are interested in acquiring some works of American painters who were influenced by the colors of light and its effect on images the artist sees. Our Impressionist movement is well documented, but the influence of our artists on American painters is not. Homer, of course, was one of the most powerful and original American painters and was called by some critics a completely American impressionist. This work is impressive, and its use of sunlight and shadows on this beautiful woman is masterful."

"Did we send you an announcement?" asked Vera, still wondering how her distinguished visitor had gotten to Salisbury.

"No," he replied. "Regrettably, we were not favored with an invitation to your very impressive exhibition, but we do follow the activities of some of your international art dealers in New York. A Mr. Friedlander owns a successful gallery in Paris, and one of his employees asked one of my colleagues if he had heard of a new Homer in Salisbury, Maryland. We called our embassy in Washington and found that our cultural attaché had indeed received your announcement. He is acquainted with Dr. Jennings, who, I believe, authenticated the painting, and we decided that this was something I should see."

Vera called Harry and made arrangements to have lunch with Raymond the next day. They found him to be a delightful companion who was very interested in how the Homer painting was discovered.

"What was it that attracted you to the beech-tree painting?" he asked Harry. "Was there something that made you suspect that this Homer was concealed beneath the picture of the tree?"

"I am not an artist," said Harry, "and I wouldn't have noticed anything unusual about the painting. What attracted me was the beech tree and the field, which looked like a place I used to hunt in Virginia, and I thought it was strange to see it way up in Maine. Vera is an artist, so I gave it to her to clean it up for me, and she discovered the concealed painting."

"Ah, yes." Raymond smiled, looking at Vera. "Vera, the lady who gives the tours … and is very attractive, is she not?"

Harry laughed. "Well, that was another incentive," he said. "I hoped Vera would get interested in touching up the picture, and we could get better acquainted."

"I applaud your motives and good taste, Mr. Walker," Raymond said with a knowing smile. "It is something we French understand."

They discussed the authentication process, and Harry told him about the help he had gotten from Sarah Burns and Dr. Jennings at the Philips Gallery and his agreement to give Philips a chance to make an offer to buy it before selling it to anyone else.

"So you see, Claude," said Harry, "if I decide to sell this painting, I must let Jennings know and give him a chance to bid for it."

"I see," he said thoughtfully. "Am I correct that you presented the documentary evidence summarized in this booklet to the Philips board?"

"I think most of the board members were present," said Harry.

"There might have been an effort to intimidate me, because they asked some pretty hard questions, but I had my daughter, who is an attorney, present the evidence and give the board her interpretation of the legal conclusions. I think the board was pretty well convinced."

"Have you had any offers?"

"No, I really haven't tried to sell it. I probably will eventually, but it is pretty exciting to have distinguished people like you coming to see me."

"What about Philips?"

"We do expect them to make an offer. I think they would like to acquire the painting, but I guess they are uncertain about how much this painting is worth."

"Do you think the concealment issue is a problem?"

"Maybe, but most of the lawyers I talked to seem satisfied with an indemnity clause lasting during the statute-of-limitations period of five years. The concealment issue works both ways. There is some concern over a possible adverse claim, but it also adds considerable glamour to the painting."

"What are you asking for the painting?"

"I haven't consulted anyone on a price. I think I will engage a professional art broker if I decide to sell it."

Raymond nodded. "I think I shall arrange to meet with Ms. Burns, your restorer, and I am acquainted with Dr. Jennings. We will have a conversation about the authentication process."

Raymond thanked Harry and Vera for the lunch and assured them that they would hear from him shortly.

After he left, Harry and Vera talked for a while about the significance of having a world-famous institution like the Musee d'Orsay interested in their painting.

Vera said, "It looks like our strategy may be working. I wonder if anyone will make an offer now."

The first bite came from an unexpected source. Art Friedlander called Harry and made an appointment to see him the next day at ten in the morning. He arrived with an entourage consisting of a secretary and two lawyers. He was a large man with a hawklike, predatory nose; gray hair; and piercing black eyes.

This will be an interesting meeting, thought Harry as they sized each other up. Art got right down to business.

"Seymour here," he said, pointing to one of the lawyers, "has a contract which I have signed and is ready for your signature. It provides that we will pay 450,000 dollars for the painting you claim was done by Homer."

"Come again?" said Harry. "You think it's a fake?"

"We don't know," replied Art. "But whatever it is, it's a piece of crap. If it is a Homer, it's one of his worst works. We've had our experts look at it, and they agree it isn't much. Frankly, I wouldn't be wasting my time here, except that I told your son I would help him market this thing."

"You know, Art," Harry said coolly, "it is very strange that I have so many people buzzing around me trying to buy my piece of shit. I guess I don't understand this business."

Art shrugged. "It's a tough business. Seymour, explain to Harry what this contract means."

Harry held up his hand. "Tell you what I'm going to do. I will fax this contract to my lawyer, and she will contact Seymour, and they can discuss the terms. No way I'm going to talk to your lawyer about what this pile of papers means."

Art stood up and glared at Harry. "All right, Harry," he said. "You have three days to sign this contract and fax the signed copy to me; otherwise, I'll withdraw it, and you will never get a deal like this again."

"I don't know about that," said Harry casually. "I just had lunch two days ago with a Frenchman from Paris, and he's up in Washington now, checking out the authentication process."

Art's ears seemed to prick up like those of a hunting dog scenting its prey. "Who was that?" he demanded.

"I think his name was Claude Raymond."

"That frog!" bellowed Art. "Don't you dare sell that painting to him.

He looks and acts real smooth, but he's a crook! He'll skin you. How did he get wind of this?"

"He said one of your Paris employees told him about it," said Harry, trying to keep a straight face. "But I wouldn't worry about it if I were you. He doesn't look like the type to go around buying pieces of crap, so if my picture is as bad as you say it is, you've got nothing to worry about."

"We've got to go," Art said. "You'd better sign this contract, Harry, and leave it to me to deal with these international thieves. Joan," he barked, looking at his secretary. "Get our Paris office on the line and find out who told Raymond about this painting. Someone is going to get fired."

With that, they stormed out of Harry's villa and roared off.

Harry laughed as they drove off. *What a character!* Maybe Art's bullying tactics worked sometimes, but Harry was pretty sure that was not how he had become so successful. *He underestimated us*, thought Harry. *In his book, Salisbury is a hick town, and he assumed he was dealing with an elderly old man who didn't have all his marbles.* But Art did know George pretty well, apparently, and George was somebody people underestimated. It had been a strange meeting, but Harry was pretty sure he would hear from Art again.

Later that evening, he got a concise e-mail from Pat informing him that she had torn up the contract Art had given him and had called Seymour and told him that if his client was interested, she would be glad to send him a draft containing terms acceptable to the seller. Seymour said he would get back to her.

Harry called George and told him about Friedlander's offer and his visit with Claude Raymond. "We're having lots of action at the exhibition, and some people have called Julie and Agnes, so the story has gotten around. What is your sense about the market for our picture now?"

"I think it's time to get a good broker. Joe Bonelli is one of the best, and he called me yesterday and said if you ever want to sell your picture, he could almost guarantee he could get over a million for it, and maybe a lot more if we put it up for auction."

"So I guess the preliminary phase is over," said Harry. "I'll call Jennings and tell him we are ready to sell and are going to a professional broker."

The news that Harry was ready to sell came as no surprise to Jennings. He asked that Harry wait a few days while he contacted his board members.

"We will give you a good price, Mr. Walker," he said, "but it may not be as much as you could get from your broker. I do want to come down and talk to you and Vera about some collateral advantages you may get if you deal with us." They agreed to meet on August 25 at Harry's villa.

The exhibition was beginning to wind down. It had been a great success. It had started slowly, but after the newspaper articles had been published, the number and the diversity of the visitors had been unexpectedly large. Harry had only the offer from Friedlander, but that seemed to have stimulated the New York market, and word had gotten around that the famous Musee d'Orsay was interested. Harry was very optimistic that he and Vera would clear over a million dollars for the painting.

In a conference call with Harry and Vera, George urged them not to act to quickly. "The interest in your painting is getting more intense every week," he said. "And I know Friedlander is going to make a substantially higher offer pretty soon."

"How do you know?" inquired Vera.

"Because he has called me three times and hung up on me each time."

"Why?"

"Because I told him he better make a good offer without a lot of legalistic crap attached and that he better do it fast, because you were thinking of giving it to Joe."

"When are you and Jennings going to meet?" Vera asked.

"I gave him until August 25 to make an offer," said Harry. "He says he wants to discuss some collateral benefits that might result if we deal with Philips."

"I'd like to get our families together to see this picture and get to know each other," Vera said. "I'd like to do it around Harry's birthday, September 20. It will be a good time to get together and discuss what we are going to do with the painting. Will this delay the engagement of the broker too long?"

"I don't think so," replied George. "The pot is just beginning to boil; there is no harm in waiting until after September 20. So go ahead with party ... but there are a lot of us. Do you have some ideas of where we can accommodate everybody?"

"The beach house sounds ideal to me," Vera said. "There are four bedrooms, and there must be some local motels that can take the rest of us. I want Pat and your wife to help plan the party. Projects like that are a great way for people to get acquainted, and I am very anxious for us to be good friends."

"Don't go to a lot of trouble and expense," Harry said. "I try to forget about birthdays now. Let's have a keg of beer and grill some hot dogs and hamburgers. The grandkids will like that."

"We'll see about that," replied Vera. "I want Pat and Jean involved in planning this party. Once they get to know me, they will see that I'm just a nice old lady and not some gold digger after your money."

On Wednesday, August 25, Dr. Jennings arrived at Harry's villa shortly after eleven in the morning. Jennings had requested that Vera be present to hear what he had to say.

"I want you both to hear my proposal, because you were both involved in the discovery of this painting, and I believe you have a mutual interest in each other." He paused and looked directly at Harry. "We are offering $900,000 for the painting. It is our best offer, and it comes with no indemnification clauses or other restrictions. If we buy it and there is an adverse claim, we will deal with it, and you are not involved."

"That's quite a bit less than our broker thinks it is worth," replied

Harry. "And my son has assured me that Friedlander is about to make us a substantial offer before we turn it over to Bonelli."

Jennings nodded. "I am sure Friedlander will make a substantial offer, and I am sure Pat will have a rousing fight to get the more obnoxious provisions out of the contract. But we aren't going to get into a bidding war. Our budget will be pretty strained to get to nine hundred thousand. What I would like to talk to you about is the collateral matters, which I think you will find interesting."

"Such as?" inquired Harry.

"For one thing, peace of mind," he answered. "You don't have to wait five years to find out if you're going to be involved in a lawsuit. For another, we have that ownership issue involving the painting of Laura as a young girl and the Rosalee Stuart paintings, and we will probably retain Pat to settle it. As you know, we were very impressed by her, and you should know she is under active consideration for a vacancy on our board."

Jennings paused and looked at Vera. "You have also become a party of interest to us, because you discovered the painting, and the fact that you are, yourself, a competent artist makes it even more interesting. Environmental issues are of great concern to the public, and we have considered having an exhibition of art with an environmental message. As you may know, there was a group of painters in the latter part of the nineteenth century known as the Ashcan School. It was led by John French Sloan. I think there were eight of them, and they concentrated on the grittier scenes of New York City, emphasizing dirt and pollution. We don't know if Homer was influenced by these artists, but he was known to love the beauty of nature and was very realistic in his paintings. The Ashcan School was early environmental art, and I understand an environmental exhibition is one of your great ambitions. Am I right?"

Vera looked stunned and nodded her head. "You have really done your homework!" she said.

Jennings smiled and leaned back in his chair. "I'm not trying to bribe you or mislead you," he said. "These are things that would flow naturally from making a deal with us. I can make no promises, but I can tell you they are worth considering."

"Your message has been received," said Harry, "and we will consider it carefully. I also can tell you that your help in uncovering and authenticating this picture is very much in the equation."

Harry called George and told him about Jennings offer.

"That is a tough one, Dad," he said. "I know you could get more money if you hired an agent, but what he is telling you about the possibilities for Pat and Vera is hard to ignore. What are you going to do?"

"I told Jennings I would think about it carefully. I'll have to talk to Vera about it. I think we would like everyone in both families to see the picture and hear what our options are before we make up our mind. Vera has been working with Pat and Jean on some sort of party."

Chapter 23:
HARRY AND VERA

VERA'S SUGGESTION OF a joint birthday party for Harry was enthusiastically supported by Pat and Jean. Everyone was coming; this was an event nobody wanted to miss. Vera had engaged all units in the Bay View Motel, a short distance from the beach house, for the nights of September 18–September 20. After some discussion, it was agreed that Gwen's family would occupy the beach house; she was the one Harry saw least and was the most suspicious of Vera. It was important to make her feel good.

Harry and Vera went down to the beach house a week before the arrival date to inspect it and get it ready for the party. It was basically in good shape, but badly in need of cleaning. Vera hired some local women to clean and a yard service to mow the lawn and prune the trees and shrubs. They stayed in the back bedrooms overlooking the bay, but were very busy and had little time to themselves. The night before the arrival date, Harry and Vera had dinner by themselves and sat on the porch in the gathering darkness of early fall.

"How do you think our kids will react to us?" Vera asked.

"Not sure," answered Harry. "But you have been burning up the telephone lines with Pat and Jean about this party. How are you getting along with them?"

"We have warmed up considerably," she said. "Pat is taking care of the drinks, and Jean has found a catering service down here specializing in local seafood. We have gotten to be real good telephone pals."

"Good," he said. "And I think you will get along with Gwen after she sees you and finds out that you have become such an important person to me. But what about your family? Am I going to be a problem to them?"

"I don't think our relationship will be a problem to them," said Vera thoughtfully. "They have lived in many different parts of the world and been exposed to a number of different cultures. The Puritan ethic of sin and damnation that is very strong in middle America doesn't influence them very much."

"Would you like to stay with me tonight?" asked Harry gently. "We're all alone."

Vera leaned over and kissed him. "Yes, I would like to, very much," she said softly, "but not now. We have to get all such thoughts out of our heads and get me safely and chastely in one of those units at Bay View long before Gwen gets here."

"You're right, as usual," sighed Harry.

The guests began arriving on Thursday afternoon. Vera's daughter, Nancy, and her son, Jim, were arriving at BWI late and had made arrangements to stay overnight in the Baltimore area before driving down the next morning. The youngest, Melonie, decided to drive down that evening and arrived at Bay View about 2:00 a.m., and had breakfast with her mother on Friday morning. Harry and Vera welcomed his children as they began arriving from Baltimore and New York. Nick and Gwen took an early flight from California and came in at about seven o'clock.

Gwen was dressed to the nines and looked gorgeous and a little combative when she met Vera. Her attitude brightened a little when she was informed that her family was staying with Harry at the beach house.

"I do hope I haven't inconvenienced you, Vera," she said, critically eyeing Vera's outfit of a casual cotton blouse and designer jeans.

"Not at all, Gwen. Harry and I are old friends, and this painting has brought us together again, but we are of that age when we both need our own space, and I am very happy to be with the others at Bay View."

For the next half hour, Gwen grilled Vera about her connections to Harry in high school and how they had met in the park. When Vera told of the rude remarks Harry had made about her ass and sagging bazooms, Gwen tried to suppress a loud giggle.

"Dad!" she said, trying to sound horrified, "did you really say those mean things about Vera?"

"Well," he said defensively, "she was leading me around by the nose for a couple of days, acting like the little teaser she used to be, so I got a little irritated."

Both women began to laugh. "I still get mad every time I think of it," gasped Vera, "but that's Harry; that's your dad!"

"Yes," agreed Gwen, "that's Dad. You have to take him as he is; he isn't going to change."

Gwen began to tell stories about Harry from her childhood. "He was always like a pistol about to go off," she said.

"I'm glad you are having such a good time gossiping about my many character flaws," groused Harry. "But don't you think you should introduce Vera to the rest of your family? And maybe she would like to say hello to Pat and George."

"Oh, I didn't mean to monopolize you, Vera," she said happily. "Meet Nick and my kids. We heard all about you from Nick's brother, Spiro; he said you were a real charmer. Oh, here comes George and Pat." Gwen was gracious and relaxed and enjoyed her role of introducing Vera to other members of the family.

Friday was "get acquainted" day. Gwen and Nick were very interested in Nancy and Jim and were already making plans for a joint Christmas and New Year's Eve party. Some of the grandchildren rigged up the sailboat and enjoyed sailing around the marshy islands in the bay. Others took a swim and went crabbing off the dock. Patrick and Henry had brought their fly rods and took a rowboat to a small rock outcropping near shore and managed to catch several undersized trout and flounder, which they released. Harry was surprised and pleased at how well they handled their rods and the length of their casts. It was a beautiful, warm late-summer day with a nice breeze off the bay, which kept the temperature at a reasonable level and the bugs off the lawn.

During the afternoon, the painting arrived from Salisbury State, accompanied by three competent-looking men who would remain on the premises while the painting was being displayed.

Howard had told Harry that he was sending down professional security guards. "They will work with the sheriff's office and will spot any suspicious strangers—and, if necessary, deal with them. You will hardly notice them, but they will be around."

Harry's painting of a flock of canvasback ducks in flight, whichbe had bought at a Ducks Unlimited auction, was taken down from its place over the fireplace, and the Homer was hung there very carefully and with reverent ceremony by Vera. All of the family members gathered around to look at it, and the beauty of the painting and the gorgeous woman in the garden touched everyone, even those who were not interested in art. Vera told the story of the Mystery Woman and how they had uncovered her identity and of Homer's great and long-lasting love for Laura Ashton.

"There is another oil painting in Virginia showing Laura as a young girl during the Peninsula Campaign of the Civil War," said Vera, her eyes bright with the excitement of displaying the painting and telling the story of Homer's love affair. "This was Homer's first meeting with Laura, in about 1862. It shows clearly his admiration for her. When Laura grew into the beautiful woman shown here, you can feel the intensity of his love. This is a love affair that spanned more than fifteen years and ended tragically for him when she married someone else. As his later artworks show, he never got over the disappointment."

"Oh, Mother!" exclaimed Nancy, Vera's oldest daughter. "What an exquisite love story … and to think it was you and Harry who not only discovered this painting but also the story behind it. It's so exciting."

"It is fabulous, Mom," agreed Jim Harrison. "It's like a true detective story—stranger than fiction."

"And Mother!" exclaimed Melonie, Vera's youngest. "I have never seen you look so beautiful!"

Vera stood in front of the painting, her face glowing with animation and her remarkably lovely eyes blazing with passion and excitement. The gray hair, the wrinkles, the spreading hips, and the sagging, pendulous bosoms were all there, but no one noticed. What they all saw was a very feminine woman, talented and intelligent, full of vitality and love of life. She did indeed look beautiful.

Harry was almost moved to tears. He stood looking at Vera with so much pride and affection that it caught Gwen's attention. She could feel the bond between them and saw the way they looked at each other with such admiration.

"Well, Dad," she said. "I don't know what it is about you two, but you seem to be good for each other. I haven't seen you looking this well in twenty years."

After a round of cocktails, the bus Vera had ordered came and took them to a local restaurant, where the party planners had reserved a private dining room and a seated dinner for twenty-six people. When the bus left, Harry noted with satisfaction that one of the invisible security men was patrolling the grounds near the road; another was stationed near the dock, intently watching some slow-moving motorboats nearby. The third was somewhere in the house. They were a great comfort to Harry.

September 20, Harry's birthday, was clear, but hot and humid. The breeze off the bay had died down, and he was afraid they would have to move the party indoors. He put the heat pump on the cooling cycle and closed up the windows to cool off the house and make it comfortable if the heat was too much outside. The caterers arrived at about three, set up their outdoor grills, and hooked up the beer keg. Several cases of wine arrived, and the wine and beer bar were well stocked with ice and sturdy paper cups. Much to Harry's relief, a strong thermal current sucked in cool air off the bay at about four thirty and dropped the temperature about ten degrees.

The two non family guests, Howard Cohen and Sarah Burns, arrived

248

early and went immediately into the great room to view the painting before the others came. By six o'clock, the party was in full swing. The beer flowed copiously and was delightfully cold and bitter—just right for a hot summer day. Vera and Harry enjoyed themselves acting as hosts for the party and relating their experiences in Maine and Virginia while uncovering the story of the Mystery Woman. Then it came time for Harry's birthday roast. George, Pat, and Gwen gave hilarious accounts of what it was like growing up with their father.

"There's so much material here, I don't know where to begin," said George, "but I think I'll start with that girlie show dad took us to Las Vegas. There I was, barely fourteen and just beginning to realize that boys and girls were different, and suddenly the differences were on display—close up!" He went on to describe in lurid detail all aspects of the show.

Pat told of the time Harry had asked her what a male chauvinist was, and then described how Harry fitted the definition perfectly.

Gwen told of her first date, when she was in ninth grade.

"I was so excited," she said. "My date was a junior in high school, and he really liked me. So I invited him over to dinner before the dance. Dad kept staring at him and asked him if he ever had a haircut. I was so embarrassed! Then he told me if I ever brought him home again, he would throw him out."

"That was the worst dog you ever brought in," commented Harry, "and you really brought in some dandy losers. Thank God for Nick!"

Then came the gifts: a bag of prunes, a bottle of Geritol, another bottle marked Viagra Plus, and then what Harry called the unkindest of all: a package of Pampers. It was a hugely entertaining show.

As Harry stood up to make his rebuttal speech about the difficulties involved in raising retarded children, he suddenly felt dizzy and started to fall. George caught him and helped to his seat.

"You okay, Dad?" he asked, his face showing great concern.

"I don't know," he muttered.

Vera came up and took his arm and led him into the house. "You are everyone's hero tonight, big boy, but you have had enough beer, and you need to lie down a while." She helped him into the family room, where he lay down on the sofa with a light blanket over him. When she came out, she could see how distressed the other family members were.

"When he gets too exuberant, his heart sometimes gets irregular, and that causes him to feel dizzy," Vera said. "He has to rest and calm down, and usually it corrects itself in about an hour. It's happened a few times before, and I guess I will have to try to be a little firmer in keeping him from getting too high."

Pat nodded in approval. "We're counting on you to take care of him, Vera; he seems to forget he is not forty-five years old anymore."

"I intend to take very good care of him," replied Vera, "and I think this might be a good time to explain to all of you how much this relationship means to us." For the next fifteen minutes, she explained how their lives had been enriched and their horizons expanded since they met.

"We aren't contemplating marriage now," she said. "I adore Harry, but he occupies a different place in my heart from John Harrison, with whom I lived for over fifty years and with whom I had my children. And I know Harry is very fond of me, but I will never take Mary Ellen's place, nor do I want to. We do love each other and need each other, but in different ways." Her moving speech seemed to satisfy all of the family members.

About an hour later, Harry came out into the great room, looking a little pale but otherwise steady. He looked around the room and saw the family members were sitting looking at the picture and drinking iced coffee or wine. The grandchildren were outside visiting the ice cream truck that Jean had ordered, and the caterers were packing up and getting ready to leave.

"Sorry about my little flameout," said Harry. "Looks like I kind of pooped out the party."

Jim Harrison laughed. "I think we're all a little pooped, Harry. Between the dinner last night and tonight's birthday bash, I'm all partied out. We were sitting here wondering what you are going to do about this painting. Do you mind telling us about it?"

"Yes, let's talk about that," he said. "First I want to make clear that Vera and I are equal partners on this deal. Whatever we get, we split equally. Anyone have trouble with that?" Harry was gratified to see no signs of surprise or disapproval.

"Okay then, here are the options. I have a firm offer from the Philips Gallery for $900,000. There are no strings attached; if there is an adverse claim, they will deal with it. The other option is to hire a professional dealer to market the painting, and George has identified Joe Bonelli of New York as one of the best. Joe's fee depends on the price he gets for the painting, so he will be motivated to get us the best price. He has assured us that he would be able to get at least a million for it, and if he could make a deal with one of the big auction houses, it could be a lot more. A third option is to wait a while and see if Art Friedlander will make an offer. George thinks he is working on an offer that may have some contingencies attached."

"He will make an offer," said George. "He wants that picture badly. I'm a little surprised he hasn't sent it down now. But I think he will insist on an indemnity clause for five years and an escrow of a couple of hundred thousand to cover legal fees if there is litigation. Art is a tough New Yorker, and he is always looking for an edge, but he wants that picture, so he will back down on most things. But the indemnity and escrow might be hard to eliminate."

"I don't think either Friedlander or any buyer from our agent will back down on the indemnity clause," said Pat. "Litigation is a distinct possibility. I think we can win, but our case is by no means a slam dunk."

"And five years at my age is a long time," commented Harry.

"What are the collateral benefits if you take the Philips offer?" asked Gwen.

"They are considerable," answered Harry. "Vera becomes an interesting artist to Philips, since she discovered this Homer. They are considering an exhibition of paintings with an environmental message, and that is Vera's great passion," he added, turning toward Vera.

"I'm not saying a word, Harry," she said softly. "Such an exhibit is one of my life-long ambitions, but we both could use the extra money."

"And then there is Pat," Harry said, looking at her with pride. "You should have seen her sock it to that snotty board, and they were impressed. If we deal with them, Pat will probably be hired to work out the ownership issues involving the painting of the Mystery Woman as a young girl and the Rosalee Stuart paintings, which have become much more valuable now that this painting has surfaced. Jennings says she is also under consideration to fill the vacancy on their board."

"There's another perk, Dad," interjected Pat. "I have had some preliminary discussions with Agnes and Julie about creating a trust to take title to all of the paintings, and we would work out a fair division of ownership between them. They were very receptive to the concept, and do you know who they want as trustee?"

"Vera," answered Harry.

"No, they want you."

"Me?" he said. "I know nothing about art."

"Doesn't matter. They think you are absolutely honest and a good businessman." She paused and giggled slightly. "And Agnes thinks you're pretty cute."

This brought howls of laughter from the other guests. Harry's eyes brightened as he remembered the unexpected embrace from Agnes at their last meeting.

"Yes," he said enthusiastically, "I know she does, and Vera better be good to me, or I might run off with Agnes."

"Ha!" snorted Vera. "I have met Agnes, and she is a handsome and lusty forty-five-year-old. You wouldn't know how to handle her. You better stick with this old lady." This brought a roar of approval from the group.

Harry held up his hand.. "Okay, okay, I get the point, and I kind of like this old lady, too. Now, seriously, do any of you have any advice for us? Help us out here. What should we do?"

After a long moment of silence, George finally spoke up. "Dad, this is a decision you and Vera must make, and whatever it is, we will all support it. But you must know which option I think all of us hope you will take."

Harry looked a little bemused. "I guess I do," he said. "Pat has even anticipated me by contacting Julie and Agnes."

Pat was unperturbed. "We know you pretty well, Dad," She said gently.

"Those collateral benefits are important to us," he said. "But it is awfully hard for me to leave what might be a half million dollars on the table. I'll just have to sleep on it. And speaking of sleep, I am all done in, and I think I better get to bed. I'll see you all in the morning before you leave."

"We're all of us done in, Harry," said Nancy, "and thanks so much for all you have done to get us acquainted. We're all looking forward to getting to know the Walker family better, and it is so good to know our mother is so happy with you."

"Thank you, too, Nancy," said Harry, giving her a big hug. He blew a kiss to Vera and went upstairs to his room. The other guests left shortly after, and the party was officially over.

On Sunday, the West Coast contingent left early to catch afternoon flights from BWI. Gwen and the Harrison family were already talking about the joint Christmas and New Year's Eve parties and insisted that Harry and Vera must come out west for at least a week. George and his family left in midmorning for the tedious drive to New Jersey, and Pat and Peter left for Baltimore after lunch.

Vera and Harry were alone. She moved back into the beach house after checking out of Bay View at noon. The security guards took down the Homer painting and returned it to Salisbury State to be held in the secure vault until they decided what they would do. They spent the afternoon picking up debris from the party, washing sheets and towels, and straightening out the guest rooms. It was hot and sticky, and some ominous-looking storm clouds were building up in the northwest.

"Looks like we may get a thunderstorm tonight," observed Harry. "Want to go over to Talbert's for dinner?"

"Let's eat some leftovers here tonight," said Vera. "I am tired and feel like I'm somewhere off in space. I just want to take off my shoes and lean back and think about the wonderful week we enjoyed."

"Me, too," agreed Harry. "I'm still a little shaky after last night. Guess I had a few too many beers?"

"Yes, you did."

"Your kids a little put off by that?"

"No, everyone likes you, Harry. You are exuberant, and sometimes you think you are still a big stud and can drink everybody under the table. That's how you are, but you are also very attractive."

"What about you? Can you put up with my occasional overindulgence?"

"I absolutely adore you, Harry. I love that macho spirit, but it's going to be my job to step on you from time to time if you start drinking too much."

"Do that, Vera," he said. "I'll listen."

They sat there on the porch, holding hands and watching the storm clouds build up. They talked about how well their families had gotten along and about their remarkable experiences in discovering the Homer—and, even more notably, in unraveling the story behind the painting.

"So, Vera, how do you think we should proceed? Are you ready to leave a couple of hundred thousand on the table?"

"My family never had a lot of money," she said slowly. "The Foreign Service has many advantages, and the pay is good, but we always lived close to the edge. So money is important to me." She hesitated for a minute. "But what Jennings implied could result from dealing with Philips just can't be measured in dollars."

"I agree," he said.

"But do you think that is just a lot of talk?" she asked. "Do you think he can or will deliver?"

"I have been wondering about that myself," he said. "Jennings is a highly respected man. I am well aware he can't promise anything, since whatever he recommends must be approved by his board. But he isn't a person who would mislead us, and I can't think of any reason his board wouldn't go along with his recommendations. So, yes, I think he will deliver."

A low rumble of thunder interrupted their thoughts, and a cool breeze sprang up from the north.

"We better close up the house," said Harry. "This might be a strong squall."

After closing up the windows and securing the doors, Harry kissed Vera and said good night. "I can't even try to seduce you tonight," he said. "I am played out." He went into his bedroom, put on a thin pair of summer pajamas, and sat looking at the spectacular display of lightning over the bay.

"Hello, honey," he heard a soft voice say behind him. He looked around and there was Vera in a lovely bright yellow nightgown, looking at him with such radiant eyes it took his breath away.

"Vera," he said hoarsely. "What are you doing here?"

"I am coming to bed with you, Harry," she said softly. "It has been such a wonderful and emotional week for me. I don't think I can sleep. I need you—tonight."

Harry looked dazed. "Vera, I'm awfully tired too," he said a little desperately. "It's been tough week on us both, and I don't think ... well, I'm not sure I can ... you know ... I don't think I can ... take care of you," he blurted out.

Vera giggled delightedly. "Harry, all I want is for you to hold me; I'm not interested in anything else." She began to turn back the sheets and spread of the big king-size bed. "Now turn off the light and get into bed."

A sudden gust of wind rattled the window shade, and a few drops of rain fell on the floor.

"I better close that window," muttered Harry. "We'll get wet."

"Leave the window open; I like to listen to the storm. Just turn off that light and get in here with me."

Harry turned off the light, and in his best macho growl, he said, "All right, Antonelli, you asked for it! Here I come—get ready!" He heard a smothered laugh as he got into bed and pulled her into his arms. He could feel her soft arms embrace him, and he nestled down against her large but surprisingly firm breasts. He smelled the wonderful scents of a woman: a hint of flowers and a musky scent of warm milk and honey. He sighed deeply and immediately fell asleep.

The blinds rattled again, the wind howled, and rain splattered against the floor. Vera pulled the bedspread up to her chin and stroked Harry's old white hair, and they slept.

Epilogue

This is a good time to leave Harry and Vera, asleep in each other's arms. They had endured many difficult and tragic events before they found each other in their autumn years. Many more happy experiences and difficult decisions await them. No doubt some readers will be disappointed that their romance did not reach the fulfillment that we wanted them to enjoy. But using our imagination about what might have happened the next morning is more exciting than the most graphic and lurid description.

We know Harry and Vera will make a deal with the Philips Gallery, and we are pretty sure this will be a wonderful opportunity for Vera and will plunge Harry into the strange and often bizarre world of art, art critics, historians, and artists.

And what of their evolving romance? Does sleeping together on this night represent a big change in their relationship? Absolutely! The embers of romance still burn in their hearts, even at their age, but they burn with a different intensity. A geriatric love affair is different than one between younger couples. So what will they do? Will they marry, and get involved with the many legal issues, like prenuptial agreements, that a second marriage involves? That is uncertain, but we know they will decide what is best for them with advice from their families. This is a new and exciting chapter in their lives, and they are enjoying every day of it.